OUTLAW TOWN

Chancy tensed to go for his six-gun. He would draw and shoot and throw himself to one side at the same time. With luck, Reid would miss but he wouldn't.

But Reid made no attempt to go for his own six-shooter. Glaring, he stalked up and made as if to jab Chancy in the chest. But he glanced at the batwings and lowered his arm. "You're damn lucky, boy."

"Stop calling me that."

"We're men, the both of us," Ollie said. He had taken a step to the left and his hand was close to his holster.

"Stay out of this, idiot," Reid said.

"I'll do no such thing," Ollie replied. "He's my pard."

"He can't do better than a jackass like you?" Reid said.

For Chancy it was the last straw. And since Reid wasn't going for his hardware, he didn't go for his. Instead he punched him on the jaw.

Ralph Compton

OUTLAW TOWN

A Ralph Compton Novel
by David Robbins

A SIGNET BOOK

SIGNET
Published by New American Library,
an imprint of Penguin Random House LLC
375 Hudson Street, New York, New York 10014

This book is an original publication of New American Library.

First Printing, January 2016

For more information about Penguin Random House, visit penguin.com.

ISBN 978-1-101-99020-9

Printed in the United States of America
10 9 8 7 6 5 4 3 2 1

The Immortal Cowboy

This is respectfully dedicated to the "American Cowboy." His was the saga sparked by the turmoil that followed the Civil War, and the passing of more than a century has by no means diminished the flame.

True, the old days and the old ways are but treasured memories, and the old trails have grown dim with the ravages of time, but the spirit of the cowboy lives on.

In my travels—to Texas, Oklahoma, Kansas, Nebraska, Colorado, Wyoming, New Mexico, and Arizona—I always find something that reminds me of the Old West. While I am walking these plains and mountains for the first time, there is this feeling that a part of me is eternal, that I have known these old trails before. I believe it is the undying spirit of the frontier calling me, through the mind's eye, to step back into time. What is the appeal of the Old West of the American frontier?

It has been epitomized by some as the dark and bloody period in American history. Its heroes—Crockett, Bowie, Hickok, Earp—have been reviled and criticized. Yet the Old West lives on, larger than life.

It has become a symbol of freedom, when there was always another mountain to climb and another river to cross; when a dispute between two men was settled not with expensive lawyers, but with fists, knives, or guns. Barbaric? Maybe. But some things never change. When the cowboy rode into the pages of American history, he left behind a legacy that lives within the hearts of us all.

—Ralph Compton

Chapter 1

"Where the blazes are we?"

Chancy Gantry gazed out over the sprawling expanse of brown country they were passing through. "That's a good question." He tilted his head skyward and squinted at the blazing sun from under his hat brim, but only for a moment. The glare hurt his eyes. "All I can tell you is we're heading north."

"That's not where, pard," Oliver Teal said with a grin. "That's a direction."

Chancy grinned. Ollie and he had been partners for going on six years. They were both from San Antonio, but that was about the only thing they had in common. He was tall and lanky; Ollie was short and broad. He had straight black hair and brown eyes; Ollie had reddish hair with a lot of little curls, and wide, frank green eyes. His chin sort of came to a point; Ollie didn't have much of a chin at all.

Their taste in clothes was different too. Chancy went in for plain work clothes and a hat with a single crease. Ollie liked to wear a brown rawhide vest even in the hottest weather, while his hat had a crease in the center and two more to either side.

They didn't tote the same revolvers either. Chancy was fond of a Remington. Ollie favored a long-barreled Colt.

There was one other difference between them. One that wasn't obvious. One they never talked about. Ollie Teal, since birth, had been what folks politely called "slow in the head."

"We're somewhere in Indian Territory," Chancy clarified.

"The Injuns can have it," Ollie said. "It's a heap of nothingness."

"From what I hear, they don't want it either," Chancy said. "The government made them come here."

"That's the government," Ollie said. "Always telling folks what they should do even when the folks don't want to do it."

Chancy changed the subject before his friend started on his usual rant. Ollie's pa had been conscripted during the War Between the States, and Ollie, a youngster at the time, never forgave the government for taking his pa away even though Ollie had been one of the lucky few in that his pa made it home in one piece. "Ten days or so and we should be in Kansas."

"Addy told me this morning that he heard the trail boss say it was more like fourteen or fifteen days."

Chancy couldn't wait to reach the railhead. Back in Texas the notion of taking a herd north had been exciting. A trek of over seven hundred miles, with all sorts of dangers along the way. He'd imagined tangling with Comanches, or having to stop a stampede, or running into owl-hoots. All sorts of things could have gone wrong. But nothing did. The drive had been as uneventful as a Sunday stroll in a San Antonio park.

It was Chancy's first trail drive, and if he had to pick one word to describe it, that word would be dull.

Lucas Stout was the reason. Stout had a reputation as one of the best trail bosses around. He had a knack for finding water and grass, and got the cattle to market with few losses. Not only that, but he had a knack for overseeing men too. No one ever gave Lucas Stout trouble. Not twice, they didn't. Small wonder that hardly anything ever went wrong on any of his drives.

"What's that?" Ollie suddenly said.

Chancy looked up.

In the distance riders had appeared, their silhouettes distorted by the heat haze. They were hard to make out until they came closer. There were seven, all told, and they spread out as they came.

"Why, speak of the Devil," Ollie said.

"What?" Chancy said. It galled him a trifle that his friend had the eyes of a hawk and could make out things a lot farther off than he could.

"Injuns, by gosh."

Chancy sat straighter and placed his hand on his Remington. "Are you sure, pard?"

"Well, they've got long hair and some of them have bows, and their faces are kind of dark." Ollie paused. "I never did savvy why we call them redskins, though. They're not really red. But then we're not really white, are we? We're sort of pink."

"One of us should ride back and let Stout know," Chancy suggested. They were riding point, well ahead of the fifteen hundred longhorns.

"What if they're hostile?"

Chancy scowled. He'd never fought Indians. For that matter, he'd never fought anyone. Of the fourteen cowboys on the drive, not counting the cook, only two were any shucks with a six-shooter. Jelly Varnes shot two men once in a saloon fracas. And then there was Ben Rigenaw. Gossip had it he'd killed at least three and wounded a few more. Maybe he had and maybe he hadn't, but the matched pair of Remingtons he wore wasn't for show.

"I reckon you're right," Chancy said, drawing rein. "We hold our ground and see what they want."

Ollie followed suit. "Three of those redskins have bows. One has a lance. He'll be the one to watch out for."

"Since when are you an expert on Indians?"

"I know a lance is a lot bigger than an arrow," Ollie said. "If that redskin raises his arm to throw, we should plug him."

"Listen to you," Chancy said. "Wild Bill Hickok."

"So what if I've never shot anybody?" Ollie said. "I'm not about to let them stick me."

Chancy studied the Indians as they drew near. Truth was, he couldn't tell one tribe from another. But he could tell old from young, and with one exception, the seven were long in the tooth. Over half had gray hair, and were scrawny to boot. Four wore leggings, the others a mix of white clothes that had seen better days. "They don't look very fierce."

"Neither does a dog until it bites you."

Sometimes, Chancy reflected, his pard said the silliest things. "Keep your six-gun holstered. We don't want to provoke them."

"Could be they're already riled," Ollie said. "Three of them have arrows nocked."

It could be caution on the part of the redskins, Chancy reflected, or it could portend trouble.

"They lift those bows, we better shoot."

Chancy prayed it wouldn't come to that. He plastered a smile on his face to show he was friendly, but none of the Indians returned it.

The warriors drew rein about ten feet out. The youngest, in the middle, wore a black hat with a round crown and cradled a Sharps rifle in the crook of an elbow.

Chancy held his left hand up, palm out, and said, "How do you do, gents? We're friendly if you are."

"What makes you think they speak our lingo?" Ollie said. "They probably only know their own. Or that finger-talk Injuns do."

"Doesn't hurt to try," Chancy said.

The warrior in the middle gestured sharply. "We want cows."

"How's that again?" Ollie said.

"We want cows," the warrior repeated.

"I don't blame you," Ollie said. "They beat pigs. Pigs don't give milk and taste too salty. I've always liked cow meat more than pig meat. Chicken meat too, for that matter. Snake meat I can do without. I won't eat any critter that crawls."

The warrior cocked his head as if confused, then said, "One cow for each." And he pointed at every single warrior in turn.

"I don't happen to have any cows on me at the moment," Ollie said.

"No cows," the warrior said, "you not go by."

"Well, that's rude," Ollie said. "You and your geezer friends should move out of the way before our outfit gets here. Some of them won't be as nice to you as we are."

"Cows," the warrior said, and thumbed back the hammer on his Sharps. "Or you be sorry."

Chapter 2

"I think he means it," Ollie said.

Chancy couldn't believe it would come to bloodshed. Neither he nor his pard were red haters. A lot of people hated Indians because they'd lost love ones to arrows and tomahawks. Others hated just because red wasn't white, which never made any sense to him. He was about to suggest they should go easy when hooves drummed behind them. Glancing over his shoulder, he smiled in relief. "Thank the Lord."

"What?" Ollie said. He hadn't taken his eyes off the warrior with the Sharps.

"Lucas Stout and two more," Chancy said.

Ollie grunted in satisfaction. "Mr. Stout won't take no guff. He's got more grit than any hombre I ever met."

Their trail boss was as big as his reputation. Six feet four, with broad shoulders and a beard he kept cropped close. The way he carried himself, even his hat and his clothes, gave the impression he'd been born a trail boss straight out of the womb. He always had a no-nonsense look, and anyone could tell that here was a man it wasn't smart to trifle with.

The two punchers with him were Addison and Mays.

Addy had been born in New York, but no one held that against him since his family had moved to Texas when he was three, so he'd been raised mostly Texan. He was nearly as tall as Stout but all bone and sinew. He'd also been on more trail drives than anyone except the trail boss and Ben Rigenaw.

Mays was the youngest in the outfit. Only seventeen, he'd

nonetheless been at the cowboy trade for more than two years and could hold his own when it came to riding and roping. He was like a young pup, always eager to please. He was also, although no one would come right out and admit it, the handsomest. He didn't have much experience with females, though, and some of the hands were plotting to throw him into the lion's den, as it were, when they reached Wichita, and the sporting houses.

Lucas Stout reined up in a swirl of dust and Stout regarded the Indians with no more emotion than if they were a passel of townsmen come calling.

"Glad to see you, boss," Ollie said. "These here Injuns are demanding cattle or they won't let us pass."

"Why, the nerve," young Mays said.

"They get hungry, boy, the same as everybody else," Addy said.

"So what?" Mays said. "And don't call me boy, you old goat."

Chancy smothered a chuckle. The two always playfully prodded each other. That Mays liked to call Addy "old" tickled him. Addy was only twenty-five.

The warrior with the Sharps was staring at Lucas Stout as if he sensed that Stout was the head man and the one to deal with. "You give us cows?"

"Now that it's five to seven, he's asking instead of telling," Ollie said.

"Hush," Lucas Stout said.

Ollie didn't hide his surprise, but he hushed.

"How many?" Stout said to the Indian.

The warrior gestured at his companions. "One for each."

"No," Stout said. "How many of you altogether? Women and kids too."

The warrior said something in his own tongue to one of the older men and he answered. Taking his left hand off the Sharps, the warrior held up five fingers four times, plus two more.

"You can have three cows," Lucas Stout said.

"Seven."

"Three and that's all," Stout said firmly. "It's enough to feed all of you, and that's the best I'll do."

"You're giving them cows?" Mays said in amazement.

"You can hush too," Stout said.

"Six," the warrior said.

"Three."

"Five."

"Three. And if you say four, you don't get any."

The warrior looked at the older Indians and held up three fingers and several of them smiled. Facing Stout, he nodded. "Three. Not skinny cows, like some give. Cows with meat."

"I said they'll feed you and they will," Stout said. He turned to Addison. "Ride back and pick the three. Not the leaders. Three of those as like to straggle."

"Will do, boss," Addy said. Reining around, he tapped his spurs and galloped off.

Chancy had to hand it to their trail boss. Stragglers were a nuisance. The hands were constantly goading them to keep on the move. Getting rid of three made their job easier.

"It'll take a bit," Stout said to the Indian. "The herd is a ways back."

"We wait," the warrior said.

Lucas Stout motioned at Chancy and the rest and reined over to one side. Leaning on his saddle horn, he said, "I don't like the delay but it can't be helped. Might as well relax a little."

"I can't believe you're giving them cows," Mays said. "They're just mangy Injuns."

"You have a lot to learn," Stout said. "Indians are people too."

"And you plumb flabbergast me, boss," Mays made bold to say. "Why not have Rigenaw and Jelly Varnes come up and shoo these redskins away whether they want to be shooed or not?"

"Is that your answer?" Lucas Stout said. "Gun work?"

"They're stealing from us, is what they're doing. It's not right."

Chancy was considerably surprised the youngster was questioning their trail boss's judgment. He reminded himself that when he was younger, he sometimes let his tongue do his thinking too.

"Look at them," Stout said. "At how their clothes hang on their bodies. They're starving. Their people are starving. The women. Their sprouts. Three cows will keep them alive for a while."

"You're being nice to them on purpose?" Mays said, sounding as if the notion astonished him.

"Ever hear of do unto others?" Stout said.

"I still think you should bring Rig and Jelly up."

Lucas Stout shook his head as if disappointed. "Ben Rigenaw doesn't pull on someone without cause. Jelly might. He can be reckless. He's trying to prove himself and hasn't learned the lessons Ben has."

"What lessons are those?" Mays asked.

"That a man on the peck is looking for an early grave. You don't last long as the cock of the walk if you fly up on the barn and crow about it. Sooner or later someone will get tired of your crowing."

"I think I savvy," Mays said. "But still. You're bending over backward for a bunch of redskins."

"Bending isn't the same as breaking," Stout said.

Chancy figured that would be the end of it, but the young puncher wouldn't let it drop.

"My grandpa used to the say the only good Injun is one that's six feet under." Mays stared at the warriors as if he had half a mind to plant them himself.

Lucas Stout had apparently had enough. "Your grandpa was a jackass."

"Here, now," Mays said. "What gives you call to talk about him like that? You didn't know him."

"Haters, boy," Stout said, stressing the "boy." "I've run into their kind all my life. They hate anyone who's different. They hate because of skin. They hate because of religion. They hate for no reason at all other than they don't like something. From cradle to grave, they hate, hate, hate. And you reckon that's the right way to be?"

"Well, no, I suppose not," Mays said uncertainly.

"I'll have no truck with haters," Stout said. "I live my

life how I please and mind my own business, and I expect those who work for me to do the same. If you're a hater, keep it to yourself."

"I didn't mean . . . ," Mays said, and stopped. "It's just that my grandpa . . ." He stopped again.

"That's all right," Stout said. He stared to the south. "Addy better hurry with those cattle. We can't dawdle at this."

"What's the rush, boss?" Ollie said. "Those Injuns aren't any threat."

"We have a bigger problem than a handful of starved Indians," Stout said, and grew grim. "It could be we'll lose one of us before we reach Wichita."

Chapter 3

Chancy Gantry thought it was almost comical how the warriors practically drooled over the three cows. Their eyes lit up and one of them rubbed his stomach, and the one who had done all the talking came over and offered his hand to Lucas Stout, white-fashion. When they rode off, they were about the happiest Indians Chancy had ever seen.

The trail boss told Chancy and Ollie to push on while he and the others returned to the herd. Stout's parting words were "You're doing fine, gents. Keep it up."

Once they were alone again and riding point, Ollie snickered and said, "How can we not do fine? All we're doing is following the herds that have gone before us."

There was more than one trail north from Texas. Some were used more than others. The Chisholm Trail, one of the earliest, was so popular that at times the herds were lined up one after the other for miles. The trail they were following was an offshoot that shaved a little time. A lot of herds had been up it before them. The ground was pockmarked with thousands of prints, and dry droppings were everywhere. The previous herd, Chancy figured, had gone by not more than a few days ago.

"This is easy to do," Ollie went on. "I like it when things are easy. When they're hard, I have to think more, and my ma always said I shouldn't ever try to think too much because I'm sort of slow at it."

"Not that slow," Chancy said.

"You know who Stout was talking about, don't you?" Ollie said. "The one we might lose?"

Chancy nodded. The puncher's name was Finger Howard. Finger was called that on account of when he was a baby, a rat gnawed one of his fingers almost down to the bone. The flesh never did regrow all the way.

"Last night Finger was curled up in a ball and gritting his teeth and trying not to groan," Ollie mentioned.

"I saw," Chancy said.

"Stout says it's Finger's appendix. I never heard of it, so I asked Lester Smith and he said it's some kind of wormy thing we have inside us."

"Wormy thing?"

"Lester's own words. He says it's at the end of our, what do you call them, intestines? And that it wriggles around a lot like a worm."

"I wouldn't put a lot of stock in anything Lester says," Chancy said. "He was the one who told us that you can tell how much milk a woman can give a baby by the size of her breasts."

"Lester says it's common sense. The bigger the jugs, the more they can hold."

"It's not true, I tell you," Chancy said. "My aunt had no jugs to speak of, and she gave her baby milk by the gallon. My uncle used to joke that she was a regular cow."

"Well, something is sure wrong with Finger Howard, and if it's not his worm, I don't know what it is."

The miles fell behind them as the morning crawled like a turtle.

Chancy was recollecting his days as a boy on the farm when his hawk-eyed partner cleared his throat.

"What in Sam Hill is that?"

Chancy looked up.

Off to the north something shimmered and sparkled, casting gleams of sunlight. It wasn't all that big, but it was bright.

Ollie rose in his stirrups for a better look. "Ain't that something? I've never seen the like. What can it be?"

Chancy was at a loss too. "Beats me. Maybe it's more Indians."

"Injuns don't sparkle," Ollie said. "And it's not moving, whatever it is. It's just standing there."

Chancy's curiosity got of the better of him. "Let's go see."

They used their spurs, trotting side by side. The cattle trail, Chancy noticed, passed right by whatever was sparkling. Once again, his friend's eyes made out what it was before he could.

"Why, it's a blamed sign."

"A what?"

"Are you hard of hearing? It's a sign. In the middle of nowhere. And it's got words and everything."

Words weren't all it had. Over four feet high and three feet wide, it had been firmly nailed to posts embedded in the ground. Pieces of broken glass had been stuck around the edges, which accounted for the sparkling.

"That's some trick," Ollie said. "I bet they did it so their sign can be seen from a ways off."

Chancy was more interested in what the sign said in large black letters. "Don't that beat all?"

"What's it say?" Ollie said. "You know I can't read worth a lick."

"Prosperity—" Chancy began.

"How's that?" Ollie interrupted.

"Are you going to let me read it or not? That large word at the top is *Prosperity*."

"What do you suppose it means? What's prosperous about the middle of nowhere?"

Chancy stared at him.

"What?"

"Let me finish." Chancy turned to the sign again. "'Prosperity,'" he read. "'One mile west. Plenty of—'"

"Why, it must be a town," Ollie interrupted a second time.

"I could hit you."

"What did I do?"

Reading quickly, Chancy said, "'Prosperity. One mile west. Plenty of food and drink. Water and graze for herds. Come one, come all. Spend the night or a week. Everyone welcome.'"

"Why, that's right friendly," Ollie said. "Who knew there was a town hereabouts?"

"I wonder," Chancy said.

"You wonder if someone put up the sign to trick folks?"

"Do you ever listen to yourself?" Chancy replied. "Who would go to all the bother of toting those posts and that slab of wood all the way out here just to fool people?"

"What were you wondering, then?"

"A town might have a sawbones."

"You're ailing and didn't tell me? What's the matter? Is it those headaches you get from time to time? I doubt a doc can do much about those. Some people just naturally get headaches and there's nothing anyone can do."

Chancy shook his head. "You beat all, pard. Do you know that?"

"What?" Ollie said, and jerked as if he'd been stung. "Oh. You meant a sawbones for Finger Howard and that wormy thing in his gut?"

"It's worth paying this town a visit, don't you think?"

"One of us should ride back and tell Lucas Stout. Although he must know a town is here. He's been up this trail before."

"Odd he didn't mention it," Chancy said.

"Maybe he forgot," Ollie said.

"Have you ever known the boss to forget anything?"

"No."

"Then I doubt he'd forget a whole blamed town."

"We'll flip a coin to see who goes," Ollie said. He patted his pockets. "Do you have one?"

"We'll go together," Chancy said. "You shouldn't be on the loose alone."

"I'm not dumb, you know," Ollie said indignantly. "My ma told me I'm not. I may be slow sometimes, but I pick up on things."

"If by slow you mean molasses, then that's you, sure enough," Chancy joked.

"I hope you're right about the sawbones," Ollie said. "It would spoil the drive if Finger dies."

"Would it ever!" Chancy said.

Chapter 4

It was well-known that settlements and towns were springing up all over the place. The East bulged with people, and a lot of them were heeding the advice of someone whose name Chancy couldn't recollect to "Go West, young man." Or young woman. Farmers by the drove were flocking to the fertile plains. Miners were pouring into the Rockies to work the new silver, gold, and lead mines. Then there were the butchers and haberdashers and clerks and whatnot who figured they could earn as good a living in a Western town as in an Eastern town, and besides, life west of the Mississippi River was new and different.

The railroad had a lot to do with the influx, just as it did with the cattle trade. Without the rails, cattlemen couldn't get their herds to Eastern markets. Those same rails brought people and goods from back East. So did stagecoaches and wagon trains, but it was the railroad that was widely regarded as the pinnacle of enterprise.

Some towns sprang up so fast it was as if one day they weren't there and the next they were. Which was an exaggeration, but it fit Lucas Stout's reaction when he set eyes on the sign decorated with the broken bits of glass.

"Prosperity? Never heard of it," Stout said. "It wasn't here the last time I came through. But you're right, Gantry. It could be there's a doc, and we could use one. The only thing is . . ." He stopped and twisted in his saddle.

The herd had come up, all fifteen hundred head, or thereabouts, and the fourteen hands. Plus the cook with his wagon. The cattle had stopped and most of the hands were out on the flanks and at the rear to ensure that none strayed off.

With horns on the cows and the steers that could stretch up to seven feet from tip to tip, and over eleven feet on a big bull, longhorns were aptly named. They packed a lot of meat on their bony frames. Five hundred pounds or more for a cow wasn't unusual. Steers and bulls weighed a lot more. Good meat too, not stringy or rangy. Small wonder that longhorns were highly prized for Eastern tables.

"Something wrong?" Ollie asked when the trail boss didn't go on.

"I have a decision to make," Lucas Stout said.

Chancy could guess what it was. Should they take the entire herd to Prosperity? Or leave it and just take Finger Howard?

As if to prove him right, Stout remarked, more to himself than to them, "I'll have to send someone along. He's in no shape to go by himself."

"Are you talking about Finger Howard?" Ollie asked.

"No. President Grant."

"You're joshing. He doesn't know cows. From what I hear, all he knows is cigars and being a general."

Stout looked at Chancy. "Does he do this often?"

"All the time," Chancy said.

"Do what?" Ollie said.

Just then several punchers joined them, Addy and Mays and Finger Howard himself. Howard looked terrible. He was pasty and slick with sweat, and he was gritting his teeth against the pain. He had both hands on his saddle horn as if he was afraid he might fall off.

"Addy said you wanted to see me?" Finger said to Stout, speaking with visible effort.

Lucas Stout nodded at the sign. "We're hoping there's a sawbones. Chancy and Ollie will take you there."

Chancy's pulse leaped a little. The town might have a saloon, and maybe doves to boot.

"No need to go to all that bother on my account," Finger said. "I can make it by myself."

"Like hell," Stout said bluntly. "And I decide what to do, not you. We're ahead of schedule, so we can take a day or two to see that you're tended to, and then we'll move on."

"I'm obliged, but—" Finger began.

Stout held up a hand. "I haven't ever lost a hand on a drive and I don't aim to start with you. That appendix has to come out or you can die." He turned to Chancy. "You and your pard see to it. If there's no doc, or no water or graze for the cattle like that sign claims, one of you come let me know. I'm not taking the herd unless there is." He glanced at the sun. "We'll wait. It shouldn't take you more than an hour to get there and back."

"Half that if we hurry," Ollie said.

Stout nodded at Howard. "Finger can't ride very fast. It wouldn't do to kill him getting there."

"Let's go," Chancy said, and clucked to his roan. He was eager to find out about the saloon. He held to a walk. Ollie came up on one side and a few seconds later, Finger Howard on the other.

"I hate this," Finger said.

"You can't help getting sick," Chancy said.

"My ma used to blame getting sick on baths," Ollie remarked. "She said that if you take too many, it makes you poorly."

"I can't remember the last time I had a bath," Finger said.

Neither could Chancy. But then, anyone with a delicate nose had no business being a cowhand. "If you need us to stop, say so."

"I don't," Finger said. The next moment he closed his eyes and groaned.

"It's bad, isn't it?" Ollie said.

"You shouldn't ought to remind him of it," Chancy said.

"What difference does it make?" Ollie replied. "He'll hurt whether I do or I don't."

"Enough about how I'm feeling," Finger said.

"Sure thing," Ollie said, and with his next breath added, "I wouldn't have reckoned a little worm can cause a body that much trouble."

Large drops of sweat trickling down his brow, Finger blinked at Chancy and said, "Would you shoot him for me?"

"Gladly," Chancy said.

Chapter 5

The new town of Prosperity liked signs. The three cowboys came on another after going only a short way. It didn't have bits of glass, but it was on a higher pair of posts so no one would miss it.

"'You're halfway there,'" Chancy read. "'Supplies. Drinks. And more. Keep on coming.'"

"The sign says that? 'Keep on coming'?" Ollie said.

"It does," Chancy confirmed.

"Why, it's like they're talking to us. Who writes a sign that way? Usually signs are just words."

"It's a good thing you're not my pard," Finger Howard said. "You would drive me loco in no time."

"Why say something mean like that?" Ollie asked.

Chancy hazed the subject before they got into a spat. "Where's your own pard anyway?" Finger's saddle partner was Jelly Varnes.

"Stout sent Jelly and Rigenaw back on drag," Finger said. "On the off chance those Injuns we ran into weren't happy with the three cows he gave them and came after more."

The three of them rode on, Ollie commenting, "Those Indians try anything, Ben Rigenaw will gun them dead."

"Rigenaw would warn them if he could," Finger said. "Jelly is the one who'd shoot them as quick as look at them."

"You say that about your own pard?" Chancy said in mild surprise. He was even more surprised that Finger Howard was willing to talk at all, as much pain as the man was in.

"We are what we are," Finger said.

"What's that mean?" Ollie said. "We're cowhands. It's why we work with cows. Usually shooting Injuns isn't part of the job. It's not like we're Injun fighters or anything. Now, if we were army scouts, it'd be different. We'd tangle with a heap of redskins then."

"Jelly has his fancy six-gun and you have your mouth," Finger said.

Ollie's face scrunched up in confusion. "Everybody has a mouth."

"Sad to say," Finger said. He sighed and shook his head and drops of sweat went flying. Doubling over, he hissed like a struck snake.

"Is it getting worse?" Chancy asked.

"It's not getting better."

They covered the next half mile in silence. Around them, the brown of the dry countryside belied the claims of Prosperity's signs. Then, out of nowhere, they came to the crest of a low ridge and drew rein. Below, a gentle slope descended to a valley green with grass and scattered stands of trees. In the distance the blue of a small lake gleamed like a sparkling jewel. Between the ridge and the lake were buildings lining a single street. Horses were tied to hitch rails, and a couple of people were moving about.

"Well, I'll be dipped in tar and covered with feathers," Ollie declared. "I'd never in a million years have guessed this was here."

Neither would Chancy. But a body never knew what lay over the next hill or the far horizon.

A few yards away stood another sign. This one read YOU HAVE FOUND IT! PROSPERITY JUST AHEAD! COME ON DOWN!

"I never heard of anywhere so fond of signs as this place," Ollie said after Chancy read it to him.

"Let's go," Finger said, and gigged his claybank.

They weren't quite to the valley floor when Chancy, squinting hard, made out SALOON on the false front of one of the buildings. He imagined slaking his dry throat with a couple of glasses of bug juice, and smacked his lips in anticipation.

"I sure hope Stout lets us have a little fun while we're here," Ollie said.

Feeling guilty that he had been thinking the same thing, Chancy said, "We're here for Finger. Anything else is gravy."

"For a place that calls itself Prosperity," Finger said, "it's not much of a town."

Chancy had to agree. Only three of the buildings were of any size. The saloon, and what must be a livery stable, and a general store. Most of the rest were cabins. The street was empty now, the place as still as a graveyard. He gazed off toward the lake and noticed something else. "I don't see any cattle. No other herds are here."

"Good," Ollie said. "We don't have to worry about ours getting mixed up with any others."

Finger Howard groaned louder than ever and bent his forehead to the claybank's neck.

"Hang on, Finger," Chancy said,

"I'm trying."

"Here," Chancy said, and snatched Finger's reins. Finger didn't resist or object. Riding faster, Chancy led the stricken puncher to the near end of the dusty street. He ignored another sign on the outskirts.

The cabins appeared deserted. Not one person looked out any of the windows or came to a doorway to see who was coming into town. The hitch rail in front of the saloon was lined with mounts, and two more were tied at the rail at the general store across the street. Further down the double doors to the stable were wide-open, and the heads of horses poked over some of the stalls.

"Where are all the people?" Ollie wondered.

The saloon's batwings creaked and out ambled a man in a small hat and a well-worn vest with a six-shooter high on his hip. He had a ratlike face speckled with dark stubble. He took a few steps and raised his arms as if to stretch, then saw them and gave a mild start. Wheeling, he hurried back inside.

"What was that all about?" Ollie said.

The answer came when men poured out of the saloon. Six, seven, eight of them. All but one stopped and stared.

A portly man in a bowler and Hessian boots strode briskly to meet them, smiling broadly.

"Gentlemen, gentlemen! I'm Mayor Broom. On behalf of the good citizens of our fair town, welcome to Prosperity."

Chancy drew rein. "Our friend," he said, gesturing, and got no further.

Mayor Broom took one look at Finger Howard and drew up short. "My word. That man looks terribly ill."

"It's his worm," Ollie said.

"His what?" Mayor Broom said.

"His appendix, our trail boss thinks," Chancy clarified. "We're hoping you have a sawbones."

"Ah. Don't you worry." Mayor Broom came to the claybank and patted Finger Howard's leg in reassurance. "We don't have a doctor, but we do have someone with a lot of medical experience. He was in the army during the war and helped with the wounded and whatnot. He's healed a lot of us of various ailments."

"We need to see him right away," Chancy said.

"Of course," Mayor Broom said. "Put your fears at rest." He took the claybank's reins from Chancy. "You've come to the right place, gentlemen. Prosperity is here to serve your every need, whatever those needs might be."

"You make it almost sound like heaven," Ollie joked.

"Better that than hell," Mayor Broom said, and laughed heartily.

Chapter 6

Chancy Gantry was puzzled no end when Mayor Broom hustled toward the stable, tugging on the claybank's reins every few steps even though the claybank wasn't balking. Finger Howard was still hunched low, his left hand gripping the claybank's mane. His body quaked now and again.

Chancy was deeply worried. Finger and he were only acquainted through their work, but he liked him. Finger was easy to get along with, which was more than Chancy could say about some of the others. "Why are you taking us to the livery?" he demanded to know.

"That's where Dodger is, most likely," the mayor replied.

"Who?" Ollie said.

"The one I was telling you about. His first name is Laverne, but he doesn't use it much. He was the one in the army. He helped the surgeons cut people up."

"Who'd want to do a thing like that?" Ollie said.

They were almost there when out of the shadows inside limped an apparition. He walked stooped over. An empty sleeve hung where his left arm should be, and his left leg ended in a wooden peg. Long hair hung from under a wool cap, partially concealing the left side of his face, which was badly scarred. On his right hip was a bowie. The hilt of another jutted from the top of his right boot.

"Dodger!" Mayor Broom exclaimed. "We have a gentleman who is dreadfully ill."

"We think it's his worm," Ollie said. "That little wriggly thing in his gut."

The man called Dodger had mismatched eyes. The right

was normal, but the left was narrowed by a thick scar across the eyelid. Both fixed on Ollie and Dodger looked him up and down. "Wriggly thing?"

"His append-something," Ollie said.

"Quiet," Chancy said, and appealed to Dodger. "Would you look at our friend and see if you can help him?"

Dodger limped to the claybank. "How long have you had the pain?" he asked Finger Howard.

"Pretty near a week now," Finger said without looking up. "Came and went at first, but now it doesn't go away."

Dodger grunted. "Get your friend down," he directed, "and lay him on his back."

"In the middle of the street?" Ollie said.

"I need a quick look. Could be his appendix has burst. If that's happened, there's not much I can do."

Chancy swung down and motioned for Ollie to help. Together, they carefully lowered Finger, who grimaced and shook uncontrollably as they eased him from his saddle.

"Sorry for any pain we caused," Chancy said.

"Not you," Finger gasped.

"Move aside," Laverne Dodger said, and shouldered Ollie out of the way. Ollie opened his mouth to protest but must have thought better of it. Dodger kneeled on his good leg and pried at Finger's shirt buttons. "Help me get this off."

"You're undressing him?" Ollie said.

"Can't examine him with his clothes on," Dodger said impatiently.

"But in the street?" Ollie said.

"Your friend is a nuisance," Dodger said to Chancy as Chancy squatted to lend a hand. Chancy undid several of the buttons and Dodger told him to undo Finger's belt buckle too and then had him pull Finger's pants down past his hips.

"Hold on there, mister," Ollie said. "What if there are ladies out and about?"

"In Prosperity?" Dodger said, and snorted.

Chancy glanced up and was taken aback to find they

were hemmed on three sides by onlookers. Only men, though. Close to twenty, those from the saloon, apparently, and others. Something about them pricked at the back of his mind but he shook it off and concentrated on Finger and on Laverne Dodger. "You were in the army, the mayor told us."

Dodger was peeling Finger's shirt away from his body. "Medical corps. I was studying to be a doctor. Would have been one too if not for the cannonball that did this." He wagged his left shoulder, and the empty sleeve swung back and forth.

"You should pin that up," Ollie said. "You might get it caught in something."

Dodger bent and placed his right hand flat on Finger's abdomen. It was red from inflammation, and swollen. He gingerly probed, stopping whenever Finger groaned. "Have to check, mister," he said. "Have to make sure."

"Do what you need to," Finger got out.

Chancy admired how professional Dodger was. The man seemed to know just what to do, and had a light touch, like a lot of doctors. The examination went on for two or three minutes, until Dodger sat back on his heel and his peg, and nodded. "What the verdict, Doc?" Chancy asked.

"I don't think it's burst yet, but I won't know for sure until I've cut him open," Dodger said.

"You're fixing to operate?" Ollie said.

"Unless you want to do it."

"Why, I'd plumb kill him."

"Then I guess it's me," Dodger said. Turning to the mayor, he said, "I didn't count on anything like this."

"We do what we have to," Mayor Broom said.

"You're asking a lot," Dodger said.

"It's only neighborly," Mayor Broom said. "We do this for them, they might see fit to bring their herd." He glanced sharply at Chancy. "You gents *are* with a herd, aren't you? I distinctly heard mention of a trail boss."

"Thanks for reminding me," Chancy said, and jabbed his thumb at Ollie. "Go report to Stout. Tell him how things are. That Finger is being looked after, and there's plenty of graze and water for the cattle."

"Why, bless you, son," Mayor Broom said.

"I'm only doing what my boss told me to do," Chancy said.

Dodger glanced at the mayor, and then at Finger Howard's distended belly. "Same here," he said.

Chapter 7

Chancy Gantry had never heard of anyone being operated on in a stable. Usually surgeries were done in a doctor's office. But the closest thing to a sawbones Prosperity had was the peculiar Laverne Dodger, and Dodger insisted there wasn't a minute to waste. "I've got to go right in," was how he put it.

Under the mayor's direction, four townsmen carried Finger Howard into the stable and placed him on a horse blanket that Dodger had another man spread out. The horse blanket didn't look any too clean, but Chancy figured it beat operating on Finger in the dirt.

Finger was getting worse by the minute. He constantly trembled and uttered small sounds of agony. He dripped sweat. He looked at Chancy in silent appeal when Chancy hunkered and placed a hand on his shoulder.

"We'll have you well in no time."

"I hope so," the stricken puncher said. "I feel awful poorly."

"Would you like some whiskey?" Chancy knew that doctors sometimes used it to dull pain.

Finger closed his eyes and gave his head a slight shake. "I feel like I'm burning up."

Chancy pressed his palm to Howard's wet brow. He'd never felt a forehead so hot.

Laverne Dodger limped a couple of steps toward the rear of the stable. Pausing, he said to Chancy, "Come with me, cowpoke."

"What for?" Chancy was loath to leave Finger's side.

"Do you want to save your friend or not?" Dodger said, and clomped off.

"Watch him, will you?" Chancy said to the mayor, and quickly caught up to the disfigured stableman. "What do you need me for?"

Dodger's face, the right half, was set in grim lines. "I want you to understand so there's no hard feelings, after."

Chancy didn't like the sound of that. "Understand what?"

"It might be too late. When an appendix is infected enough, it can turn the whole body septic, they call it. It's where the blood goes bad, and once that happens . . ." Dodger shrugged.

"You're saying we can't save him?"

"I'm saying I'll try my best, but don't get mad if it's not enough. I can only do so much."

"We'll leave it in God's hands," Chancy said.

"God?" Laverne Dodger glanced sharply at Chancy. "Have you taken a good gander at me, cowpoke? I stopped believing the day that Reb cannonball turned me into a ruin of the man I used to be."

"It was the Confederates who fired the cannonball," Chancy said. "You can't blame God for that."

"Like hell I can't."

Chancy was uncomfortable slighting the Almighty. "I admit you have it rough, but you're still breathing and that should count for something."

"You're almost as dumb as that pard of yours."

"I won't be insulted," Chancy bristled.

"What will you do? Hit a cripple?" Dodger said, and laughed bitterly. "Go ahead. Show everyone how tough you are."

"I'd never," Chancy said, and added, "You've let that cannonball sour you on life, is your problem."

To his surprise, Dodger laughed again, only this time in amusement. "I take it back. You're not dumb. You're blind. You look but you don't see."

"I don't know what in tarnation you're talking about," Chancy admitted.

"Forget it, cowboy. I'm having a bad day, is all."

By then they had reached the tack room. Dodger entered and moved to a far corner where a cabinet stood. He opened the door, leaned in, and stepped back holding a large black leather carrying case covered with dust. "Carry this for me, would you?"

Chancy didn't mind. The bag was heavy, and the man did have only one arm. He hefted it, and realized, "Why, this is a doctor's bag."

"You're not completely blind," Dodger said, and started back out, chortling to himself.

"Where did you get it?"

"I was in medical school, a year shy of getting my degree, when the war broke out. I was young and stupid and against slavery, so I volunteered and the army put me in the medical corps, and here I am."

"Why didn't you go back and finish your schooling?"

"Blind as a bat," Dodger said half under his breath. "Look at me, cowboy. Look real good. I can't hardly walk and I can't hardly see out of one eye and with only one hand I can't hardly do half the things doctors have to do to practice medicine."

"It's no cause to give up."

They were halfway up the aisle and Laverne Dodger almost stopped but muttered something and continued. "Out of curiosity, have you always herded cows for a living?"

"I was raised on a farm," Chancy said. "Wanted to see some of the world, and since I'd been around cows all my life, I figured herding them was something I could do and see some of the world at the same time."

"That's your whole life right there? Cows?"

"More or less," Chancy admitted, wondering what the man was getting at.

"Figures," Dodger said, and didn't elaborate.

The mayor was waiting for them. He must have shooed everyone else out because they were beyond the double doors, looking in. "I sent Ira Reid for hot water and Carter for whatever clean towels he can find."

Dodger grunted.

"Anything else I can do?" Mayor Broom asked.

"You can try prayer," Dodger said sarcastically.

"Don't start on that again," Mayor Broom said.

Chancy set the black bag down next to Finger Howard, and kneeled. Finger barely stirred when he touched his arm. "How are you holding up?"

Finger's eyelids fluttered and his throat bobbed. "I reckon I'm not long for this world."

Chapter 8

Chancy reckoned that the large black leather case contained instruments and whatnot. He was right, and he was wrong. The cantankerous Dodger took out a long wooden box that once must have been highly polished but now bore nicks and scrapes and other signs of heavy use. Dodger worked two small levers and the box swung open on brass hinges. Inside were two trays. The top tray held a saw—at which Chancy winced—along with scalpels and scissors and other things. The bottom tray contained probes and instruments he'd never set eyes on. Under the bottom tray were clamps and needles and more.

As Dodger rummaged in the tray, mumbling under his breath, Mayor Broom made as if to leave.

"I don't think I want to see this. Blood when a man is shot is one thing. Watching someone be cut open is another."

"You're not getting off that easy," Dodger said sourly. "I need four men to hold him. The cowboy here and three others."

"Surely you don't expect me to take a part?" Mayor Broom said.

"This was your idea."

"Yes, but," Mayor Broom said, and didn't go on.

Chancy kneeled beside Finger Howard and put his hand on Finger's shoulder. Finger didn't open his eyes. Chancy gently shook him, but Finger didn't move. "Something's wrong."

"He's in the final stages," Dodger said. "There's still hope. If the worm, as your simpleton partner called it, hasn't burst. If the poison hasn't spread through his system. If he's strong enough to handle the surgery."

"If, if, if," Chancy said.

"I know," Dodger said.

Outside, voices were raised, and the onlookers parted to admit a man carrying an armful of towels. None were folded. It looked as if he had scooped them up from wherever he found them. The man himself was as untidy as the towels. His clothes were rumpled, the hair that hung from under his hat stringy, his face grimy. "I found some, Broom," he said.

"That's Mayor Broom to you, Carter," Broom replied. "I'll thank you to remember that."

Carter looked at Chancy and at Finger. "Sure thing. Mayor Broom, it is." He let the towels fall at the mayor's feet.

Dodger picked one up and frowned at a brown stain. "I don't suppose it occurred to you that they should be clean?"

"It's the best I could do," Carter said. "Who keeps a clean towel around anyhow?"

Chancy saw his point. The cowhands on the trail seldom washed their towels. For that matter, they seldom used any.

"These will have to do," Mayor Broom said.

Another commotion outside resulted in another man entering. He was toting a large pot by the handle with both hands, and didn't look happy. He had to be in his forties, with gray at the temples, and wore a Smith & Wesson on his left hip, rigged for a cross draw. He was cursing and loudly declared, "Watch out! This damn thing is hot!"

Chancy had to move out of the way as the newcomer set the pot down much too hard, and water splashed every which way. A few drops splattered on Finger's arm, and he groaned.

"That was dumb," Chancy said.

The newcomer's dark eyes flashed with anger and he snapped, "What did you just call me?"

"You got some on my friend," Chancy said. "You're too careless by half, mister."

"I will gun you where you stand," the man said, coiling as if to draw.

"No," Mayor Broom said. "You won't. Simmer down, Reid."

"You heard him," Reid snarled. "He called me dumb."

"No. He said what you *did* is dumb. He called you careless and he's right. You are." Mayor Broom became stern. "And you *will* simmer down or I'll send for Ives. Would you like that?"

At the mention of the name, Ira Reid slowly let his body relax. Shaking his head, he said, "No need for that."

"Remember where you are and what this is," Mayor Broom said. "We have a herd on its way in."

"About time," Reid said.

"Go outside with the others," Mayor Broom said, "and behave yourself."

"No," Laverne Dodger said. He was sorting through his scalpels. "I told you I need four men to hold the patient down. You and the cowboy take an arm. Reid and Carter take a leg."

"The hell you say," Reid said.

"We don't save him," Dodger said, "the herd might not come."

Chancy didn't understand why they were so anxious about the cattle. A moment's reflection, and he reasoned that they must rely heavily on passing herds for their livelihood. He put it from his mind.

"I can't believe you want me to lend a hand," Mayor Broom said.

"You have to do your part, the same as everybody else," Dodger said. Shifting on his only heel, he lightly pressed his fingertips to Finger's belly. "He's swollen something fierce. When I cut him, the smell will be rank. Just so you know."

"I hope I don't get sick," Carter said.

"You do, you turn the other way," Dodger said. He

waggled the scalpel and dubiously remarked, "I haven't cut on anyone in years."

"Let's hope you haven't forgotten how." Mayor Broom said.

"Amen to that," Chancy added.

Chapter 9

If Chancy lived to be a hundred, it would please him considerably if he never remembered a single minute of the horror that followed. He'd seen badly hurt men before. Like that time a bull gored a puncher. Or the time his cousin fell out of a tree and broke his leg and the shattered bone sliced clear through the skin. Or when a neighbor accidentally cut off a couple of fingers with an ax while chopping wood for the fireplace.

This was something else, something horrible to witness, something surgeons did all the time but he could never do in a million years.

Laverne Dodger didn't waste any time. He took a deep breath and made a swift cut low on Finger's abdomen. There was a hiss like escaping air, and blood and a vile yellow fluid oozed out.

"The stink," Carter said, and made as if to retch.

"Don't you dare, damn you," Dodger said.

Chancy averted his face. It wasn't the smell so much as the sight that nauseated him. The sounds were almost as gruesome: bubbling and squishing, and worse.

"Lord help us," Mayor Broom gasped. He too had turned his face away, and was pressing his mouth and nose to his sleeve.

"How long is this going to take?" Reid wanted to know.

Without looking up, Dodger said, "I have to cut the appendix out, then sew his intestine, then stitch the wound."

"How long, damn it?" Reid snapped.

"A while," Dodger said.

Chancy shut his eyes and breathed shallowly and thought

of pleasanter times. Of growing up on the farm, of his ma and pa, the best parents a body could ask for. Of his four brothers and three sisters. They were a close-knit family. His whole life until he went off on his own, he'd shared a bedroom with his two older brothers and never minded a bit. Fact was, sleeping in a bunkhouse or out on the prairie with the other hands for company wasn't much different.

Chancy remembered the pies his ma used to bake. Cherry was his favorite. She used the tart kind, and they always made his mouth pucker. She also made the best biscuits this side of anywhere. Smeared with butter, they were so soft and delicious they'd melted in his mouth.

He recollected his first ranch job. How green he'd been. He could ride well enough back then, and he was a passable roper, but when it came to cattle, he hadn't known as much as he thought he did. Longhorns and dairy cows weren't the same critters. And going into the brush after a longhorn that didn't want to be brought out was an education in itself.

Chancy thought of Felicia, a girl he'd been sweet on. Leaving her had been hard, even after what had happened. He'd courted her, taken her to church socials and the like, and finally mustered the courage to ask for her hand in marriage. It had shocked him clear down to his toes when she informed him she would think about it, and shocked him even more the very next day when she told him marriage was out of the question, then and forever. When he'd asked why, Felicia said her pa didn't think he'd ever amount to much, and she could do better.

That she went along with it cleaved his heart in two.

Chancy never let on, though. He'd looked her in the eye and said that he thought he'd asked for her hand, not her pa's, and if she'd let her pa run her life, she wasn't the woman for him anyhow. Walking away had taken every ounce of grit he possessed.

Since then, Chancy hadn't given females much thought. As far as he was concerned, he was shed of them. Ollie liked to tease him and claim that when the right gal came along, he'd find out it was easier to give whiskey up than it was to give up women.

That Ollie, Chancy reflected, and inwardly smiled. He would be the first to admit his pard wasn't the brightest candle on the table, but as friends went, Ollie stuck through thick and thin, and that was what counted. Chancy knew he could rely on him, no matter what.

Such as that time Chancy dismounted to check for sign and a longhorn came charging out of the brush. It had him dead to rights. But Ollie jabbed his spurs and yipped and hollered and caused it to shear off. When Chancy thanked him for saving his life, Ollie grinned and said, "Shucks. That's what pards are for."

Chancy later repaid the favor with an incident involving a rattlesnake. They'd been out after strays and Ollie's mount nearly stepped on a rattler. The snake coiled and rattled, and the horse reared. Ollie was thrown. He landed so close to the snake its darting tongue almost touched him. All it would have taken was a flick of the rattler's head, and its deadly fangs would have sunk into Ollie's neck. Seeing his pard in peril, Chancy had drawn and fired. He wasn't much of a shot. Certainly he wasn't in the same class as Ben Rigenaw or Jelly Varnes. But Lady Luck smiled on him, or maybe she smiled on Ollie, because his desperate shot cored the snake's tiny brain and it rolled over and showed its belly to the sky.

Ever since, Ollie was convinced that Chancy was one of the best shots alive. Chancy told him time and again that he couldn't pull off that shot again if he lived a million years, but Ollie said he was just being modest.

Chancy recalled their visit to Dallas not long after that. How they'd gone there figuring to have a high old time. Dallas was supposed to be wild and woolly, but if so, that was in the past. It was as peaceful as a spelling bee. They'd made the rounds of a few saloons and turned in before midnight. The only excitement, if you could call it that, was when a woman who looked to be older than his ma approached them and asked if they wanted to treat her to a few drinks and whatever else they might have in mind. Ollie thanked her but said he'd preferred someone with fewer wrinkles. She almost hit him.

Suddenly Chancy became aware of a hand on his arm.

"You can let go," Laverne Dodger said.

"What?"

"It's over."

"It's only been a few minutes."

"Hellfire, cowboy," Dodger said. "I've been at it over an hour." Exhaustion marked his features, and beads of sweat sprinkled his brow.

Chancy gave a start. He'd been so lost in his memories he'd lost all track of time.

The others had already risen and stood back. The mayor had his bowler off and was mopping his face with a handkerchief. Reid stood with his thumbs hooked in his gun belt. Carter looked green around the gills and was rubbing his stomach.

As for Finger Howard, he was breathing fine and wasn't as pale. His belly, Chancy was happy to see, was a lot less swollen. The stitches were neatly done, and except for smears of blood around the incision and a few small scarlet splotches here and there, you could hardly tell he'd been cut.

"I'll be switched," Chancy said in amazement. "You'd have made a great doc, Dodger."

"Thanks." Dodger smiled sheepishly, "I reckon I haven't lost my touch."

Mayor Broom smiled and clapped him on the back. "We are all in your debt, Laverne. This will put us in good with their trail boss, I bet."

"Why is that important?" Chancy asked.

Instead of answering, Mayor Broom said, "We're looking forward to making his acquaintance. Him and the rest of your outfit. Aren't we, boys?" He motioned at the men outside, and every last one smiled or nodded.

Chancy had seldom seen such a friendly bunch.

Chapter 10

Under the mayor's guidance, half a dozen townsmen carefully carried Finger Howard to a nearby cabin and deposited him on a bed.

Chancy was grateful but couldn't help remarking, "Whoever lives here won't mind? We don't mean to put anyone out."

"Don't you worry," Mayor Broom assured him. "The folks who live here are gone right now."

To Chancy, it didn't look as if anyone did. Despite the bed and a table and a couple of chairs, the cabin had an empty feel. There wasn't even a cupboard, or any sign of habitation. Just a lot of dust.

"Trust me, Mr. Gantry," Mayor Broom said. "The good people of Prosperity are happy to meet your every need."

Dodger had come along, his peg thumbing loudly on the cabin floor. "I'll check in on your friend regular," he promised. "To make sure his fever stays down and the swelling goes away."

"In fact," Mayor Broom said to Chancy, "you can stay here yourself. Bring your horse over and make yourself to home."

"What I could use right now," Chancy said, "is a drink."

Carter was one of those who had helped bring Finger over, and he grinned and nodded. "Now you're talking. A bottle would help me forget all the blood and that terrible smell."

"You'll have two drinks at the most, and that's all," Mayor Broom said. "You know how you are after a bottle, and we don't want you misbehaving when our guests arrive, now, do we?"

Chancy marveled at the mayor's gall. The man had no right to tell another how much he could drink. He marveled even more at how meekly Carter gave in.

"Whatever you say, Broom. I reckon I wasn't thinking. But you know how much I like bug juice."

"You'd suck it down from dawn until dusk if you could."

"Dusk, hell," Carter said, and cackled. "I'd suck it down plumb to midnight."

Some of the others laughed.

The mayor led the exodus out. Other onlookers had followed, and he stepped to one side and addressed them all. "Pay attention. I'll only say this once. We have a herd on the way. The first in a while to stop. I want everyone on their best behavior. Whatever they want, we give them. You're to be polite and courteous at all times."

"Do we lick their boots too?" Reid said.

"I mean it," Mayor Broom said. "None of your crustiness or you'll answer to Ives."

Chancy perked his ears. There was that name again. "Who is he? You've mentioned him before."

"He sort of keeps the peace around here," Mayor Broom said.

"Ives is the closest we have to a lawman. You could say he's our tin star even though he doesn't actually wear one."

That struck Chancy as strange, but then again, "You have a doc who isn't a doc, and look at how well he does."

"Thank you for the praise," Laverne Dodger said.

"Exactly my point," Mayor Broom declared. "We like to keep things informal, Mr. Gantry. To do as the Bible says and love our neighbors."

"You're laying it on too thick," Reid said. "He can tell just by looking at us that none of us are Bible-thumpers."

"I could kick you," Mayor Broom said angrily. To Chancy he said, "Pay him no mind. Reid was born a grump and his disposition hasn't improved any since he came out of the womb."

Carter erupted in mirth, and Reid glared.

"Now enough of this," the mayor said. Coming over, he draped his arm around Chancy's shoulder. "What say we repair to the saloon and you can have a drink on us and wash down all the trail dust you must have swallowed on your way up from Texas?"

"Mayor, that's the best offer I've had in a coon's age," Chancy said eagerly. He let His Honor usher him down the street. The batwings creaked noisily as they entered.

Chancy inhaled deeply and smiled. Saloons all smelled the same. The liquor, the cigar smoke, the spittoons, and sometimes, like now, the scent of perfume, were enough to drain his worries away like water down a hole in a barrel. He stopped and drank it in.

There was the usual bar, and tables for cards and dice. No piano, though, which was a shame, since Chancy liked music. Several men were ranged along the bar and a few others were playing cards. At the back, at a table by himself, sat another man.

None of them interested Chancy as much as the two female visions who peeled themselves from the bar and sashayed toward him. "Doves, by golly," he said in delight.

"Of course," Mayor Broom said. "What kind of saloon would it be if there weren't any?"

One was a blonde, the other a brunette. The blonde had curls and bright red lips and was plump in the middle and heavy in the thighs, but she had about the nicest smile anywhere. The brunette's hair hung straight. She was thin and had bumps for breasts, but her legs were long and nice, and she swayed her hips saucily.

"What have we here?" the blonde said in a sultry voice that tingled Chancy's spine.

"Where'd you find this handsome fella?" the brunette said.

"Ladies, permit me to make the introductions," Mayor Broom said. "This here is Chancy Gantry, Texas cowboy." He nodded at the blonde. "Chancy, I'd like you to meet Della Neece. This other gal is Margie."

"Margaret Hampton," the thin dove said. "But I don't like Margaret. I like Margie better."

"A pleasure," Chancy said.

"Not yet it's not," Della said, taking hold of his arm and playfully snuggling against him. "But it might be later if you play your cards right."

Margie took his other arm and giggled in his ear. "We're friendly as anything once we've had enough to drink."

Chancy thought he must be dreaming. "A dove on either arm. I must have died and gone to heaven."

The ladies laughed and Della gave his arm another squeeze. "Why, listen to you, you silver-tongued devil."

"I like a man who flatters a gal," Margie said.

Chancy grew warm all over.

"Ladies, ladies," Mayor Broom said. "I hate to spoil your fun, but in case you haven't heard, there's a herd on the way with a lot of other cowpokes who will want female companionship. Don't lavish it all on Mr. Gantry."

Chancy could have punched him.

"Which reminds me," Mayor Broom said. "How many hands are there, exactly? Just so we know."

Chancy didn't see where it mattered much. "Fourteen. And the trail boss and the cook."

"So sixteen? That's good. That's real good."

"How so?" Chancy asked.

"We wouldn't want there to be too many for us to handle," Mayor Broom said, and winked and grinned.

Chapter 11

Ollie Teal returned in less than an hour. He wasn't alone.

By then Chancy had downed a couple of drinks and was feeling happy with the world and everyone in it. The doves were a delight. They talked and joked and helped him forget the ordeal with Finger. He was so absorbed in his whiskey and the ladies that he didn't pay much attention to what was going on around him until he happened to glance to the rear at the man at a table by himself.

It was as if a glass of cold water had been thrown in his face.

The man radiated menace, like a cougar about to pounce. He wore a wide-brimmed black hat, a black vest, and a black shirt. His hair was black too and hung to his shoulders. His face was downright cruel, with eyes that glittered flint. Above the table poked the pearl handles of matching revolvers worn high in twin holsters. Colts, from the looks of them.

Chancy paused with his glass almost to his mouth. "Who in the world?" he blurted.

Mayor Broom had been hovering the whole while, and he quickly stepped in and said, "That there is Ives, the gent I was telling you about."

Out of the corner of his eye, Chancy saw Della give an involuntary shudder.

"You can see why we let him keep the peace," the mayor continued. "You might say he's our resident gun hand. Although, truth to tell, all the boys are pretty handy with a pistol."

It wasn't until that moment that Chancy realized every

man in the place, with the exception of the mayor, was heeled. Even the bartender had a revolver strapped around his waist. Most towns, only some of the men went around armed.

The mayor saw him looking. "I know what you're thinking, Mr. Gantry. But look at where we are. Indian Territory, with hostiles everywhere. Outlaws too and ruffians of every stripe, who flock to the territory because there is so little law." He gestured at the saloon-goers. "To keep trouble at bay, we stay prepared. I've personally asked our good citizens to always wear their sidearms. As a precaution, you understand?"

"Makes sense," Chancy supposed.

"It works," Mayor Broom said. "We haven't had a lick of trouble. Oh, rough characters wander by now and then, but they think better of acting up and go their merry way."

"Or get planted," Carter said, earning a harsh glance from Broom.

Chancy had forgotten the man was hanging around. He was about to ask how many men they'd had to plant when the batwings swung open and in strode Lucas Stout with Ollie Teal in tow.

Chancy set down his drink so fast he sloshed some on his hand. Wiping it on his pants, he went over. "Boss. Finger has been taken care of."

"So Ollie told me," Stout said.

"I was waiting for you to get here," Chancy said by way of explaining his presence in the saloon. As it turned out, he was worried over nothing.

Mayor Broom was coming toward them and offering his pudgy hand. "Mr. Stout, isn't it? Trail boss for the Flying V, Mr. Gantry has informed me. I can't tell you how pleased we are that you might bring your herd to our little paradise."

"Is that so?" Stout said, shaking hands.

"Feel free to graze your cattle where you like, and help yourself to the water from our lake. Anything you and your men want, anything at all, you have only to ask and we'll try our best to accommodate you."

"That's right friendly," Stout said.

"Oh, it's more than that," Mayor Broom said. "As you've no doubt guessed, much of the business we do stems from men like yourself. We don't have a railhead to offer, as Wichita does. So we offer what little we do have in the hope you'll be free with your spending."

"And fill your pokes while we're at it."

"Our secret is out," Mayor Broom said, and laughed. "Give us credit for being honest about it."

"You're that," Lucas Stout said. He scanned the drinkers and the cardplayers and his gaze fixed on the man in black at the far table.

As usual, Mayor Broom was quick to notice. "That's Ives. As I've explained to Mr. Gantry, he sort of keeps the peace around here. He's our resident gun hand, as it were."

"I have a couple of my own," Stout said.

"Oh?"

The trail boss looked over his shoulder. As if it were a signal, the batwings opened and in sauntered Jelly Varnes. A few steps behind him came Ben Rigenaw.

Jelly was only a couple of years older than Chancy. A happy-go-lucky sort, he was always smiling. He smiled while he worked. He smiled while he ate. Rumor had it he smiled when he shot someone too. He had a round face, almost babylike, with sparkling blue eyes and hair the same color as Della's and just as curly. On his hip nestled an ivory-handled, short-barreled Colt with which he was uncommonly proficient.

In Chancy's opinion, and that of some of the other hands, Ben Rigenaw was quicker. On a couple of occasions Rigenaw and Jelly had practiced together, shooting at bottles and such, and while Jelly might disagree, it was plain that Rigenaw was a shade faster. Not only that, Chancy always had the impression the older man was holding back.

Rigenaw was in his thirties. He had brown hair, cut short, and brown eyes that hinted at uncommon depths. He had been a cowboy nearly all his life and had been on several trail drives. His experience with cattle was second only to Lucas Stout's, and maybe Addison's. His experience with pistols was second to none. Like Ives, Rigenaw was a two-gun man. They were rare. Most men could draw and shoot with the hand they used most. To do it with two hands, at the same time and with equal accuracy, took special skill. Rigenaw preferred Remingtons with rosewood grips, and he was a wizard with both. His clothes were ordinary cowpoke duds, bought at a general store. His only condescension to fashion was a large silver belt buckle in the shape of a wolf's head, and tassels that hung from the bottom of his holsters.

Chancy once asked him about the wolf and Rigenaw replied that he wore the buckle because he used to "howl at the moon when I was younger and dumber." The holsters with the tassels had been given to him by a "female friend," which was all Rigenaw would say about it, and no one was about to pry.

Jelly Varnes stopped next to Lucas Stout and stared at the back table. "Well, lookee there, boys," he said with his inevitable smile. "A rooster among the hens."

"Among what, now?" Mayor Broom said.

Ives met Jelly's stare with a quirk of his lips that might pass for a smirk.

Ben Rigenaw came to a stop on Stout's other side. He too stared at the man in black.

Ives lost all interest in Jelly. Focused solely on Rigenaw, he rose, pushing his chair back with his foot. His hands loose at his sides, close to his Colts, he came toward them smiling. But on him the smile was as warm as a frigid blast of Arctic wind.

"Ives!" Mayor Broom said. "I'd like you to meet Mr. Lucas Stout and some of his cowhands."

Up close, the man in black was taller and wider than Chancy had imagined. He didn't know what to expect, but it certainly wasn't what Ives said.

"Welcome to Prosperity, gents. Where only the good die young."

Chapter 12

Mayor Broom uttered a nervous bark. "What kind of thing is that to say to our guests? Be civil, if you please."

Ignoring the mayor, Ives stared only at Ben Rigenaw. "Not often I run across any like us."

Rigenaw didn't respond.

"You ever have a hankering to prove you're the top of the heap, I'll be here," Ives said. He had a low, gravelly voice that made Chancy think of a grizzly hungry for raw meat.

Again Ben Rigenaw didn't reply.

"Enough of that kind of talk," Mayor Broom said.

"Wolf got your tongue?" Ives said to Rigenaw, and flicked a finger at Rigenaw's belt buckle. "Or is it that you don't stand up for yourself?"

"When I have to, I do." Rigenaw broke his silence.

Jelly Varnes had lost his smile. "What am I? Chopped liver? I stand up for my own self. Ask anyone. Or try me. Anytime."

"Listen to you," Ives said. "You'd be easy to rile."

Mayor Broom took half a step between them. "Gentlemen, gentlemen. What's all this talk of riling? We're friends here, or we soon will be. Prosperity is nothing if not hospitable, and I hope you give us the chance to prove it."

"Hospitable," Ives said. Another quirk of his mouth, and he touched his hat brim and went on around Ben Rigenaw, nearly brushing against him, and out the batwings.

"You have to excuse him," Mayor Broom said. "He's not as sociable as the rest of us. Some people are that way, I'm afraid." Broom had the temerity to pluck at Lucas Stout's sleeve. "Why don't I treat you to drinks all around and we can become better acquainted?"

"There will be time for drinks later," Stout said. "Tonight, after we've bedded the herd and set up camp."

"Then you've made up your mind. Excellent. But why bother with a camp when you can have a roof over your heads?" the mayor said. "We have cabins to spare. Enough for all of you if three or four bunk together."

"It would be nice to have a roof for once," Ollie said hopefully.

"We stay with the herd, except for Finger and whoever I pick to be with him," Lucas Stout said.

"Your man is being well looked after, I assure you," Mayor Broom said. "Ask Mr. Gantry."

Chancy nodded. "The fella who operated on him is keeping a close eye on things."

"Even so," Stout said.

"Whatever you deem best," Mayor Broom said. "You're a cautious man, Mr. Stout. And I don't blame you, being in charge of a herd and the punchers and all. I have this town to watch out for, so I'm the same way."

Chancy smothered a snort. The mayor had all the caution of a patent medicine salesman.

"We'll see you later, then," Lucas Stout said, and wheeling, he strode out with Ben Rigenaw right behind him. Jelly gave the shelves of liquor a longing look and jingled after them.

"Lucky devil," Ollie said to Chancy. "Getting to have a drink already."

"We'd best catch up," Chancy said.

Their boss and the gun hands had stopped past the overhang and were surveying the main and only street.

"What do you think?" Lucas Stout asked Ben Rigenaw.

Rigenaw shrugged. "We see his kind everywhere."

"Is it bluster or for real?" Stout said.

"He didn't strike me as full of hot air," Rigenaw said. "Reckless neither. We should be all right so long as the mayor keeps him in line."

"Should be," Stout said dubiously.

"Shucks, boss," Jelly Varnes said. "He causes any trouble, I'll deal with him for you."

"Not you," Rigenaw said. "Me."

"I'm not no slouch," Jelly said.

Stout nipped their disagreement in the bud with "Neither of you is to skin your six-shooter unless I say so or he goes for his mother-of-pearls first. Savvy?"

"I hope he does," Jelly said. He gazed past them, and stiffened. "Good Lord. Take a gander at the scarecrow."

Laverne Dodger had hobbled out of the stable and was making for the cabin where Finger Howard had been taken. With his scarred face, his missing arm, and his peg leg, the comparison wasn't unwarranted.

"He's the doc," Chancy said. "His name is Dodger. He got blown up in the war."

"He'd give an infant nightmares," Jelly said.

"That man saved Finger's life," Lucas Stout said. "So I'll say to you the same thing the mayor said to that Ives. Be civil."

"It's not as if I was going to go over and ask him if he scares babies for a living," Jelly said.

"That would be mean," Ollie said.

"Although he could likely take over for the bogeyman and make a fortune at it," Jelly said, and his smile bloomed.

"Damn you, Varnes. Don't make me tell you twice," Stout said.

Grinning, Jelly held his hands up, palms out. "I'm only joshing. I'll mind my p's and q's like everybody else."

"I've always wondered about that," Ollie interjected.

"About what?" Lucas Stout said.

"Why only the p's and the q's? I never had any schooling, but even I know there's a whole, what do you call it, alphabet. Why not mind our c's and our r's? Or those a's and those z's?"

Lucas Stout sighed and shook his head. "You are a wonderment, Teal."

"I am?" Ollie said.

"Want me to shoot him?" Ben Rigenaw said.

Chancy laughed mightily.

"Why waste the lead?" Lucas Stout said, and motioned for them to head up the street.

Dodger had reached the cabin, seen them coming, and stopped to wait.

"Are you saying none of you ever thought about that p and q business?" Ollie said.

"Drop it," Stout said.

"Maybe have Chancy shoot him," Rigenaw said. "Ollie is his pard."

"I don't know how he does it," Stout said.

"Who does what?" Ollie said.

Laverne Dodger acted surprised when Lucas Stout thrust a hand at him and pumped his arm with vigor.

"Mr. Dodger, I believe it is. I hear I have you to thank for saving Finger Howard. We're all of us obliged. Anything I can do for you, anything at all that's in my power, you only have to ask."

"That's decent of you," Dodger said.

Stout fished in his pocket and brought out his poke. "How much do we owe you?"

Dodger hesitated, then said, "Not a cent."

"A sawbones always charges."

"I'm a stableman," Dodger said.

"Who saves lives when he's not forking hay," Stout said. "I haven't been to a doc in ages, but twenty dollars should cover it."

"I couldn't."

"I insist."

"I won't, I say, and don't try to make me take it."

Clearly puzzled, Lucas Stout slid his poke into his pocket. "If thanks is all you want, then it's thanks you'll get. But at least let us buy you a drink or three tonight at the saloon."

"I will do that," Dodger said, and opened the cabin door. "After you, gents. If he's asleep, try not to wake him."

Finger Howard was out to the world. The incision was red and puffy, but otherwise the swelling was gone. His color had returned, and he wasn't sweating nearly as much.

"My prognosis is a full recovery," Dodger said as he pulled the blanket to Howard's chin.

"How long before he's back on his feet?" Lucas Stout asked. "Better yet, how long before he can sit a horse?"

"In a few days he'll be walking fairly fine," Dodger said. "I'd give him a week, though, before he's ready to do any riding."

"We can't wait around that long."

Laverne Dodger said a strange thing. "It's for the best that you don't."

Chapter 13

After a spectacular sunset, Prosperity turned into a rip-roarer.

Every man in town, or so the mayor mentioned, made a beeline for the saloon. Chancy reckoned there were close to forty. Add to that the seven trail hands Lucas Stout let come in—the rest had to stay with the herd—as well as the cook, and the saloon was jammed.

Then there were the women. Della and Margie weren't the only doves who worked there. An older gal called Cora joined them. So did a vision of loveliness by the name of Missy Burke.

Missy was the youngest of the doves, the same age as Chancy and Ollie, with lustrous chestnut hair that fell in waves past her shoulders, a face an angel would envy, and a figure that took a man's breath away. At least it took Chancy's. Her face was exquisite: oval, with a smooth complexion, dazzling green eyes, and lips as full as ripe strawberries. When she smiled, he would swear her teeth gleamed.

Chancy was pouring himself a drink when Cora and Missy came in through the back, and his mouth dropped. He couldn't take his eyes off Missy. Moving as gracefully as a swan, she smiled and nodded at men she knew, and received a hug from Della, who squealed, "Missy Burke! Where have you been all day?"

Someone nudged Chancy's elbow and Ollie snickered and said, "You catching flies?"

"Don't you see her?" Chancy blurted.

Ollie looked over. "Which one?"

"Are you blind?" Chancy said. "The young one in the blue dress."

"She's all right."

Chancy tore his gaze from the ravishing embodiment of womanhood. "All right? She's more than all right. She's the prettiest girl I ever saw."

"And you're not even drunk yet," Ollie teased.

Chancy finished pouring and took a gulp. He savored the taste and the warmth, but they were nothing compared to the feeling that had come over him. He imagined himself going over and taking her hand and introducing himself, imagined spending the evening with her, and many more evenings besides. She was so beautiful any man would be happy to be in her company. "I bet she's married."

"Huh?" Ollie said.

"A girl as pretty as her, she has to be hitched."

"And her husband lets her flaunt herself in a saloon?" Ollie said. "And people say I'm the one who is a mite slow between the ears."

Chancy had to admit his pard had a point. As a general rule, married gents didn't like other men pawing their wives. "If that's true, I have died and gone to heaven."

"How many drinks have you had?" Ollie asked.

"What's that got to do with anything?"

"Oh, nothing. Only you haven't even met her yet and you act like you're in love."

"Blazes, you're right. Here. Watch my drink." Chancy set it down and threaded through the merrymakers to where Missy Burke stood talking to Margie. He was behind her and to get her attention he lightly tapped her on the shoulder, saying, "Pardon me, ma'am."

"Yes?" Missy Burke said, turning. She gave a start, and looked him up and down, her cheeks coloring. "Who might you be?"

"I'm—" Chancy began, and his throat froze up. He tried to speak, but nothing came out. To make it worse, his body became red-hot, and he broke out in a sweat.

"Yes?" Missy Burke said again.

"I . . . ," Chancy said.

"Are you all right?"

A familiar laugh added to Chancy's embarrassment. Ollie had come over and was holding both their drinks.

"You have to excuse my pard, ma'am. He doesn't get to hobnob much with gracious ladies like you. I'm Ollie Teal and his handle is Chancy Gantry. His full name is Chancellor Floyd Gantry, but he hates the Floyd and thinks Chancellor sounds foreign, so he only uses Chancy. I'd never have known, only he got drunk one night and told me all his secrets. Or as much of them as he remembered, I reckon, before he passed out."

Missy Burke put a hand to her throat and smiled. "Oh my. Aren't you something?"

"Me, ma'am?" Ollie said. "I'm a puncher, is all. I work as a trail hand for now. Chancy too. He talked me into it. Said we'd get to see some of the world and make some extra money. So far we haven't seen much except some countryside and a few towns like this one, but I expect that will change when we get to Kansas. They say Wichita is as wild as anything, and a sight worth seeing."

Missy Burke looked at Chancy. "Does he always go on like this?"

Chancy coughed, and found his voice. "Only when he opens his mouth." Her laughter sent a tingle through him clear down to his toes. "But as pards go, he can't be beat."

"Why, thank you, Chancellor," Ollie said.

Missy Burke appeared delighted. "You two are cautions. I'm glad we've met. There aren't many here as young as me."

"There's one younger in our outfit," Ollie said. "His name is Mays. He doesn't even have peach fuzz on his chin yet."

"I'd be grateful if you'd let me buy you a drink," Chancy said.

"It's why I'm here."

Chancy gave her a quizzical look.

"To entice men into buying drinks and spending their money in other ways." Missy caught herself and, to Chancy's immense joy, slipped her arm through his. "Why don't we go to the bar? It's a little more private."

Chancy didn't see how, but he was eager to comply.

"Can I come too?" Ollie asked.

"You certainly may," Missy Burke said. "You're his pard, aren't you? And a lot of fun, besides."

"I am?" Ollie said, and blushed a deep red.

Missy hooked her other arm in Ollie's. "The three of us will spend a little time together and get better acquainted."

"Gosh, ma'am," Ollie said. "A lady's never taken my arm before."

"Not even your mother or your sisters?"

"My ma mostly took a wooden spoon to me when I did something that didn't suit her, and my sisters hardly ever touched me." Ollie paused. "Say, how did you know I even had any?"

"A lucky guess," Missy Burke said.

"I wish I had your brains," Ollie said. "Most of my guesses end up being wrong. Like that time the butcher filled a jar with marbles and said whoever guessed how many there were would win a side of beef. Ma made all of us guess and wrote our guesses on slips of papers so we'd have more chances to win."

"How did you do?" Missy asked when he didn't go on.

"I guessed there were forty-two marbles in the jar."

"And how many were there?"

"As I recollect, one hundred and seventy-three."

"Oh my. You were a ways off."

"My ma wasn't pleased. But she had to write my number down because the butcher was right there. When we got home she took her spoon to me. I couldn't sit for half a day."

"That was terrible of her."

"I don't blame her so much," Ollie said. "She liked to say that since I wasn't born with brains, she'd beat them into me. She sure tried her best."

"Your own mother."

"I didn't have any other. If I'd had, the other one would probably have beaten me with her spoon too. I was lucky to have any backside left when I got too old to be spooned."

Missy laughed, but Chancy didn't think it was humorous. "You shouldn't be talking about backsides and such."

"Why not?" Ollie said. "Everybody has one."

They reached the bar. Amazingly an empty space opened, and Missy Burke steered them into it and let go of their arms. "Now, then. What's your poison?"

Chancy was about to point out that they already had drinks when Jelly Varnes appeared out of nowhere, planted himself in front of Missy Burke, and pushed his hat back on his head so his curls spilled out.

"What do we have here?"

Chapter 14

Chancy Gantry felt a surge of anger. Resentment so keen it pierced him like a knife.

"Shoo," Ollie said. "She's with us."

"Not anymore she's not." With a grand flourish, Jelly clasped Missy Burke's hand, raised it to his lips, and lightly kissed her knuckles.

"Goodness gracious," Missy said.

"I'd enjoy making your acquaintance, ma'am," Jelly said, "and expect you'll enjoy making mine."

"Aren't you humble?" Missy said.

"He's not showing good manners," Chancy said. "Make yourself scarce, Varnes."

Jelly and Missy both looked surprised.

"What's gotten into you, Gantry?" the young gun hand said. "Why take that tone with me?"

"He's smitten," Ollie said.

Chancy—and Jelly—and Missy all said, "What?" at the same time.

"Why, we've only just met," Missy said. "He doesn't know me well enough to be smitten."

"It doesn't take much," Ollie said. "I've seen gents smitten by a whiff of perfume."

Jelly Varnes laughed. "Don't this beat all?" He tilted his head and studied Chancy, and laughed again. "Tell you what, though. We both ride for the same brand and you've never given me cause to dislike you, so I'll let this pass. You can have some time alone with the lady. But don't expect to hog it. Some of the rest of us might be interested." He winked and grinned at Missy Burke and ambled off.

"He thinks he's everything," Ollie grumbled.

"Oh, I don't know," Missy said. "He's rather handsome."

Chancy's ears began to burn. For a short while he had forgotten they were in the middle of a crowded saloon. There had been only her and him and Ollie. Everyone else had faded into the background, as if they weren't really there. Jelly shattered that illusion. Suddenly the voices around them swelled, and he became all too aware of the press of bodies.

"Nothing to say, Chancellor?" Missy said.

"I'd rather you called me Chancy."

"I don't know. I like Chancellor. It has a dignity about it," Missy said. "My real name is ordinary."

Chancy was reluctant to pry, but his pard had no such qualms.

"What is your real name, ma'am?" Ollie asked.

"Promise not to tell?" Missy said.

"I promise not to tell other people," Ollie said.

"Who else is there to tell it to?"

"My horse."

"I beg your pardon?"

"I talk to my horse a lot. Especially when I'm riding herd alone and there's no one else to talk to. I tell him things I'd never tell anyone else. So I can't promise I might not tell him your name."

"Ollie, you're precious," Missy said, and reaching up, she brushed a finger across his cheek.

"Good Lord, ma'am," Ollie said, and turned even redder than before. "Warn a fella when you're fixing to do that." He coughed and fidgeted, then said, "You haven't said what your name is."

Missy lowered her voice. "Geraldine."

"Geraldine?" Ollie practically hollered. "What's wrong with that? I have an aunt named Geraldine. And there was a lady over to the county seat, the wife of a baker. She was named Geraldine too. It's right popular."

"I've never liked it," Missy said. "The same way Chancellor doesn't like his."

"Wait a minute," Ollie said. "How did you get from Geraldine to Missy? Shouldn't it be Gissy?"

Missy squealed with glee and clapped her hands.

"What's gotten into her?" Ollie said to Chancy.

"You, you lunkhead."

Missy was shaking her head and chuckling. "When I was little, Ollie, my pa used to call me his little miss. That stuck, and when I got older, they dropped the 'little' and I became Missy."

"Names sure are peculiar," Ollie said. "I had another cousin called Abimelech. Who names a fella that? We called him Frank on account of he liked it best of all the men names he'd ever heard."

"You don't say."

Chancy realized he'd hardly said a word except when Jelly butted in. He figured he'd better say something soon to show Missy he could hold up his end of a conversation. It needed to be something smart. Something clever. Taking a breath, he said the first thing that came into his head. "How would you like to go out with me sometime?"

"You and me?" Missy said.

"I don't think he means me," Ollie said. "We go practically everywhere together as it is."

Chancy made bold to do as Jelly had done, and grasped Missy's hand. "Yes, you and me. Just the two of us."

"Are you saying you want to court me, Chancellor?" Missy asked as if he must be loco.

Chancy didn't even have to think about it. "I reckon I am," he said, nodding. "If you're not attached to anyone else, that is."

Missy grinned. "The only person I'm attached to is me."

"I'm attached to my horse," Ollie said.

"Please hush," Chancy said. He was still holding Missy's hand, and the feel of her skin, so soft and so warm, set him to tingling anew. "What do you say, Miss Burke?"

"Aren't you formal?" Missy said, and laughed, but it wasn't a mocking laugh. "No one has ever asked to court me before."

"How can that be?" Chancy marveled. He'd have expected every man she met to want to.

Missy bit her bottom lip, glanced quickly around, then

said quietly, "Why not? But we have to keep it between ourselves. Reid finds out, he'll take a switch to me."

"Reid?" Chancy said, remembering how crusty and unfriendly the man had been. "What's he got to do with it?"

"He runs the saloon for Broom," Missy said. "He's my boss."

"Damn," Chancy said before he could stop himself.

"How about if you come by at noon tomorrow?" Missy proposed. "I'll have an hour or so free."

"I'll be here," Chancy vowed.

"And you." Missy addressed Ollie. "You'll be quiet about it?"

"Can I tell my horse?"

Missy snorted, and put a hand over her nose. "Yes, you may."

Ollie grinned. "Then your secret is safe. My horse won't tell a soul."

Chapter 15

It was all Chancy could think about the rest of the night. He got to enjoy ten more minutes with her, talking about where she came from (Indiana) and how she had ended up in Prosperity (Della brought her and the other girls). He would have talked to her the rest of the night, but Reid came striding up.

"What's going on here, woman? I pay you to mingle. You've been with these two long enough."

"They bought me a drink," Missy said, holding it up.

"Only one?" Reid said. "And I see a lot of other hombres with empty hands." He gripped her wrist and gave her a push. "Mingle, damn it, before I get my dander up."

Chancy's already was. "Let go of her."

"Chancellor, don't," Missy said.

"Chancellor?" Reid said.

Chancy shoved him, hard. So hard Reid stumbled a couple of steps and bumped into others, and had to grab a chair to keep from falling. His cheeks flushed, and as he straightened, he moved his hand close to his Remington. "You miserable cowpoke," he snarled. "No one lays a hand on me."

"You were laying a hand on Missy," Ollie said.

"Keep out of this, jackass," Reid snapped. He pushed a man to make room and took another half step back. "Whenever you think you're man enough, cowboy."

"Reid, no," Missy said.

"Shut the hell up, girl," Reid snarled without looking at her. "This is your fault for not doing your job." He fell into a slight crouch, his fingers splayed. "Don't keep me waiting, boy."

Chancy was thunderstruck. He'd never been in a shooting affray. The closest he'd come was once in Texas when he'd witnessed a shootout between two drunks, neither of whom could hit the broad side of the saloon unless they stood next to it. Other drinkers had broken them apart before they did any harm.

"Say something," Reid said. "Or are you too busy wetting yourself?"

Chancy moved a step out from the bar.

"Pard, no," Ollie said.

Missy's eyes went wide with fright. "Both of you. There's no need for this. None whatsoever."

"I won't tell you again to shut up," Reid growled. "This cowpoke laid a hand on me."

Chancy's mouth had gone dry and his heart was thumping in his chest. "You shouldn't have manhandled her."

"She works for me, boy. I can do any damn thing I want."

Chancy became aware the saloon had gone quiet. Word had spread, and a roomful of statues were awaiting the outcome.

"Jerk that smoke wagon, boy," Reid taunted. "Or should someone do it for you?"

Chancy girded himself to draw. He had no idea how fast Reid was, but that didn't matter. He had to prove himself, to show Missy, and everyone else, he wasn't yellow. He was on the verge of swooping his hand to his own Remington when the unexpected occurred.

Mayor Broom stepped between them. "That will be quite enough," he said to Reid. "I leave the saloon for five minutes and look at what happens."

"Out of the way," Reid rasped.

"You know that's not going to happen," Mayor Broom said, "and you know why. I'll thank you to control yourself and go outside for some fresh air and simmer down."

"He laid a hand on me."

"He's with the herd," Mayor Broom said.

"I don't care."

"The rest of us do."

"I don't care," Reid said once more.

"We don't get that many. We have to be hospitable. I've made that perfectly plain and everyone agreed."

"Move out of the way."

To Chancy's considerable surprise, the mayor stayed put.

"Listen to me, Reid. You can't let your temper get the better of you. You gave your word, remember? The same as everyone else. I expect you to abide by it. *He* does too. And you don't want to make him mad, do you?"

Chancy figured the mayor must be talking about Ives.

"Damn it, Broom," Reid said. "You and your tricks."

"This isn't one of them," Mayor Broom said. "This is man-to-man. A request, if you will. Back off, or else."

Chancy wasn't quite sure what they were arguing about. Part of it had to do with him, but another matter was at stake, a more important matter, from the way the mayor talked. He decided to apologize. It might smooth Reid's ruffled feathers, and no one would think less of him.

But suddenly someone else was there. Ives, the one in black, the two-gun man with the pearl-handled Colts. He seemed to materialize out of thin air. His hands were at his sides, and his posture was as relaxed as if he were in a pew in church. He smiled that icy smile of his and said as mildly as anything, "Problem?"

Reid went rigid.

"No," Mayor Broom said.

"Sounds like a problem to me," Ives said. He gazed about the room. "Looks like one too. You could hear a pin drop in here."

"I've taken care of it," Mayor Broom said.

"Have you, now?" Ives squared on Reid, and now his body was as taut as wire and his voice as hard as quartz. "Why is it always you? This makes, what, two or three times now? The last was over your cut."

"Ives, no," Broom said.

"No more out of you," Ives said without looking at him. "This is between Reid and me."

"I'm not looking for trouble with you," Reid said.

"You make trouble for everyone else, you make it with me," Ives said. "That's how it's always been." He paused. "You have two ways to go. Fill your hand or drag your tail."

"That's no choice."

"It's all you've got. Your six-gun, or you say you're sorry."

Reid gestured at Chancy. "To *him*?"

"And everybody else, for disturbing the peace."

Chancy didn't expect Reid to do it. The man was too mad. Yet, to his astonishment, Reid straightened and his shoulders slumped, and he said loudly so everyone would hear, but to no one in particular, "I'm sorry." Then, tucking his chin to his chest, he barreled out of the saloon as if he couldn't get out of there fast enough.

"Trouble over," Ives declared.

Mayor Broom wasn't pleased. "Join me out back, would you? We need to have words."

"That's one thing you're good at," Ives said, but he went along.

The spell was broken. A few men swore. Others laughed. Hushed conversations broke out, and people moved again.

"That Ives must be hell on wheels," Ollie said.

"Is he ever!" Missy Burke said. "Whatever you do, don't tangle with him or he'll bury you."

Chapter 16

Chancy would have liked to ask her a million questions about her life before she came to Prosperity and whatever else he could think of, but Missy excused herself and went off to mingle.

"She sure is nice," Ollie remarked.

"The nicest." Chancy watched her, feeling absolutely fine for all of half a minute. Then someone blocked his view.

"Outside," Lucas Stout said.

"Uh-oh," Ollie said.

Chancy followed the trail boss through the batwings and out into the cool of night. Stars filled the sky and in the distance a coyote yipped.

"What was that all about?" Lucas Stout said. "As if I can't guess."

Chancy clamped his lips tight.

"Listen," Stout said. "A good trail boss never pries into a hand's personal life. Except when it affects the outfit. And this does. We'll only be here another day at the most, and when we go, we have to leave Finger behind. He'll be under their care. We want to part company on good terms. Savvy?"

"I know all that," Chancy got out.

"Then why were you about to throw down on Reid?"

"It wasn't his fault," Ollie said. "That other fella grabbed hold of Chancy's girl and it riled him."

"Your girl?" Stout said.

Chancy felt himself grow warm for what had to be the fifth or sixth time that night. "We only just met."

Lucas Stout sighed. He closed his eyes and rubbed them, then stared up at the stars. "I've never seen it to fail. On every drive there's always one or two who fall head over spurs for some filly who catches their eye."

"She's the prettiest gal I ever saw," Chancy said.

"Of course she is. And she almost got Reid or you shot."

"That wasn't her fault."

"You're right," Lucas Stout said. "It's yours. I don't expect my men to be paragons of virtue, as a parson might say. But I do expect them to use common sense. I told everyone back at camp that we're all to be on our best behavior while we're here. Anyone hankers to howl at the moon, they can do it in Wichita after they've been paid and the outfit can't be blamed for their antics."

"I didn't mean to cause trouble," Chancy said. "It just happened."

"Gantry, you're young, but I've always thought you had a good head on your shoulders. Don't go chasing a skirt you'll never see again. And no gunplay, you hear me? Not without more cause than you had in there."

For some reason Chancy's memory flashed back to the time he was eight and his pa took him to the woodshed. "I won't get into any more trouble, Mr. Stout. I promise."

"I hope you keep it," Stout said. He glanced to one side, into the shadows. "I'm heading back to camp. Are you coming?"

Chancy was startled to see Ben Rigenaw come out of the dark. The gun hand had been there the whole time.

"Well, howdy, Ben," Ollie said. "You sure are sneaky."

"You want some advice, Teal?" Rigenaw said.

"From you?" Ollie said. "Why, sure. There's no one I respect more. What's it about? Have I been talking to my horse too much?"

"Has it ever kicked you in the head?"

"My horse? Why would he do a thing like that? He likes me as much as I like him. Besides, I wouldn't own one that's a kicker. I knew a man who got his brains bashed out once by a mustang. I like my horses tame and easy to ride."

"My advice, Teal," Ben Rigenaw said, "is to keep a close eye on this pard of yours. I saw the whole thing, and that Reid doesn't strike me as the kind to turn the other cheek."

"You were there? I didn't see you. But then I was looking at that Reid at first, and then at that Ives. He sure is fearsome."

"For some he might be."

"Not for you? I reckon not, as good as you can draw and shoot. If I was as quick as you, I wouldn't be scared of anything. Except maybe grizzlies. I used to have nightmares about being eaten by a bear. When I was little, we had a neighbor whose dog got ate, and I saw what was left. I've been afraid of bears ever since."

"Ollie?"

"Yes, sir?"

Rigenaw gazed up and down the street and at the buildings around them. "You and your pard be careful. There's something about this place I don't like. It doesn't feel right."

"Feel right how? Like a coat that's too small?"

"Like when you hear a rattler but can't see it."

Chancy figured that Rigenaw meant Reid and Ives. "We won't get into any more trouble. I've given my word."

"See that you don't," Lucas Stout said. He wheeled toward the hitch rail and said, "You coming?" over his shoulder.

As Ben Rigenaw turned, he paused and said quietly, "Watch your backs, boys."

The trail boss and the gun hand swung onto their mounts, and Stout raised his reins.

"Be at the herd by midnight."

"We will," Chancy said. He was eager to go back into the saloon and be near Missy Burke.

"That Rigenaw sure is nice," Ollie remarked.

"You think everybody is."

"That's not true," Ollie said indignantly. "That Ives is mean as anything. And Reid is always on the peck."

"Is that a fact?" someone said from across the street, and a figure moved toward them.

Chancy swore.

The light spilling from the saloon window lit the hate-stamped features of Ira Reid.

Chapter 17

Chancy tensed to go for his six-gun. He would draw and shoot and throw himself to one side at the same time. With luck, Reid would miss but he wouldn't.

But Reid made no attempt to go for his own six-shooter. Glaring, he stalked up and made as if to jab Chancy in the chest. But he glanced at the batwings and lowered his arm. "You're damn lucky, boy."

"Stop calling me that."

"We're men, the both of us," Ollie said. He had taken a step to the left and his hand was close to his holster.

"Stay out of this, idiot," Reid said.

"I'll do no such thing," Ollie replied. "He's my pard."

"He can't do better than a jackass like you?" Reid said.

For Chancy it was the last straw. And since Reid wasn't going for his hardware, he didn't go for his. Instead he punched him on the jaw.

The blow knocked Reid back a step, but he didn't go down. Fury gripped him, and he started to lower his hand to his Remington but once more glanced at the batwings. "No," he snarled. "Ives would gun me for sure." He pried at his belt buckle, saying, "You want fists, fine by me. They can't hold that against me. Not when you started it."

Chancy prided at his own belt.

"What are you doing?" Ollie said.

"Stay out of this," Chancy said.

"You heard the trail boss. Stay out of trouble, he told us."

Chancy was tired of Reid's insults. He got his gun belt off, wrapped the belt around the holster, and shoved them at Ollie. "Hold these for me."

"Pard, you shouldn't," Ollie said.

Reid had his own gun belt off and was draping it over the near end of the hitch rail. "I'm going to enjoy this."

"You like to hurt folks?" Ollie said.

"Who doesn't?"

Chancy raised his fists as he had seen some men do, but he had barely set himself when Ira Reid was on him. He blocked a right jab, but a looping left caught him low in the ribs and pain exploded up his side. Grunting, he backpedaled. Reid came after him. He countered a cross and was jarred by a blow to his cheek.

Reid was good with his fists, and knew it. "What's the matter, boy?" he gloated. "We're only getting started."

Hunching his shoulders and holding his elbows in front of his gut, Chancy thought he was ready, but the next flurry nearly overwhelmed him. For every punch he blocked, another got through. He was hit on the chin, on the ribs again, on the temple, on his ear. That last hurt the worst even though it only grazed him.

Ira Reid laughed. "I'd heard you Texicans are pitiful with your fists, but you take the cake."

Chancy's anger got the better of him. He closed in and swung, but he was reckless and his swing was too wide. Reid easily blocked, and the next instant it felt as if a hammer slammed into Chancy's stomach. He doubled over, saw a fist sweeping at his face, and jerked aside barely in time.

Simultaneously a shout came from the saloon. A head was poking over the batwings.

"Everybody! Come see! There's a fight!"

Boots pounded, and there were more yells.

Reid had been about to come at Chancy again, but he stopped and regarded the people pouring from the saloon with unease.

Chancy could guess why. He was grateful for the reprieve. His gut hurt so much he couldn't straighten.

Mayor Broom emerged, followed by Ives. Ives made as if to step into the street, but the mayor held out an arm, stopping him. "Hold on. Let's hear what this is about."

Reid was quick to say, "I didn't start it. The cowpoke did. And we're not using our guns."

"I can see that," Mayor Broom said. "Is he telling the truth, Mr. Gantry? You're the cause of this ruckus?"

"He insulted my pard," Chancy said, "and I hit him."

"That was awful sweet of you," Ollie said.

Ives gave him a strange look. "Sweet?"

"Sure. Like when someone says bad things about a lady you're with. You'd fight for her, wouldn't you? Like my pard is fighting for me."

Embarrassed, Chancy said, "You don't need to say any more."

"I'm not done," Ollie said. "More people should be sweet like you. It'd make the world a better place. My ma used to say that she fell in love with my pa because he was so sweet and I should go through life trying to be the same. Be sweet as sugar, she'd say, and then pinch my cheek and kiss me on the head."

Ives cocked his head from side to side as if studying a new sort of creature. "Are you sure you're a Texan?"

"How's that again?" Ollie said.

"I'm told your outfit is from down Texas way," Ives said, "but I never saw a Texan who acts anything like you."

"There aren't as many as sweet as me."

Reid had been glowering this whole while. "Can I get on with this, Broom? I want to pound him while my dander is up."

The mayor looked at Chancy. "Ordinarily I wouldn't permit it. But since you admit you're to blame, and since no six-guns are involved, I'm afraid I'll have to give my consent. Nothing personal, you understand, Mr. Gantry?"

"Let's do this," Chancy said. He wanted to get it over with. And hope that Lucas Stout didn't hear about it. But he'd forgotten that Ollie and him weren't the only hands there.

"Kick his slats in, Gantry!" Jelly Varnes whooped.

"You can do it!" Drew Case shouted.

"Show him what you're made of!" young Mays hollered.

"I already know the answer to that," Reid said. "You're made of mush." And sneering confidently, he waded in.

Chapter 18

Chancy had never traded punches with another man before. He'd never wanted to. By nature he had a peaceable disposition. His folks, like Ollie's, had impressed on him from an early age that he should try to get along with everyone, and he supposed that had stuck.

And now that his initial anger had faded, he felt a sudden lack of confidence. Reid was older. Reid *had* done this before. And Reid was hell-bent on beating him to a pulp.

It was all Chancy could do to defend himself as Reid unleashed a furious flurry that nearly drove him to his knees. He blocked. He twisted. He tried to sidestep. But punch after punch landed. Unless he rallied, he would be beaten senseless.

A blow caught him on the side of the head, and he reeled. He realized his hat was gone. But that was the least of his worries. He managed to avoid a straight arm to the face by throwing himself to one side. For a few seconds he was in the clear, and his gaze happened to drift to the onlookers and to alight on Missy Burke.

She stood with her hands clasped to her bosom, worry lighting her face. Her eyes caught his and something seemed to pass between them. He had a sense that they had touched minds, somehow. A sense that she was rooting for him, that she cared if he won or lost. And she yelled as loudly as the men were doing. "Hit him!" she screeched. "Knock him down!"

Something happened. A grim resolve came over Chancy, and a surge in confidence. He raised his arms higher and waited, and Reid came at him swinging. Chancy blocked a cross, then drove his right fist into Reid's gut with all the power in his body, driving in with his legs and whipping himself half around. He heard Reid grunt. It was music to his ears. He saw a look of shock on Reid's face. It added fuel to his inner fire. He swatted a weak counter and hit Reid twice on the chin so fast he wasn't even sure he threw the punches. Reid was jolted onto his bootheels and flapped his arms to steady himself, leaving himself wide-open.

Chancy showed no mercy. He pressed his attack, landing a solid right to the ribs, a left to the face, a right to the stomach that he buried almost to his wrist, a left to the face and a right to the face and another left and suddenly there was no one to hit, no one in front of him. He stopped swinging and blinked in confusion and saw Reid lying unconscious at his feet. "What?" he blurted.

People were cheering and clapping, and Jelly Varnes patted him on the back and Mays did the same on his shoulder. Addison was there. Ollie grabbed his arm and pumped it.

"You did it, pard!"

Chancy looked at Missy Burke and she smiled the finest smile any female had ever bestowed on him. He wanted to say he had done it for her, and it occurred to him that she knew that. He smiled back, and tasted blood.

And then Mayor Broom and Ives came up, blocking his view of Missy.

His friends faced them, standing on either side, backing him. Jelly Varnes stared hard at Ives.

"What?" Chancy said.

Mayor Broom frowned down at Reid. "He brought that on himself, the fool."

"I wouldn't have reckoned you had it in you, cowboy," Ives said.

"It was a fair fight," Chancy said.

"That it was," Mayor Broom agreed. "And I want to be sure there are no hard feelings. You and these others shouldn't hold Reid's actions against the entire town. The rest of us are happy to have you here, and invite you to stay as long as you'd like."

"It's not up to us," Chancy said. "It's up to the trail boss."

"I realize that," Broom said. Smiling, he held out his hand. "To be clear. No hard feelings?"

"Not from me," Chancy said, shaking hands. "Except at him." He nodded at Reid.

"We're going to have a long talk with him once he comes around," Mayor Broom said. "His shenanigans have to cease."

The mayor gave orders to several others and they lifted Reid none too gently and carried him into the saloon.

Chancy looked for Missy, but she was gone.

"We have to get you to camp, pard," Ollie said.

"No," Chancy said. He wanted to go talk to Missy.

"Listen to him," Jelly Varnes said. "You're a mess."

"I am?" Chancy said.

"You took a terrible beating," Addison said. "You need to be cleaned up. See how bad it is."

"That's right," Mays said.

Chancy thought of Lucas Stout. "I'd rather get cleaned up here."

"Don't buck us on this," Addison said. "You're heading back, and we'll go with you in case Reid has friends. I saw some giving you dirty looks. They're not all willing to forgive and forget like the mayor."

Reluctantly Chancy gave in. Ollie brought his horse, and together the five of them rode out of Prosperity and across the valley toward the lake.

Chancy thought about Missy. How pretty she was. And how he couldn't wait to see her at noon tomorrow. He'd never looked forward to anything so much in his life.

He wondered what was happening to him. He'd only just met her. Yet he was head over heels.

He'd heard of men being love-struck, they called it, but he'd never imagined it would happen to him. When it came to women, they were nice and all, but he'd had no interest in finding a gal of his own. Falling in love was the last thing on his mind. Until now.

They passed a lot of their cattle, and punchers riding herd. The light of the campfire illuminated the chuck wagon parked nearby, and part of the horse string. Ben Rigenaw and Lester Smith were hunkered by the fire, drinking coffee. Smith was the talker of the outfit, a teller of tall tales, like the time he'd been to California and seen a grizzly as big as a Conestoga, or the time he went to Utah and saw the Great Salt Lake, and claimed there was so much salt in the water he could walk on it.

Any hope Chancy had of not attracting notice when they arrived was dashed when Lester Smith stood and said in that loud voice of his, "Well, look who's back!"

Ollie didn't help matters by exclaiming as they dismounted, "My pard was in a fight. You should have seen it. He walloped the other fella good."

The simple act of climbing down brought a wave of pain. Chancy winced and turned and stopped cold.

There stood Lucas Stout. "A fight?"

"Uh-oh," Ollie said.

Chapter 19

Morning broke clear and chill, despite it being early summer. Chancy lay awake listening to the sounds of Old Charlie, their cook, going about making their morning meal. Old Charlie was a character, as they liked to say. Cantankerous as anything, he regarded the chuck wagon as his personal domain. No one was allowed to go near it when Old Charlie was cooking. If he asked a cowpoke to do something, like, say, fetch a pail of water, that cowboy better well do it, or else.

For all his crankiness, Old Charlie was well liked. His coffee was thick enough to float a horseshoe and his food mouthwatering. He was a wizard with a frying pan, a master with a Dutch oven.

Chancy heard the clang of a spoon on a pot and glanced over. The simple movement caused him to wince. He hurt from head to toe. The beating he'd taken was worse than he'd realized. But the agony was worth it. The beating had spared him from being fired.

Lucas Stout hadn't been happy to hear about the fight. Not as first. But then Ollie and Jelly and the others made it plain that Reid had been to blame, that he had braced Chancy and almost gone for his six-gun.

"My pard and me were just standing there minding our own business and he marched up mad as a wet hen," was how Ollie related it.

Stout had given Chancy a penetrating look, then said, "I won't hold this against you. I gave you an order not to get into more trouble, but you can't be blamed when a man comes after you."

"Thanks, boss," Chancy had said in great relief.

Even better, the beating had gotten him out of work for a while. The blood on his face from his nose and his mouth, and all the dark bruises, to say nothing of his half-swollen left eye and the fact that his bottom lip had puffed up to twice its normal size, had prompted Lucas Stout to relieve him of riding herd for a spell. He was to take it easy until further notice. Ordinarily Chancy would resent any suggestion that he wasn't man enough to do his job. But now he had a secret reason not to, involving the lovely lady he couldn't stop thinking about. He couldn't sneak into town if he was riding herd.

The sun wasn't up yet and already he was looking forward to noon and his meeting with Missy. Getting to town still posed a problem. He wasn't supposed to leave camp without permission.

For now Chancy was content to lie there and spare himself worse pain. His eye hurt and his mouth hurt and some of the bruises were particularly sore. In the middle of the night he'd rolled over and made the mistake of bumping his bottom lip, and it had throbbed like the dickens for the longest while.

It was a well-known fact that Texans by and large disdained fistfights. They preferred to resort to their six-shooters. Now Chancy understood why. Fistfights left a man hurting for days.

Even so, he was glad he hadn't had to pull on Reid. He'd never shot anyone, and heard tell that once a man did, it changed him. He didn't see that Ben Rigenaw or Jelly Varnes were all that different. But they were *treated* different. Once a man acquired a reputation as a man-killer, others tended to walk easy around him.

Chancy put man-killing from his mind and thought about his meeting with the lady who wouldn't leave his head. The question he should be asking himself was, to what end? What did he aim to do about her? They'd talk, most likely, and what then? Stout had let it drop that the herd would head north in one more day. What did he hope to accomplish with regard to Missy Burke between now and then? Chancy asked himself. What could possibly happen in twenty-four hours? She'd fall in love with him and beg him not to go and they would marry and raise kids and live happily ever after?

Chancy forgot himself and snorted at how silly that sounded. It caused his swollen eye and lip to act up.

They hardly knew each other. All seeing her again would do was make him pine for her on the trail.

Maybe the smart thing to do, Chancy mused, was not to. Make a clean break now, before it went any further. He'd pine for a bit and then get on with his life.

"How are you feeling, pard?"

Chancy hadn't noticed Ollie sit up. "A few aches," he allowed, "but only when I breathe."

Ollie chuckled, then yawned and scratched his head and jammed his hat on. "You look like you've been stomped by a bull. Your face is more black and blue than whatever color we really are."

"Whatever color?" Chancy said.

"We talked about this before. Most folks say we're white, but my grandma used to say we're really pink, which makes no sense, since pigs are pink and we look nothing like pigs."

Chancy started to grin and caught himself. "I can always count on you to start my day off right."

"How do I do that?"

"By being you."

"Who else would I be?" Ollie said. Casting off his blanket, he scratched his armpit. "We should have Laverne Dodger take a look at you. Could be all those punches rattled your brain."

And just like that, Chancy had an excuse for going into town. He didn't have to sneak in. He'd come right out and ask Lucas Stout if he could go see the sawbones. "Pard, you are a marvel."

"If I am it's news to me."

Others were waking up, and a general stir was about the camp.

"You know," Ollie said as he began to roll up his bedroll. "I was thinking last night before I fell asleep. We sure were lucky to find a town like Prosperity."

"It didn't take much finding," Chancy said. "They're right on the cattle trail."

Ollie didn't seem to hear him. "But it sure is a strange town. I don't mean because the doctor isn't really a doctor and their lawman isn't really a lawman."

"What are you prattling about?" Chancy said.

"The women."

"What about them?"

Ollie looked over. "Didn't you notice? Except for Missy Burke and Della and those other doves, there aren't any. I didn't see another female anywhere. No sprouts neither."

Now that Chancy thought about it, he hadn't either.

"Isn't that strange? What kind of town doesn't have wives and kids running around?"

"I've never heard of one," Chancy admitted.

"There you go," Ollie said.

Chapter 20

Chancy couldn't get that out of his head. It nagged at him the rest of the morning. He'd never heard of a town without women. Doves didn't count. Sometimes saloons had them; sometimes they didn't. But towns always had ordinary females: wives and single women and little girls. The more he thought about it, the stranger it seemed. He made up his mind to ask Missy about it when they met.

Getting there proved easier than he'd reckoned. Ollie inadvertently helped.

Shortly after breakfast, Lucas Stout and Rigenaw came over. Stout, never one to mince words, took one look at Chancy and remarked, "You look like hell, Gantry."

"Doesn't he, though?" Ollie piped up. "Maybe I should fetch him to that sort-of sawbones in Prosperity and let the doc have a look at him."

"He'll live," Rigenaw said.

Ollie persisted. "The doc might have some medicine for the swelling. My pard can't hardly eat with his lip swollen like that, and he can't hardly see out of his left eye. It's swelled almost shut."

"I was hurt worse when I was thrown by a bronc," Rigenaw said. "And I never saw a doc."

Chancy feared that the gun hand would talk the trail boss out of it.

"No," Lucas Stout said. "It's a good idea. It'll save me an extra trip in. They can leave in an hour or so and check on Finger Howard while they're there and report back on how he's doing. I didn't figure to go in until this afternoon."

"If Finger is doing all right, why not leave today?" Rigenaw said.

"The cattle and the horses can use the rest. And there's all the graze and water. They'll be well fed and rested for the final push to Wichita."

"Sounds smart to me," Ollie said.

Stout and Rigenaw looked at him.

"What?" Ollie said.

Chancy could have hugged him. But so as not to seem too eager, he said, "Are you sure it's all right, Mr. Stout? I'm no shirker. I'll do my share of the work."

"You're off herd duty for the day," Lucas Stout said. "Tonight, though, you'll take a turn. So be rested up by then."

"I will," Chancy promised.

"You young ones," Rigenaw said.

"What about us?" Ollie said.

"In my day we weren't pampered. When we were hurt, we got right back up and went back to work."

"That doesn't sound smart," Ollie said.

Rigenaw stared at him, then snorted and grinned. "The Lord must be fond of simpletons."

Ollie laughed. "My ma used to say the same thing to me when I was little. Then she'd pat me on the cheek and tell me how much she loved me. She stopped saying it when I got older. I figured it was because I stopped being a simpleton."

"You figured right, Ollie," Lucas Stout said.

Ben Rigenaw reached up and pinched his nose and closed his eyes and uttered an odd sort of sound.

"You all right, Ben?" Ollie asked. "You sound like you're getting a cold."

"Oh Lordy," Rigenaw said.

For the first time ever, Chancy saw the gun hand burst out in hearty laughter. Rigenaw walked away still laughing and motioning with his arm at Ollie as if he were swatting flies.

"It must be that town," Ollie said. "Everybody's acting a mite strange."

"You go in with your pard," Lucas Stout directed. "Stick with him the whole time."

"I'll stick like glue," Ollie said, smiling. "Although just not as sticky."

Lucas Stout turned, then glanced over his shoulder at Chancy. "You're lucky to have him for a partner. You know that, don't you?"

"More than anything," Chancy said.

"What's so special about me?" Ollie said. "All of us got pards. Rigenaw has Lester Smith. Addison has Mays. Jelly has Finger Howard. Parker has Webb. Lafferty has Collins. Drew Case has Long Tom. There are pards all over the place."

"Explain it to him," Lucas Stout said, and walked off.

Ollie turned to Chancy.

"How do I put this?" Chancy said. "Not all pards are as nice as you."

"That's true, I reckon. Lester Smith talks your ears off with his tall tales. Mays is young and has fits of temper. Drew Case thinks he's mighty tough. Lafferty spits tobacco all over the place. And Webb is always picking his nose and eating the boogers. I don't know how Parker stands that. Every time I see it, I pretty near get sick to my stomach."

"You and me both," Chancy admitted.

"Stout should make it a rule," Ollie said. "No booger-eating on the trail drive. I might talk to him about it."

"Why cause trouble?"

"I suppose."

The next hour was a test of Chancy's patience. He day-dreamed about Missy, and fidgeted. He was so obvious about it that at one point Ollie, who had just brought him a cup of coffee, gave him a worried look.

"Do you have ants in your britches?"

"Not that I know of."

"You ought to check. You've been squirming around like they are eating you up."

When it was time to go, Ollie insisted on saddling both mounts and brought the horses over. "I got you the dun with the easy gait."

"I'm obliged," Chancy said. He wouldn't have thought of that. Pushing off his blankets, he rose. Every muscle in his body protested. His ribs spiked with pain and his swollen eye throbbed. A groan escaped him.

"It's a good thing we're getting you to that doc," Ollie said.

Chancy had a better medicine in mind. Sweeter medicine. With lustrous hair and the prettiest face anywhere.

Ollie held the dun's reins out. "I just had a thought, pard. Now you'll get to keep your date with Missy Burke."

Keeping a straight face, Chancy looked at him and said, "I hadn't even thought of that."

Chapter 21

It was the longest ride of Chancy's life. He swore he could see Missy's image floating above the town, beckoning him with her smile.

In the light of the new day, Prosperity might as well be a ghost town. Only a couple of horses were at the hitch rails. Not a sound came from the saloon. A single door to the stable was open partway.

"Where is everybody?" Ollie wondered. "Most towns, the people are up and about by now."

Chancy shrugged. "Maybe they like to sleep in hereabouts."

"The whole town?"

Just then a short man in an apron came out of the general store and threw a washbasin of water into the street. He saw them and smiled and called out, "Howdy, gents. You're welcome to come in and take a look. I might have something you need."

"I could use some socks," Ollie said. "All the ones I got, my big toe pokes out. Why is it always the big one?"

Chancy thought of Missy Burke. "I'd like to pay that store a visit my own self. Let's go in."

"Shouldn't we find the doc first?"

"Laverne Dodger can wait," Chancy said. "I'm not going to keel over from a beating."

"I hope not. I'd hate to have to break in a new pard. The three I had before you didn't stay my pard very long."

This was news to Chancy. "You had pards before me? I didn't know that."

"Like I said, they didn't last long. The first one said I

was too much of a chatterbox and the second one said he had to go to St. Louis to visit his sick grandma and I never heard from him again."

"What about the third one?"

"He just gave me a peculiar look one day and laughed and rode off. To tell you the truth, I was commencing to think I'm a jinx when it comes to pards, and then you came along. Now I know I'm normal."

"You're that," Chancy said.

The general store didn't have a little bell over the door that tinkled when the door opened, like most. It didn't have the same smell either. Most general stores had a sort of fragrance about them from the items they carried. Pickle and tobacco smells, for instance. This one had a musty odor. The shelves were sparsely stocked, with a couple with town clothes and a couple with foodstuffs and a few more with tools and whatnot.

Then Chancy got to the back and stopped in amazement.

Taking up half the rear wall were shelves crammed with hats and boots and pants and shirts and belts. Cowboy duds, all of it, work clothes for the most part, the kind he and the others wore.

"What's all this?" Ollie said.

Chancy hadn't realized the short man in the apron had come up until he stepped in front of them.

"My trail drive collection, I call it. I carry the biggest between Kansas and Texas."

"You can say that again," Ollie said. "I never saw so many used shirts and pants in all my born days. Where'd you get it all?"

"Oh, here and there," the store owner said. "If you and your friends have any you can spare, I'll take them off your hands."

"Take it how? You want them free or do you pay for them?"

"I'll pay, of course."

Chancy was flabbergasted. In all his travels he'd never come across a store that bought used clothes.

"Well, now I've heard everything," Ollie said.

"You're making more of it than there is," the man said.

"Mister, everything about this town of yours is peculiar."

"How so?" the man said, his tone hardening.

Puzzled, Chancy gave him a closer scrutiny.

The proprietor had a square face with a lot of stubble, unusual in a store owner. Most shaved regularly or trimmed their beards to give a good impression to their customers. The man's apron was stained and dirty, and his clothes weren't much better. His boots were scuffed and his expression at the moment was anything but friendly.

"I asked you a question," the man said to Ollie.

"You don't have no women, for one thing. I never yet saw a town without females."

"There are doves at the saloon—" the man began.

Ollie broke him off.

"I meant normal women."

The man scowled. "Some of the men have wives. They don't get out and about much, is all. Not in the heat."

"That right there is strange," Ollie said. "Womenfolk like to parade around, no matter how hot it is. My ma and my sisters always did."

"Good for them," the man said.

"I didn't catch your name," Chancy said.

"I didn't give it," the man replied. "But it's Welker." And for some reason he glanced above the counter where a shotgun with sawed-off barrels hung on hooks on the wall.

"You have anything for ladies?" Chancy asked. "Doodads and such?"

The tension went out of Welker, and he smiled. "Gone courting, are you?"

"I have a sweetheart I want to send something to."

"You do?" Ollie said.

"Hush," Chancy said.

"I don't have a lot, but if you'll follow me," Welker said, and let them around to a glass case.

In it were pocket watches and pipes and a money clip, and on the bottom shelf, a few rings and a bracelet and a couple of necklaces.

"Not much to choose from," Ollie remarked.

"You're a grouser, aren't you?" Welker said.

"Well, there isn't," Ollie said.

Chancy frowned. Everything in the case looked used. Some of the pocket watches had scratches; the stem of a pipe was chipped, the bowl of another dark from all the tobacco used. The rings didn't have much appeal, and the bracelet was large enough to fit around a horse's leg. One necklace, though, had a shiny if thin chain, with a tiny silver heart. "That one might do."

Welker opened the case and brought it out, handling it roughly, as if he didn't care if it broke.

"How much?" Chancy asked as he examined the links and the heart. They were in good shape.

"Four bits," Welker said.

"That's all?" Chancy figured it would be more.

"I'm being generous. Or are you a grouser like your friend?"

"Four bits, it is."

Chancy paid and carefully slid the necklace into his pocket. He imagined Missy's face lighting up when he gave it to her, and went out walking on air. "That was a steal."

"I didn't like him," Ollie said. "He was rude. Calling us grousers."

"Some folks provoke too easy," Chancy said.

"And some keep secrets from their pards."

"Do you mean me?"

"None other," Ollie said, sounding hurt.

"When have I ever kept a secret from you?"

"I never knew you had a sweetheart somewhere. Who are you sending that necklace to?"

Chancy laughed and pointed at the saloon.

"Why are you . . . ?" Ollie stopped, and then he laughed too. "Oh. I should have guessed. Every now and then I can be dumb."

"Can't we all?" Chancy said.

Chapter 22

Chancy supposed he should pay a visit to Laverne Dodger, although he'd rather cross the street to the saloon and see if Missy was there. First, though, he would follow orders. He bent his boots to the cabin where Finger had been placed, entered without knocking, and drew up short in consternation.

The room was filled to overflowing. The mayor was there. So were Ives and three other townsmen. The mayor seemed as surprised to see Chancy and Ollie as Chancy was to see all of them.

"What's this?" Ollie said.

"Mr. Gantry. Mr. Teal. We weren't expecting you," Mayor Broom exclaimed. Smiling, he came over, his hand extended. "How are you? If you don't mind my saying, Mr. Gantry, you look a little worse for wear after that fracas last night."

"I came in looking for Dodger," Chancy said. "And to see how Finger is doing for our trail boss."

"Mr. Howard is coming along quite nicely," Mayor Broom said. "Dodger was by earlier. Your friend's fever is down and the swelling is gone. Dodger expects Mr. Howard to make a full recovery barring any unforeseen complications."

"Any what?" Ollie said.

"We should go," a man by the bed said.

The speaker wasn't dressed like a townsman. He wore a wide-brimmed black hat similar to Ives's, but his shirt was blue and his pants were checkered. High on his right hip was a Starr revolver, tilted slightly back. The Starr models had seen a lot of use during the Civil War but since then had lost ground in popularity to Colts, Remingtons, and Smith & Wessons.

"Yes, we should," Mayor Broom said.

"Who's he?" Ollie asked.

"The handle is Krine, cowboy," the man said. "Artemis Krine." He was handsomer than most and carried himself as if he was aware of the fact. "You'd do well to remember it."

"Why should I bother?" Ollie said.

Krine smiled. "Let's go," he said, and walked past them out the door.

Chancy didn't know what to make of it when Ives and the others followed him as meekly as could be. "That hombre tells you what to do and you do it?"

"Mr. Krine is the founder of our fair town," Mayor Broom revealed. "He doesn't hold an official position as I do, but he nonetheless has considerable sway over how things are done."

"He has sway over Ives too?"

"Why wouldn't he?" Mayor Broom said, then grinned. "Ah. You don't understand why Ives would let someone tell him what to do, given his proficiency with pistols?"

"Something like that," Chancy said.

"Three reasons. First, because Mr. Krine, as I've indicated, is the brains behind Prosperity. Everything you see here was his idea. Second, Mr. Krine and Ives are friends, and more than friends. In your parlance they might be termed pards."

"Chancy is my pard," Ollie said.

"How wonderful for you," the mayor said.

"What's the third reason?" Chancy asked.

"Oh." Broom moved to the door and paused in the doorway to grin at them. "The third reason is that Mr. Krine is as fast as Ives, if not faster. Were they to go up against each other, not that they ever would, I wouldn't presume to wager on the outcome."

"Goodness," Ollie said. "How many gun hands do you have in this little town of yours anyhow?"

"Our fair share, I suppose." Broom touched the brim of his bowler and departed humming to himself.

"What's a fair share of gun hands?" Ollie said.

"Forget them," Chancy said. He went to the bed and placed his palm against Finger's forehead. It was cool to the touch. Lifting the blanket, he inspected the wound. It too was as the mayor claimed. The swelling was down and the flesh around the stitching wasn't as red.

"Should we wake him?" Ollie whispered.

"I am awake," Finger Howard said.

Startled, Chancy dropped the blanket and took half a step back. "Consarn you, Finger."

"You spooked my pard good," Ollie said, and laughed.

Finger's eyes were open, but his eyelids were fluttering. His throat bobbed and he licked his lips and got out, "Feel woozy. They gave me something."

"Medicine," Ollie said. "You need it. They had to operate. Your worm-thing was set to burst."

"No," Finger said, licking his lips some more. He feebly raised his hand and tried to clutch at Chancy. "Listen . . ." Gasping, he got no further.

"Are you in pain?" Chancy said, moving closer. "Is something wrong?"

"It's them," Finger said, so softly they barely heard him.

"Them who?" Ollie said.

"Them," Finger said again. His eyes opened and he suddenly gripped Chancy by the wrist. "I heard what they said."

"What?" Chancy said in confusion.

"That mayor and those others. They were talking about another herd. Saying strange things."

"There's that word again," Ollie said.

Chancy motioned for him to keep quiet. "Strange how?"

"The store," Finger said. His eyelids were fluttering again, and his hold on Chancy's wrist weakened.

"The general store? What about it?"

"Look there," Finger said. "You'll find . . ." He tried to go on, but his body slumped and he exhaled and went limp.

"Is he all right?" Ollie asked in alarm.

"How do I know? I'm no doc." Chancy felt for a pulse, which was good and strong, and checked again that the fever was down. "He seems to be, but we'd better fetch Laverne Dodger."

"What was that business about the general store?"

"Beats me," Chancy said. "He wasn't talking sense. Must be whatever they're giving him."

"I'm glad they're not giving me any," Ollie said.

Chapter 23

The stable was as quiet as an empty church. Chancy hollered but received no reply. Entering, he stopped. Hardly any sunlight penetrated, and he waited for his eyes to adjust to the darkness.

Beside him Ollie sniffed a few times. "I've always liked the smell of a stable. The horses and the straw and the manure."

"You like the smell of manure?"

"When it's fresh."

"And you say this town is strange?" Chancy joshed. He went a little farther and called out, "Dodger? You in here? It's Chancy and Ollie. We'd like to talk to you about our friend Finger."

"And check my pard while you're at it," Ollie yelled. "That Reid fella beat on him pretty awful."

In the shadows, something stirred. Someone mumbled, and out of a stall hobbled Laverne Dodger, a half-empty whiskey bottle in his hand. "You two shouldn't be here," he said, slurring his words.

"Didn't you hear us?" Ollie said. "We need you."

"I heard you. But you really shouldn't be here." Dodger halted and took a swig, then wiped his mouth with his sleeve. "I like you boys. You've treated me decent."

"How else would we treat you?" Ollie said. "My ma always said to treat folks like they were pies."

"Pies?" Dodger said.

Ollie nodded. "Everybody like pies, don't they? So you treat folks like something you like."

"You're surely something," Dodger said, and chuckled.

"I don't think I'd be here if I was nothing," Ollie said.

"What's this about your friend?" Dodger asked.

"He woke up for a bit," Chancy replied. "Sounded like he was raving."

"It's the mayor's fault he woke up," Ollie said. "Him and all those others being there. Their talking probably did it."

"Broom was in the cabin?"

Ollie nodded. "With Ives and somebody called Krine and some others. You'd think they'd never seen a sick fella before."

"Damn," Laverne Dodger said.

"What?" Chancy said.

"Let's go take a look at him." Dodger moved quickly for a man with a peg leg. He did more mumbling, and swore.

"What's the matter?" Chancy asked. "Are you upset that they woke Finger?"

"It might be sooner than I thought," Dodger said. "I figured they'd wait until tonight or even tomorrow."

"Who would wait for what?" Ollie said.

"Who else?" Dodger said.

Ollie nudged Chancy and pointed at Dodger's whiskey bottle and waggled his fingers to show he thought the stableman was drunk.

"Are you sure you're up to this?" Chancy asked. "You can't examine him right if you're in your cups."

"Hell," Dodger said. "It takes two bottles for that. This little bit"—he shook the one he held—"is breakfast."

Laverne Dodger's peg made a lot of noise on the cabin floor, but Finger Howard stayed out to the world. Dodger checked Finger's pulse and his temperature and opened each eyelid and studied each pupil, then grunted and sat on the edge of the bed. "He's all right."

"They said they gave him something," Chancy said. "What was it?"

"I don't know."

"How can you not?" Ollie said. "You're the doctor, not them."

Dodger picked his bottle up from the floor where he had placed it and took a long swallow. He glanced at the door and then from Chancy to Ollie and back again. "I meant what I said about liking you gents."

"And I meant what I said about pies," Ollie said.

Dodger lowered his voice. "Which is why I'm going to do something I shouldn't. I'm going to give you some advice."

"If it's about baths I already know it," Ollie said.

"Baths?"

"My ma told me that if a man takes too many, he gets sickly. It's not good to take more than one bath a month. You being a doctor, or almost a doctor, I figured you'd know that too."

"How do you shut him up?" Dodger said to Chancy.

"You don't."

"Listen," Dodger said. "Ride back to your camp and tell your trail boss to get the hell out of here. Drive those cattle of yours back to the main trail as fast as you can."

"We're not leaving until tomorrow," Ollie said.

"Tomorrow will be too late."

"For what?" Chancy said.

"Mr. Stout is letting the cattle rest up another day," Ollie said. "All that graze and the water is good for them."

"The grass and the lake are the lures," Dodger said. "It's what brings the herds in and keeps them here long enough."

"For what?" Chancy said again.

"I can't say any more. If I did . . ." Dodger looked toward the front door and sat bolt upright.

A shadow filled the doorway. A moment more, and in came the man called Krine, with Mayor Broom and Ives behind him. "We saw you come in," Krine said, "and wondered how the cowboy is doing."

"No change from earlier. He's doing fine," Dodger said.

"That's good to hear," Mayor Broom said. To Chancy and Ollie he added, "You boys should come to the saloon and have a few drinks. It just opened."

"I was heading there anyway," Chancy said. His date with Missy was uppermost on his mind.

"Yes, go," Laverne Dodger said. "All of you. My patient needs rest. The operation took a lot out of him."

Ollie went to say something, but Chancy gestured for him not to. They ambled out, and once in the street Ollie whispered, "Why'd you stop me? I was about to ask about that lure business."

"I don't think Dodger wanted the mayor to know he told us," Chancy said.

"What do you make of it?" Ollie said. "I'm plumb stumped."

"I don't know," Chancy admitted. "Maybe it was the whiskey talking."

"Should we ride out and tell Lucas Stout?"

"It can wait until after my date," Chancy said. He wasn't about to let anything interfere with that.

"I suppose," Ollie said. "But between you and me, pard, this place just gets stranger and stranger."

Chapter 24

Missy Burke was as beautiful as Chancy remembered. She had on a bright blue dress that he suspected she saved for special occasions. It was nothing like the dress she wore when she worked. It wasn't as tight and didn't show any of her cleavage. In fact, it was the sort any woman would wear when she was out and about. Yet on her it looked magnificent. It matched her radiant smile. "You came."

"Nothing could have kept me away," Chancy said. He'd swatted the dust from his clothes and hat and spiffed the toes of his boots and slicked his hair the best he could with spit. "Did you reckon I wouldn't?"

"A girl never knows with men," Missy said. She nodded at Ollie. "How do you do, Mr. Teal? You're very quiet today."

"How do you do, ma'am?" Ollie replied. "I'm sorry for the quiet. My pard told me I'm to shush around you so he can get in a word edgewise."

Missy grinned. "You didn't?"

"I did," Chancy confessed.

"Ollie, you can talk around me all you want," Missy said. "I find you positively adorable."

"That's kind of you, ma'am," Ollie said. "My aunt used to call me that. She also told me I was the reason she never had any kids of her own. She was a great teaser."

The last thing Chancy wanted was for Ollie to monopolize the conversation. "I was thinking that you and me could go for a stroll," he proposed. "Up and down the street. Just the two of us," he mentioned pointedly.

"I'd like to but I don't know if I should," Missy said.

"Reid has this rule about getting too personal with the customers."

"Where is he anyhow?" Ollie asked.

"At his cabin," Missy said. She put her hand on Chancy's arm. "His face is all black and blue and swollen, thanks to you. I don't think he wants to be seen in public. But if we take a stroll he might spot us out his window, and come out and give me grief. Maybe it's best if we stay here. Is that all right?"

"Whatever you want." Chancy would do anything to please her short of jumping off a cliff.

Missy indicated a corner table. The saloon was virtually empty at that time of day, and only one other table was occupied, by a man playing solitaire. "How about if we sit there and talk?"

"Just the two of us," Chancy said to Ollie.

"You don't have to beat me over the head with it," Ollie said. "I can take a hint. I'll go back to the general store. I saw some bandannas and I could use one. Mine has a hole in it."

When the batwings closed behind him, Missy said, "You're lucky to have him for a friend."

"So everybody keeps saying." Chancy realized he still had his hat on and quickly doffed it and stepped aside. "After you, ma'am." He made sure to scoot around her so he could pull a chair out for her and made it a point to gently slide it under her as she sat. Taking a seat across from her, he placed his hat on the table.

"Here we are," Missy said.

Chancy could hardly believe it. Just her and just him. "It's like a dream," he said before he could catch himself.

Missy's lovely eyes narrowed quizzically. "You're serious, aren't you? It's not a line you use."

"Line?"

"Men use them all the time. To try to get close to a gal. To make the girl think she's special so they can be free with their hands."

Chancy colored and coughed. "I'd never."

"I believe you," Missy said, and after a bit she added softly, "Will wonders never cease?"

"All I know is I like being with you," Chancy said, coming right out with it. "I haven't stopped thinking about you since we met. I couldn't wait to see you again. And now that I'm here, I half want to pinch myself to make sure I'm awake."

"You are," Missy said. "And since you're being so honest, I'll be honest with you." Her voice dropped to a husky whisper. "I haven't stopped thinking of you either."

Chancy feared he might burst into flame.

"I've never felt like this before," Missy said. "I don't know what it is about you, but you're special."

"Thank heaven," Chancy said.

Missy laughed, then looked around the saloon and pulled her chair in closer to the table. "As much as I'd like to go on about us, there's something else. And it might be important."

Chancy waited, hanging on every word.

"I've only been in Prosperity a short while. I was in Kansas City, and Della sent for me. I knew her from before. She wanted me to replace another girl. The pay is better, so I came, but now that I've been here a spell, I can't say I like it very much. I've been thinking of leaving."

"I'd take you anywhere."

Missy reached across and placed her hand on his. "I believe you would."

Chancy's throat tried to constrict on itself, forcing him to breathe through his nose.

"I've heard things," Missy was saying. "Scraps here and there. And it worries me."

"What kind of scraps?" Chancy forced himself to ask.

"About the herds," Missy said. "I was in the general store one day and Mr. Welker was talking to a man named Krine. . . ."

"I've met him," Chancy said.

"Krine runs the town, not the mayor. Anyway, I don't think they knew I was there and I overheard Welker say he got more clothes than he knew what to do with from the cowboys with the last herd."

Chancy recollected the huge pile at the rear of the store.

"Krine told Welker the clothes were window dressing, nothing more. It was the money they got from selling the herds that counted."

"Wait," Chancy said. "Krine sold a herd?"

"That's the impression I had, yes," Missy said. "Which made no sense. I went around the shelf and they saw me and clammed up, so I didn't learn any more."

"Strange," Chancy said, and realized he was using Ollie's favorite word of late.

Missy sat back. "There's something about this place. Secrets everyone is keeping from me. Maybe because I'm new and they don't fully trust me yet."

"How could they not?"

"Aren't you gallant?" Missy said. "But I thought you should know."

"I'm obliged." Chancy thought of Dodger's warning, and Finger's before that, and now this.

"What do you make of it?" Missy said. "You don't suppose you and your friends are in any danger, do you?"

"I sure hope not," Chancy said.

Chapter 25

In all of Chancy's life, there had never been moments as precious as these.

They sat and looked into each other's eyes and talked and talked and talked some more. Missy related her past, what it was like to grow up on a small farm in Indiana, and how after her folks died, with no brothers or sisters and no other kin to speak of, she'd ended up working in saloons to make ends meet.

Chancy drank in every word, every movement of her lips, every sparkle in her eyes. He could have sat there forever listening and admiring her.

Then boots pounded, and in rushed Ollie. He came straight to the table and leaned on it to catch his breath.

"What on earth?" Missy said.

"Are your britches on fire?" Chancy joked.

"I got here as quick as I could," Ollie said. "To let you know that Ben Rigenaw is in town looking for you."

"Rigenaw?" Chancy said in alarm. He couldn't conceive of a reason for the gun hand to be searching for him.

Ollie bobbed his chin. "I was coming out of the general store when him and Lester Smith rode up. They asked me if I knew where you were and I fibbed and said not exactly."

Bewildered, Chancy was debating what to do when the batwings parted yet again and in the pair walked.

"There you are," Ben Rigenaw said. "I knew if I followed Ollie he'd lead me right to you."

"Well, darn," Ollie said.

Lester Smith chortled. "Reminds me of the time I was after a card cheat up to Denver. Took me five hours to track him down, going from sporting house to sporting house. I must have asked pretty near two hundred ladies before I found one he'd paid a visit to and knew where he was staying."

"None of your stories, Lester," Rigenaw said. He walked to the table and touched his hat brim to Missy Burke. "Ma'am. Sorry to intrude but the trail boss sent me to find out what was keeping Chancy."

"I haven't been here that long," Chancy said.

"It's been over two hours," Rigenaw said. "It shouldn't have taken you more than an hour to ride in, see the doc, check on Finger, and get back."

"So Stout sent us," Lester Smith said.

"He wants you to report to him," Rigenaw said.

Missy cleared her throat. "Does he have to know about Mr. Gantry's visit with me? I'd take it as a personal favor if you could find it in your hearts not to say anything."

"I see no cause to, ma'am," Ben Rigenaw said. "He can make up his own excuse."

"I won't mention it either, ma'am," Lester Smith said. He grinned and winked at Chancy. "Lucky devil that you are."

Chancy could have slugged him.

"We'll give you five minutes," Rigenaw said, "and be waiting over at the general store." He touched his hat brim again. "Ma'am."

"I'll go with them," Ollie said considerately.

Alone with her, Chancy didn't hide his disappointment. "I'd hoped we'd have longer. I want to know all there is to know about you."

"That would take a lifetime," Missy said, and blushed.

Chancy was about to say he wouldn't mind at all, but prudence stilled his tongue. It would be unwise to be too forward and spoil things.

"When are you heading north?" Missy asked.

"Tomorrow."

"Then I guess I'll never see you again. That would be a shame. We're just becoming acquainted."

Chancy felt an invisible spike pierce his chest. "I don't want that either."

"What can we do?"

The question hung in the air for all of a minute. Then Mayor Broom entered, glanced over, and made straight for them.

"Mr. Gantry. I've been looking for you. I saw those other cowboys with your friend, but I don't know them, so I'm giving this to you. I trust you to see that it's delivered."

Chancy was taken aback when the mayor slid a hand under his jacket and held out a sealed envelope. "What's this?"

"Give it to your trail boss. Tell him there's no hurry. We'll be here when he decides to ride in." Broom smiled. "As for you, Miss Burke, you might like to know I saw Reid out and about a short while ago."

"I thank you for the warning," Missy said.

"I know how he can be. And I can't say I approve of how he treats you ladies at times." Broom headed for the bar.

"I'd better go." Missy stood. "If Reid catches us, it will be last night all over again."

"I won't settle for fists this time," Chancy said, amazed by his own bluster.

"Don't you dare swap lead over me," Missy said. "I wouldn't be able to live with myself if anything were to happen to you." With evident reluctance, she turned to go.

"About tomorrow," Chancy said.

"Yes?"

"I'll think of something."

Missy touched his cheek. "You don't think we're getting ahead of ourselves? We haven't known each other twenty-four hours."

"I would gladly take you with me," Chancy said.

"And what? I'd stay with the herd? Your trail boss isn't likely to go for that. He might let me come along as far as Wichita, but what then? I could probably find work, but what about you? Would you go on being a cowboy? Go back to Texas? Or would you do something else for a living?"

Chancy hadn't thought that far ahead. "I reckon we'd take it a step at a time."

"Are we fooling ourselves, Chancy? Can it be we're nothing more than cats in heat?"

Chancy was shocked she'd say such a thing. "I don't have the answers. I'm as confused as you."

"We'd both better think on it," Missy said. "If you can get away, come see me tonight. I might know my own mind by then." She smiled uncertainly and whisked toward the back.

Troubled, Chancy made for the batwings. Things were moving too fast. For now, he'd report to Lucas Stout and ponder on his predicament later. He hefted the envelope Mayor Broom had given him and wondered what was in it.

Chapter 26

Lucas Stout was waiting with his hands on his hips when Chancy and the rest returned from Prosperity. Before they could swing down, he stalked up to Chancy's mount. "What took you so long? You should have been back hours ago."

The last thing Chancy wanted was to have the trail boss mad at him. The last puncher who aroused Stout's ire was out of a job quicker than he could blink. Chancy had been contemplating what to do on the ride back, and he'd had a brainstorm. A way to divert Stout's anger, he hoped. "The mayor looked me up," he said, which was true as far as it went. "He gave me something to give to you."

"He did what?" Lucas Stout said.

Chancy shifted, opened his saddlebag, and took out the envelope. "Broom said it's important. He didn't say what it was." He hoped to give the impression that the mayor was the reason he'd been in town so long.

Stout held the envelope in both hands. "What in the world is this?"

"There are other things I need to tell you, but they can wait," Chancy said. He was pleased as punch when Lucas Stout turned and stepped to the fire. Alighting, he grinned at Ollie.

"What's so funny?"

"That mayor might have saved my bacon."

"Is it bacon or is it hash?" Ollie said. "I can never get the two straight. For a while there I used to say 'saved my potatoes' instead, but everybody looked at me as if I was addlepated."

"Imagine that," Chancy said.

Lucas Stout had squatted and was slitting the envelope open with a thumbnail. He slid out a folded sheet of paper, unfolded it, and commenced to read.

Ben Rigenaw and Lester Smith went closer, and others were drifting over too. They seemed to sense that something was in the wind.

Chancy went with them. He saw Lucas Stout's features harden and heard him say, "Son of a . . ."

"Problem?" Rigenaw said.

The trail boss looked up, his features etched in fury. "I don't hardly believe it. As friendly as they were and they pull this."

Two punchers, Drew Case and Long Tom, were about to carry their saddles to the string and go ride herd. They stopped, and Long Tom, the tallest cowpoke in the outfit at six feet eight inches, cleared his throat. "What is it, boss? Do they want us to take Finger off their hands before he's fit to travel?"

"If only that was all it was," Lucas Stout said. Rising, he gave the sheet of paper a violent shake. "They flimflammed us. And now they've shown their true colors."

"What did they do, boss?" Drew Case asked.

Stout held up the paper. "This is a bill. For services rendered, they're calling it. They want seventy-five dollars for Finger's operation and another twenty dollars a night for putting Finger up in their cabin."

"A night?" Lester Smith said.

"That's not all." Stout read from the letter. "Grazing privileges for fifteen hundred cattle, at three dollars per head. And for our use of water privileges at the Prosperity municipal water supply, another five dollars a head."

"Why, all that will come to . . ." Ollie began counting on his fingers.

"Twelve thousand dollars," Lucas Stout spat.

"They can't be serious," Long Tom said.

"That's not all." Stout continued reading. "City taxes on liquor consumed, forty-three dollars. City tax on the use of a public thoroughfare, nine dollars."

"Public what?" Ollie said.

"Their damn street." Stout wasn't done. "City taxes on goods bought at the general store, fourteen dollars. Consultation with municipal government, thirty-five dollars."

"They have a government?" Ollie said.

"The mayor," Chancy said, enlightening him.

Lucas Stout was practically livid. "Fee for cleaning up after out-of-town horses, seven dollars."

"Does that mean what I think it means?" Ollie said.

"Shoveling horse shit," Lester Smith said.

"There's more," Stout said. "The total comes to twelve thousand, four hundred and eighty-two dollars."

"The hell you say," Lester Smith said.

"And they expect us to pay?" Ollie said.

"They expect me to," Stout said, "as the one responsible for the herd."

"They have their nerve," Lester declared.

Ben Rigenaw nodded. "They're trying to fleece us, is what this is. It wouldn't surprise me if they've done it to other herds."

In a rush of recollection, Chancy said, "They must have." He went on to tell them about Finger, and about Laverne Dodger's warning, and what Missy had overheard, although he kept her name out of it.

"They took those other cowhands' clothes?" Parker said. "I never heard of such a thing."

"They're not getting my duds," Ollie said. "I'm not about to run around naked. I might catch a cold."

"In the summer?" Lester said.

"Our skin doesn't know what season it is," Ollie said. "And it's cold at night sleeping on the ground."

Lucas Stout smacked the paper and spoke loudly so they all would hear. "They're not getting away with this. I'll be damned if I'll let them hornswoggle us. I'm going in to talk turkey with that mayor. Chancy, Ollie, Jelly, and Drew are going with me. The rest of you stay."

"You don't want me along?" Rigenaw said.

"I need someone reliable to be in charge here," Lucas Stout said. "Send the rest of the hands out to watch the herd. Let those already out there know what's going on. Have everyone ready to move at a moment's notice. That goes for you too, Charlie," he said, addressing the cook. "I want the chuck wagon hitched by the time I get back."

"Will do," Old Charlie said.

"You're expecting trouble, aren't you, Mr. Stout?" Ollie asked.

The trail boss stared hard toward town. "I sure as hell am."

Chapter 27

For once Jelly Varnes wasn't smiling. He was as grim as everyone else. Lucas Stout was the grimmest of all. A thunderhead crackled around him, ready to explode with violence.

Chancy had never seen their trail boss so mad. He didn't blame him. The bill from the town was preposterous. There was no way in God's creation they could pay that much. No outfit could. Not before selling their cattle at the railhead anyway; the fifteen hundred head would fetch around sixty thousand dollars.

Prosperity's stunt was unheard-of. Chancy wondered how many herds they had "taxed" this way. The town hadn't been there that long, so it couldn't have been too many. He was surprised word hadn't gotten back to Texas. Something as outrageous as this scheme, word of it would have spread like a prairie fire.

He thought of all the used clothes at the general store and grew troubled, although he couldn't exactly say why.

Lucas Stout broke the silence that hung over them like a shroud. "When we get there, let me do the talking. Jelly, you're not to pull on anyone unless I say so. Understand?"

"You're the boss," Jelly Varnes said.

"Do you reckon they'll start something?" Ollie asked.

"I wouldn't think so, but you never know," Stout said. "They won't get any money if we're dead."

Without thinking, Chancy said, "They would if they killed all of us and took the herd to Wichita themselves."

Lucas Stout stiffened in his saddle and glanced sharply

over. "I hadn't even considered that. Surely not . . ." He stopped, his brow furrowed.

Ollie leaned toward Chancy. "Would they take it that far? Wipe out a whole outfit for the cows?"

"Rustlers might," Chancy said.

"But these aren't rustlers. It's a bunch of townsfolk."

"The trick they're trying to pull," Chancy said, "they might as well be rustlers. It's the same thing, only they do it with their so-called taxes."

"I never heard of the like in all my born days."

"No one has." Although now that Chancy pondered on it some, he did recollect a town or three that wanted nothing to do with the cattle trade. Their citizens saw cowboys as trouble. So they levied steep fines and otherwise gave the herds no reason to stop. But still, that was nothing compared to this.

Ollie whispered, "I'd feel better if Ben Rigenaw was along."

"Jelly is almost as quick," Chancy whispered back.

"Ben has a better head on his shoulders," Ollie whispered. "And more experience at man-killing."

Jelly Barnes half turned. "What are you two on about back there? I heard my name."

"We're just jabbering," Ollie said.

"Well, jabber some other time. It gets on a body's nerves."

"See?" Ollie whispered to Chancy.

Prosperity appeared deserted. The main street was empty from end to end. The hitch rails too, which struck Chancy as odd. There was no movement in the general store. The stable doors were closed as well.

"I don't like the looks of it," Drew Case said. He had a bristly mustache and wore a long-barreled Colt. Word was he'd been involved in a shooting affray once and wounded a man in the shoulder. But he was no gun hand. His only interest in life was cattle.

"Me neither," Jelly said.

Not so much as a fly buzzed. No dogs were roaming about, no cats slinking in the shade.

Lucas Stout drew rein at the near end of the street and

they did the same. He did something rare for him; he placed his hand on his revolver. "Keep your eyes skinned. Jelly and Chancy, you watch on the right. Ollie, Drew, you watch the left side."

"Someone should take the middle," Ollie said.

"That would be me," Stout said.

"Oh."

"Pay attention to the gaps between the buildings," Jelly Varnes said, "and to the roofs."

Lucas Stout clucked to his animal. "Spread out a little. We shouldn't bunch up."

Chancy reined slightly to the right. He was close to the general store.

"If they come at us, it will be from the saloon," Jelly Varnes predicted. "It's where I'd wait if I was them."

As it turned out, he was right but he was wrong.

The batwings did open, but the only one to step out was Mayor Broom. "Greetings!" he called out warmly. "Nice to see you fellas again."

Lucas Stout angled over and came to a stop.

No one else appeared. The saloon was quiet. The rest of Prosperity might as well be a ghost town.

"There's just you?" Lucas Stout said.

"Who were you expecting?" Mayor Broom said, and beckoned. "Come on in and have a drink. On me. I assume you're here about the bill."

"What else?" Stout said curtly.

"I can tell you're upset and you needn't be," Mayor Broom said. "Please. Climb down. You're always welcome here. And we do have that bill to discuss."

"Discuss, hell," Lucas Stout said.

"Now, see?" Mayor Broom said. "We're getting off on the wrong foot. We're grown men, and we should talk this over in a rational manner. Getting angry never helps anything."

Chancy detected rare indecision in their trail boss.

Stout gazed up and down the street, and nodded. "All right. Let's get to it."

"Excellent," Mayor Broom exclaimed happily.

About to climb down, Lucas Stout said, "Drew, stay with the horses. The rest of you are with me."

Chancy alighted. A feeling came over him that unseen eyes were on them. His gut in a knot, he followed the others in and hoped to heaven things didn't go from bad to worse.

Chapter 28

Other than the bartender, the saloon was empty too.

"Drinks are on me, George," Mayor Broom called out. "Bring a couple of bottles over, would you?" He moved to the table by the front window. "Pull up chairs, gentlemen. Make yourselves comfortable."

"I'll stand," Jelly Varnes said, and moved to where he could watch the batwings and also see anyone coming out of the hall at the back.

Chancy would rather sit but took his cue from Jelly. "I'll stand too." He stepped to the bar.

Ollie was looking around as if he didn't know what to do.

"Come over here with me," Chancy said.

The mayor sat with his back to the window and folded his hands on the table. Lucas Stout sat across from him.

"You see how easy we made this?" Mayor Broom said.

George brought the bottles and six glasses on a tray and set the tray on the table. Without saying a word, he went back around the bar.

The mayor slid a bottle over to Stout. "Your punchers can drink too. It's good whiskey."

"We're not here to drink," Lucas Stout said.

"What's your rush? We can be sociable, can't we?"

"Broom, you're loco if you expect me to pay you twelve thousand dollars."

"Now, now." The mayor opened his bottle, filled a glass halfway, and treated himself to a sip. Sighing with contentment, he took his bowler off and placed it beside the bottle. He was going bald, and the hair over his ears stuck out in little tufts. "The money isn't for me. It's for the town treasury."

"It's robbery, is what it is."

Broom's thin eyebrows arched as if he was surprised. "Why are you taking this attitude? You know as well as I do that taxes are as common as air. A town has the legal right to impose them as the town deems fit. In our case, we tax the herds that come through."

"You invited us here," Lucas Stout said. "You told us we were welcome to use your graze and your water."

"And you were."

"You took in one of my men and had your doc tend to him."

"It was the humane thing to do," Mayor Broom said. "How can you find fault with that?"

"And then you charge for everything."

"I hate to be a stickler about it, but a tax isn't a charge, per se. It's more of a compulsory contribution, you might say."

"I say you had it planned all along," Lucas Stout said. "You invited us here and went out of your way to pretend to be friendly, knowing all along that you were going to sock us with a tax bill."

"O ye of little faith."

"Keep the Bible out of this," Lucas Stout said. "You and it have little in common."

"Insults now?" Mayor Broom said, and shook his head. "I expected better of you. Despite what you might believe, I've dealt with you in good faith. We didn't have to take your sick man in. Your hands practically begged us to. And when you showed up, did I twist your arm and make you bring your herd here? I did not. I merely offered you the opportunity. You came of your own free will."

"You never said anything about the cost."

"Come, now." Mayor Broom laughed. "When is anything ever free? Apparently you assumed it was, which shows a remarkable lack of judgment on your part. How long have you been a trail boss anyhow?"

"Now who's spewing insults?"

"I don't mean to," Broom said good-naturedly. "I'm

simply trying to explain that your expectations weren't realistic. And as for the taxes the town has imposed, we're perfectly willing to work with you if you think they're a tad too much."

"A tad?" Lucas Stout growled.

"You think our fee is unfair?"

Stout bent toward him, and it was obvious he was controlling his temper. "Grazing on public lands is free. So is the water."

"Public land under the jurisdiction of the federal government, yes," Mayor Broom said. "But the land for ten miles around, and the lake where your cattle have slaked their thirst, are owned by the town. We can assess fees as we please."

"No other town has ever done anything like this."

Mayor Broom grinned. "There's a first time for everything, as they say. Who knows? Prosperity might start a trend that will sweep the West."

"Over our dead bodies."

Broom pursed his lips. "By that do you mean you and your hands, specifically? Or do you mean cowboys in general?"

Lucas Stout sat back. "You like to bandy words, don't you? You should be a lawyer."

"I was, in fact," Mayor Broom said. "But the legal profession and I didn't see eye-to-eye on certain finer points of the law, and my license was revoked."

"Why am I not surprised?"

Broom showed his first trace of anger. "Let's not make this personal. The fact remains that you are accountable for the bill that was delivered. We expect payment within twenty-four hours. After that, the fees will go up."

"All I have on me are a few hundred dollars for expenses," Lucas Stout said. "You're welcome to all of it, but that's the best I can do."

"I'm afraid that wouldn't be anywhere near enough."

"Then we're done talking. I tried to be reasonable," Stout said, and went to stand.

"Hold on," Broom said. "There's a solution that evidently hasn't occurred to you. We're more than willing to settle your bill by taking its equivalent in goods or livestock."

"I should have known," Stout said.

Mayor Broom nodded. "Cattle are going for about forty dollars a head up north, the last I heard. Three hundred of your longhorns would cover the bill in full."

"That's nearly a fifth of the herd."

"You'll still have the rest."

"No."

"It's more than fair."

"You try taking our cattle, you'll regret it."

"Please," Mayor Broom said. "Let's not resort to threats. You have twenty-four hours to think about it. Give us the three hundred head and you can leave in peace." He paused. "If you don't, this will get ugly."

Chapter 29

They had been angry when they rode in. They were mad as Hades when they rode out.

"The nerve of that no-account," Drew Case fumed. "Claiming they have every right in the world to fleece our outfit."

"You should have given me the word," Jelly Varnes said to Lucas Stout's back. "I'd have gunned him where he sat."

"He sure was a talker," Ollie said.

Chancy was as furious as the others, but he had nothing to add.

Lucas Stout turned and regarded them somberly. "We're not handing over three hundred head. They can take their taxes and fees and choke on them, for all I care. When we leave, our cattle go with us. They try to stop us and there will be hell to pay."

"There are more of them than there are of us," Ollie mentioned.

"We have enough guns to hold them off," Lucas Stout said.

Chancy wasn't so sure, but he had something else on his mind. "We're forgetting someone."

"Eh?" Lucas Stout said.

"Finger Howard," Chancy reminded him. "He's not well enough yet to sit a horse. What do we do about him?"

"Oh, hell," Stout said, and wheeling his mount sideways, he drew rein. "You're right. We can't leave him there." He snapped his fingers and smiled. "I know. We'll make space for him in the chuck wagon. He can ride with Old Charlie."

“If they’ll hand him over,” Drew Case said.

Jelly nodded. “I wouldn’t put it past them not to let us have him. It gives them something to hold over us.”

Lucas Stout thoughtfully rubbed his chin. “I was so mad I wasn’t thinking straight. Now I am. We’ll do the last thing they’ll expect. We’ll circle around and take Finger out.”

“The ride to camp might not be good for him,” Chancy noted.

“He’s tough,” Lucas Stout said. “He’ll make it.” He resumed riding but bore more to the south than the west. When they had gone about halfway to the lake, he began the loop that would take them back to Prosperity.

“What if they try to stop us?” Ollie asked.

“We don’t let them,” Stout said.

“Good,” Jelly Varnes said. “I’ve been hankering to shoot one of those buzzards.”

“It might not be the whole town,” Ollie said. “Could be it’s just the mayor.”

“Don’t you believe it,” Jelly said. “He doesn’t have the grit. You can bet Ives is backing his play, and who knows how many others?”

“There’s Krine,” Chancy said.

“Who?” Lucas Stout said.

Only then did it occur to Chancy that he hadn’t told them about the mystery man. He corrected his lapse, ending with “From what I was told, Krine is the real brains of that bunch.”

“He’ll be the dead brains if he butts in,” Jelly Varnes said.

Chancy expected Lucas Stout to speak up and say that there wasn’t to be any shooting without his say-so, but Stout stayed quiet. He’d always regarded the trail boss as the most levelheaded in the outfit, but now he saw that when the herd was threatened, Stout would do whatever was necessary, the consequences be damned.

As they drew near the south end of town, Chancy found himself wrestling with his nerves. Here they were, attempting to sneak into Prosperity in broad daylight. Someone was bound to see them. They could be up to their armpits in armed townsfolk before they knew it.

Lucas Stout led them to the rear of the stable. It hid them well enough that they reached the corral without an outcry. They dismounted, tied their animals to the rails, and cat-footed around to the side. When Stout drew his six-shooter, so did everyone else.

Chancy hoped he wouldn't have to use it. He wasn't Jelly. He didn't take delight in shooting people. He would if they left him no choice, though.

At the front Stout stopped and indicated they should hug the wall. Removing his hat, he poked his head out. "No one," he whispered. "The town is as dead as when we rode in." He gestured at Chancy. "Come up here and point out the cabin Finger is in. I can't remember of it's the second or the third."

Chancy moved past the others. "There," he said, pointing at the second. They would have to cross about fifty feet of open space to reach it.

"Where is everybody?" Ollie whispered.

As if in answer, one of the stable doors opened and voices filled the air. Into the sunlight strolled the townsmen in clusters of twos and threes. Mayor Broom, Krine, and Ives were among them. So was Ira Reid.

With a start, Chancy realized they must have been holding some sort of meeting in the stable. He ducked back before he was spotted.

"I expect all of you at the saloon within the hour," Krine called out. "Bring your rifles. If those cowboys try to slip away, they're in for a surprise."

Someone laughed, and Mayor Broom said, "Those Texans think they have twenty-four hours. We have plenty of time. We must do this right, gentlemen. Like we did with the last herd."

Chancy risked a peek. The townsmen were talking and smiling and acting as if the scheme they'd hatched was the most natural thing in the world. And for them, maybe it was. That notion started a troubling train of thought.

"Should we forget about Finger for now?" Drew Case whispered.

"No," Lucas Stout said.

"We can't reach him without being seen," Drew pointed out. "They could riddle us with slugs."

"If all of us tried they'd spot us for sure," Stout agreed. "But maybe not if only one of us goes."

"Let me," Jelly Varnes whispered.

"You're too eager to squeeze the trigger," Lucas Stout said. "It has to be someone else." He looked at Chancy.

"Oh hell," Chancy said.

Chapter 30

Chancy poked his head around the corner.

Krine and Broom and the rest were well down the street. They had gone past the cabin where Finger was recuperating. Several were entering other cabins, maybe to fetch their rifles as they'd been instructed.

Chancy pulled his hat brim down. "Wish me luck," he said, and moved into the open. His chin tucked low, he didn't rush. It might draw attention. He walked at the same gait as the townsmen and watched them from under his hat brim. At a casual glance, he might appear to be one of them.

The four leaders, as he had come to think of them, were headed for the saloon. Krine and Mayor Broom were in a heated discussion. Ives and Reid trailed behind, neither so much as looking at the other.

A man at the fifth cabin down, about to go in, stopped and looked back.

Chancy's skin prickled. He expected to hear a bellow and have the whole town come charging down the street. But the man went into the cabin and closed the door behind him.

Chancy reached Finger's cabin and was quick to do the same. Once the door was shut, he breathed a little easier. He stepped to the bed thinking he'd have to shake Finger to rouse him.

"Well, look who it is."

"You're awake!" Chancy exclaimed.

"Have been for hours," Finger said. "I'm sick of lying here." He looked past Chancy. "Where's my pard? Jelly can't be bothered to pay me a visit?"

"He's here and so are Lucas and some of the others, but they sent me," Chancy said. "We have to get you out. Things are happening." There wasn't time for a long-winded explanation.

"Fine by me," Finger said. "There's something wrong about this town."

"You already warned us."

"I did?" Finger was propped on his pillow, and sat a little higher, wincing from the pain. "I don't recollect doing that."

"You were pretty much out of it, but you did." Chancy was anxious to leave. "Can you walk yet? Can you even stand?"

"I haven't tried," Finger said. "That sawbones of theirs told me not to get out of bed for another day or two."

"It has to be now," Chancy said. "There's a war brewing, and they might take it into their heads to hold you as a hostage."

"A war? Why?"

"We'll tell you all about it once you're safe. Where are your clothes?"

"On the floor at the end of the bed. I wanted to get dressed and the doc said something about them being there, but he wouldn't let me put them on because my britches might irritate the incision, was how he put it."

The clothes were there all right, the shirt and the pants neatly folded, the gun belt with the belt wrapped around the holster, and Finger's boots.

Chancy had never helped a man dress before. He tugged the pants on as high as Finger's knees and then had Finger ease them the rest of the way. The shirt was easy. He held it open and slipped each sleeve up an arm. The boots were the hardest. They were a tight fit. They had to be. Loose boots chafed and raised blisters, even with socks on sometimes.

Finger was breathing heavily when they were done. He sat slumped on the edge of the bed. "That tuckered me out."

"Rest a minute," Chancy said, although he would rather they left right away. Someone could walk in at any moment.

No sooner had the thought crossed his mind than the latch moved and the door opened.

Laverne Dodger halted in surprise. “What’s this?” he said.

“Howdy,” Chancy said.

Dodger limped in, his peg thumping. “I came to check on my patient and find him doing what he’s not supposed to.”

“It can’t be helped.”

“No,” Dodger said. “I reckon it can’t.”

“You tried to warn us,” Chancy said. “You knew they were up to something.”

“I know exactly what they’re up to,” Dodger said. “They’ve done it before. And I’ve been part of it, until now.”

“Why the change of heart?” Chancy asked.

“I like you fellas,” Dodger said. “You’re not just a bunch of faces. I got to know you a little.” He stared at Finger Howard. “And operating on your friend there reminded me there was a time when I cared about preserving life. You ever hear of the Hippocratic oath?”

“No.”

“Well, let’s just say doctors are supposed to save lives and not take them. And they will take yours if they can.”

“The mayor says they’ll be content with three hundred head.”

“Broom can talk rings around a tree,” Dodger said bitterly.

A shadow filled the doorway and Chancy glanced over, thinking that Stout and the others had seen Dodger enter and come to investigate. But the man who appeared was the same one he’d seen go into the fifth cabin, and he was holding a leveled rifle. Big and brawny, he had a square jaw and pale blue eyes.

“What’s this?” he demanded.

“Brock!” Laverne Dodger said. “What are you doing here?”

“I’ll ask the questions,” Brock said. He nodded at Chancy. “That’s one of them cowboys. What’s he doing here? Do Krine and Broom know?”

"He came to check on his friend," Dodger said. "That's all."

"I should tell Krine."

Smiling, Dodger assured him, "He'll be leaving in a few minutes. You can go on about your own business."

Clearly uncertain, Brock started to turn, then stopped. "Hold on. Why's that other one dressed? He's not to go anywhere. I heard Broom say that with my own ears."

"He was tired of lying around in his long johns," Dodger said.

"I sure was," Finger spoke up.

"This ain't right," Brock said. He jerked his rifle to his shoulder. "None of you move until I sort this out."

Chapter 31

Laverne Dodger spread his single arm. "What the hell are you doing? Don't point that thing at me."

"I'm pointing it at the cowpoke," Brock said.

Chancy was indeed looking right down the barrel. He made no attempt to go for his six-gun. He'd have a slug through the head before he touched it. "Hold on, now," he said. "All I wanted was to see how my friend is doing."

"Put that rifle down, you yack," Finger said.

Brock kept it trained on Chancy. "All three of you sit on that bed and keep your hands where I can see them." He took a step inside, his cheek to the Winchester.

Chancy backed toward the bed. All it would take was for Brock to holler and townsmen would come on the run. "Your mayor said we could come see Finger any time we wanted."

"I'm not taking any chances," Brock said. "The last outfit that came through, we lost three men."

"Last outfit?" Chancy repeated.

Dodger hadn't moved except to hike his hand in the air. "Brock, should you be talking about this? Isn't it supposed to be a secret?"

"What is?" Finger said.

"Don't try to confuse me," Brock snapped. "Sit on the bed, Laverne, with the cowpokes."

"What will you do if I don't?" Dodger retorted. "Shoot me? Krine and Broom wouldn't like that."

"Do as I say."

That was when another shadow filled the doorway, and in sprang Jelly Varnes. His Colt was out, but he didn't shoot. Instead he smashed it against the back of Brock's head, not once but three times. Jelly hit him so hard that Brock folded without a sound, ending up on his side with the rifle half under him.

"About time," Chancy said.

Lucas Stout strode in. "We had to wait until the coast was clear. Is Finger fit to travel?"

"Why don't you ask me?" Finger said. "And, yes, I am, provided I go slow."

"We'll help you." Stout came to the bed and slipped an arm under Finger's and around his shoulders. "Chancy, take the other side."

"Go easy," Finger requested.

"Jelly, cover us," Lucas Stout said.

"With pleasure."

Together, Chancy and the trail boss, bearing most of Finger's weight, had gotten him almost to the door when Stout stopped.

"Hold on. What about the doc?"

"I'm not really a sawbones," Laverne Dodger said. He had moved aside and was tucking his empty sleeve into his belt. "But what about me?"

"I don't want you yelling to your friends and giving us away."

"I believe Mr. Gantry and Mr. Finger will vouch for me. I could have given them away but didn't."

"He's helped us," Chancy confirmed.

"Why?" Stout said suspiciously. "He's one of them."

"We all make mistakes," Dodger said. "I'm with them because the gang robbed a bank up in Kansas about a year and a half ago and Krine was shot in the leg as they rode off. The bullet needed to come out. I was working at a stable in Geary at the time and one of the outlaws happened to know me, so they brought Krine to Geary and asked me to operate on him, like I did for your hand. Krine liked my work so much he offered me a share of the gang's loot from then on if I stuck with them and tended to their medical needs."

"You keep calling them a gang," Lucas Stout said.

"Haven't you figured it out by now?" Dodger said.

"That's what they are. Outlaws. Robbers and killers, the whole bunch."

"The entire town?"

Dodger nodded. "When we first came here last spring, there were only a couple of cabins. We stopped to rest up, and a herd happened by and stayed a couple of days."

"Did your friends try to steal their cattle too?"

"No. But Broom had a brainstorm. He gave a speech, saying how he was tired of always being on the move, and living hand to mouth, and wouldn't it be nice for them to have their own town and make money legal-like? All they had to do was a little work putting up a saloon and a store and a few more, and it would bring herds in right to their doorstep."

"Outlaws, by golly," Finger said.

"An outlaw town, you might call it," Dodger said. "And they have caught you smack in their web."

"Like hell they have," Lucas Stout said.

"Listen, mister," Dodger said. "More have joined since we came and there are well over forty of them now. They won't let you leave unless you give them the cattle they want. Fight them, and they'll take your whole herd."

"What about us?" Chancy said.

"They can't take your herd if you're alive, now, can they?"

"Are you saying what I think you're saying?" Finger said.

"How many herds have they done this to?" Lucas Stout asked.

"Five so far," Laverne Dodger revealed. "Four gave them the cattle they demanded, and Krine and some of the others took the cows to Wichita and sold them."

"What happened with the fifth herd?" Stout wanted to know.

"The trail boss refused to hand over a single cow. There were about eight hundred head. And he only had eight hands."

"The gang killed them?"

"Every last cowboy. That's where all the used clothes in the store came from. Krine and his wild bunch will do the same to you if you buck them."

"Did you warn those other outfits like you're warning us?"

Dodger bowed his head. "To my shame, I did not. I didn't get to know them like I have some of you."

"That's no excuse," Stout said.

Dodger flinched.

Jelly Varnes had been watching out the door, and turned. "Did I hear right? They're outlaws? Every last mother's son?"

"You heard right," Dodger said. "They drove off the settlers who were here before them. Everyone in Prosperity except the ladies at the saloon is a member of the gang."

Jelly looked at Stout. "Does this mean I can stop holding back and shoot any of these buzzards who give us trouble?"

"Shoot away," Stout said.

"About time," Jelly said, and he smiled.

Chapter 32

Chancy figured they'd make for the stable as quickly as they could, but he was mistaken.

"Around to the back of the cabin," Lucas Stout said.

Jelly Varnes covered them. Finger grunted and grimaced but didn't complain. At the rear, they halted.

"You all right?" Chancy asked Finger.

"That took a lot out of me. I reckon I'm puny yet."

"You have to hold up," Lucas Stout said. "In another minute we'll have you on a horse."

Drew and Ollie had fetched their mounts from the corral and were hurrying along the back of the cabins toward them. Not at a gallop. The sound might draw attention. They came at a fast walk, tugging on the reins to the riderless horses.

"You'll have to ride double, Finger," Lucas Stout said.

"I sure couldn't do it on my own," Finger said.

Chancy was eager to get out of there. They had been lucky so far, but a townsman—no, an *outlaw*—might happen by at any time.

Ollie arrived with Chancy's animal. Drew Case was behind him with the rest.

"Gantry, how about if you take Finger?" Lucas Stout said.

"Fine by me." Swinging on, Chancy lowered an arm, and with him pulling and Lucas Stout giving Finger a boost from below, Finger was able to get on. "Hold tight," Chancy advised.

Finger gripped the back of Chancy's belt with both hands.

"We go easy until we're out of sight," Lucas Stout cautioned. He forked leather and raised his reins. "Jelly, what are you waiting for?"

Only then did Chancy realize Jelly Varnes was still by the cabin and looking toward the street. Suddenly Jelly pressed his back to the rear wall and put a finger to his lips. Not ten seconds later spurs jingled and around the corner came one of the outlaws. The man was heeled, and on seeing them on their horses, he clawed for his six-shooter. "Hold it right there."

Quick as thought, Jelly stepped in close, jammed his ivory-handled Colt against the man's ribs, and fired. The slug passed clear through the outlaw's torso and burst out the other side, spraying blood and gore. The blast wasn't as loud as it would have been, but it was still more than loud enough to be heard from one end of the town to the other.

Jelly darted to his horse and climbed on. The instant he was in the saddle, Lucas Stout bawled for them to ride.

Chancy didn't need to be urged. Shouts were breaking out, and it wouldn't be long before other outlaws showed up.

Racing to the west at a trot, they glanced back.

"There's one!" Ollie cried out. "He's seen that dead jasper and now he sees us."

Chancy braced for the boom of a shot. It was slow in coming, but when it did, he involuntarily flinched in anticipation of taking lead in the back. Which was silly of him. The slug would have to pass through Finger Howard first.

"Anyone hit, cry out," Lucas Stout bawled.

No one was.

Finger leaned into Chancy and firmed his hold. "All this bouncing," he said. "It's not doing me any favors."

"We'll slow once we're out of rifle range," Chancy offered. Unless the outlaws came after them, they should be safe.

Ollie veered to come alongside. "So far, so good, pard."

"Don't jinx it," Chancy said.

"I'm obliged to you for coming to get me," Finger said. "You put yourselves in danger on my account."

"You ride for the brand, the same as us," Chancy said. "We don't leave one of our own behind."

"A whole town of outlaws," Finger said. "Who would have believed it?"

"Mr. Stout can outfox those buzzards," Ollie said. "I'd stake my life on it."

"You are," Finger said.

Unexpectedly Lucas Stout, who had pulled a good twenty yards ahead, stopped and reined his roan around. Jelly Varnes and Drew Case did the same.

"He must be worried about Finger," Ollie said.

It wasn't that at all. Stout pointed toward town and said something that Chancy didn't catch. One glance sufficed to know why.

Six riders were streaming out of town after them.

"Here comes trouble," Ollie said.

An understatement, if ever Chancy heard one. His rifle was in his saddle scabbard, and he reached down to slide it out.

"No," Lucas Stout said. "You keep going with Finger. The rest of us will persuade them to leave us be."

"Persuade with lead," Jelly Varnes said. "It's the best persuasion there is." He yanked his own rifle free and jacked the lever.

"What are you waiting for, Gantry?" Lucas Stout asked.

Chancy hated to leave Ollie. Times like this, pards should be together. But then Finger was Jelly's pard, and Jelly was on his own too. The difference being that Jelly was a gun hand and Ollie was a kitten. "I wish we'd never seen that sign," he grumbled.

"Which?" Finger said.

"The one that brought us here."

"If you hadn't," Finger reminded him, "I wouldn't have gotten to a sawbones in time. I'd likely be dead now. I'm grateful that you did."

To make amends, Chancy said, "You're right. You're more important than our cattle."

"Don't let Stout hear you say that," Finger said, and laughed. Or started to. Pain caused him to grit his teeth and scowl.

"You should rest," Chancy said.

"On the back of a horse?"

Chancy was about to mention that they did it all the time while riding herd, when a flurry of shots shattered the afternoon heat.

Chapter 33

The six riders had spread out and two of them had rifles to their shoulders and were spraying lead as they rode.

Chancy didn't recognize them. It wasn't any of the leaders. Whoever they were, they were reckless. It was easy enough to hit a target when standing still, but to do it from the saddle of a fast-moving horse took skill. It was hard to hold the rifle steady and fix a bead.

Jelly Varnes laughed. Wedging his Winchester to his own shoulder, he rose in the stirrups, held himself perfectly still, and squeezed off a shot.

The foremost rifleman's head snapped back and he tumbled from his mount in a whirl of disjointed limbs.

It brought the rest to a stop. Except for the other man with a rifle. He glanced back at his fallen companion, then worked his lever like someone possessed, shooting at Jelly.

Chancy held his breath. Were it him, he'd have ducked. But Jelly stayed straight and took deliberate aim. Chancy heard him say, "Jackass."

Jelly's rifle banged.

The second shooter whipped half around, his rifle falling from arms gone limp. His horse went another ten yards or so and the outlaw pitched headfirst to the ground and was still.

The rest decided not to try their luck. One shook a fist and bellowed something. Then they reined around and headed for town.

Chuckling, Jelly sat and rested his Winchester's stock on his thigh. "Some wolves are chickens."

"That was damn fine shooting," Drew Case said.

"It's what I do," Jelly said.

"Keep doing it when there's the need," Lucas Stout said. Smiling, he reined around and gave a mild start. "Gantry? What the blazes are you still doing here? Didn't you have the sense to ride on?"

"We were watching," Ollie said.

"I wasn't talking to you," Stout said. "We can defend ourselves, but Finger can't. You should have gone on."

Their trail boss was right, and Chancy knew it. "Sorry," he said. "I wasn't thinking."

"From here on we have to stay sharp," Stout said. "They won't hold back after this. They won't pretend to be decent citizens any longer. Not after we've killed three of them. They'll come at us with everything they have."

"You make it sound like we're in a war," Ollie said.

"We are," Lucas Stout said. "I'll lay it all out when we get back. All of you have a decision to make." He didn't go on.

Chancy pointed his horse toward the lake. "How are you holding up?" he asked over his shoulder.

"I wouldn't mind resting for a spell," Finger said weakly. "Some soup and sleep would perk me considerably."

"Why soup?"

"The sawbones said I shouldn't have solids, as he called them, for a while. Something about my innards needing time to mend."

"I keep forgetting that was a serious operation."

"I don't," Finger said.

Chancy's thoughts drifted to Missy Burke. He yearned to see her again, but that was out of the question. He couldn't go near Prosperity without being shot. He imagined she'd be safe, since the ladies weren't part of the gang. But he worried for her anyway, and fell into a sulk.

The hands not on herd duty had heard the shots and were saddling horses to come to their aid. Ben Rigenaw, in fact, was about to climb on a big bay when they rode in. Several asked questions all at once but fell silent when Lucas Stout held up his hand.

"Save those for later. Right now I want Ben to collect everyone on herd. Every last hand. There's things I have to say, and we have to do it quick. We can't leave the cattle unprotected."

Without so much as a word, Rigenaw rode off.

Ollie lent Chancy a hand in easing Finger Howard off and helped bear him to the chuck wagon. Old Charlie wasn't just the cook; he was their nurse, and he spread out a blanket for Finger, then shooed them away.

Chancy went to the fire and filled his tin cup from the pot Old Charlie never let run empty, and squatted.

Ollie imitated him. "We're in for it now, aren't we?"

"Those owl-hoots will be out for blood," Chancy predicted.

"Whoever heard of a town of bad men?" Ollie said. "A whole *town*! And them being so sneaky about it."

"What else would they do? Put out a signing saying 'Bring your cattle and we'll steal them'?"

Ollie laughed. "That would be plumb dumb, and they're not that. My ma used to say that outlaws are like foxes after chickens. They have to be smart about it or they'll never get into the coop."

"Your ma is smart herself."

"That she is," Ollie said fondly. "I can't wait to see her again. Her and Pa and my brothers and sisters. I miss them fierce some days."

"To see them you have to stay alive," Chancy said. "So you be extra careful from here on out, you hear me?"

"What else would I be?"

"I know you. You're too easygoing. Too trusting."

"Shucks, pard. I'm not a dimwit," Ollie said, sounding hurt. "That time a bear was after me, I knew to run away. And I stomped a rattlesnake to death once. It was a little one, but it still took a lot of stomping."

"Now we have owl-hoots to stomp."

Lucas Stout made the same point when the rest of the hands got there. They sat in pairs: Chancy with Ollie, Rigenaw with Lester Smith, Addy with Mays, Drew Case next to Long Tom, Parker and Webb, Lafferty by Collins. Jelly sat alone because Finger was over at the chuck wagon with Old Charlie.

Lucas Stout got right to it with "I called all of you together because you have a decision to make. You know about the outlaws. They won't let us leave. They want our cattle and they'll kill every man Jack here to get them."

"Let them try!" Jelly Varnes said.

"We'll blow them to hell," Drew Case snarled.

Stout continued. "None of you signed up for something like this. You signed up to drive cattle, not swap lead with a pack of killers."

"They picked the wrong outfit to tangle with," Long Tom said.

"They get our cows over our dead bodies," young Mays called out.

Lucas Stout coughed. "I'm the trail boss. The herd is my responsibility. I'll die protecting it if I have to. But I won't force you to do the same. Each of you has to ask himself if you're willing to die for the brand as well. Because that's what it will come down to. It will be them or us. And don't expect them to come at us straight up. These are vicious man-killers. They'll shoot us from ambush. Try any trick they can think of. You might not even hear the shot that kills you."

"I'll hear it," Ollie said. "I have real good ears."

More than a few mouths crinkled in grins and smiles.

"My point," Stout said, "is that each of you must make up your own mind whether to stay and fight, or go. I won't hold it against you if you leave."

"How can you say such a thing?" Rigenaw asked, sounding offended.

"Do you reckon we're paper-backed?" Addy said.

"There's not a man here I'm not proud to work with," Lucas Stout said. "But I won't force you to take part in what comes next. It's do or die, and whether you stay or not should be up to you." He paused. "So here's your chance. Anyone who wants, light a shuck, and no hard feelings."

No one moved.

"Don't feel embarrassed if you want to go," Stout persisted. "It's better to be breathing than dead."

Chancy stayed put. He was worried, sure, but he wouldn't be able to live with himself if he deserted his pard and his friends. Plus, there was Missy to consider. Somehow he was going to see her again.

"No takers?" Lucas Stout said.

Jelly Varnes pushed to his feet. "I can't speak for the rest of these hombres, but I'll tell you something, trail boss. I'm insulted you ask. I signed on to do a job. To take this herd to Wichita. To stick at it through thick and thin. Storms, drought, hostiles, what have you. They come with the work. Outlaws too."

"Exactly right," Drew Case said.

Jelly wasn't done. "These vermin are out for our blood and you want us to tuck tail? To go around with a yellow streak down our backs for the rest of our days?" He shook his head. "A man doesn't let others ride roughshod over him. A man doesn't let them take what isn't theirs. A man stands up for himself, and for the things he believes in. He does what needs doing, and that's all there is to it."

Chancy found himself nodding along with a lot of the others. Someone even clapped.

"I shot three of those buzzards today," Jelly concluded. "And I get to shoot a lot more before this is done. Let them come after our cattle. They'll find out that when you tangle with cowboys, you bleed."

Lucas Stout appeared deeply moved. He looked at each and every one of them, and said, almost hoarsely, "Well, then. It's settled. We're going to war."

Chapter 34

Stars speckled the night sky. A wind out of the northwest rustled the grass, and somewhere an owl hooted.

By the position of the Big Dipper, Chancy reckoned it was close to midnight. Another five hours of riding herd to go.

"That was some speech, wasn't it?" Ollie remarked. "Jelly got all of us raring to spill blood."

Chancy wouldn't go that far. He was determined to do what he could to thwart the outlaws, but he wasn't as bloodthirsty as Jelly and some of the others.

"You've been awful quiet."

"I have a lot on my mind," Chancy said.

"Would that 'lot' have the first name of Missy and the last name of Burke?"

"Ha-ha," Chancy said.

"You want to be with her. I don't blame you. If I had a chance with a lady as fine as she is, I'd be pining too."

"I'm not pining."

"You sure are prickly. And that's a sign that you're pining. Prickly and pining go together, my ma always says."

"She says a lot. Or else you're making that up."

"I'd never," Ollie said.

Out of the darkness came a low laugh.

"Talk a little louder, why don't you, you lunkheads? They probably can't hear you in Prosperity."

Chancy came to a stop.

A pair of riders were sitting their horses, the younger one with his hat pushed back.

"Addy and Mays," Ollie said, drawing rein.

"Who else?" Mays said. "We're riding herd together, ain't we?"

"In pairs," Ollie said. "The boss made it clear we're not to do anything alone until this is over."

"You do as Stout tells you," Addy said. "Stout knows what he's doing." He gazed toward the distant town. Only a few lights gleamed, as late as it was. "This is bad, boys. As bad as it gets."

"They're just outlaws," Mays scoffed.

"They're killers," Addy said. "Some of them anyway. And you should never take a man who will kill you lightly."

"We have killers of our own," Mays said. "Jelly and Rigenaw. Drew Case shot somebody once too, I heard."

"My pard is a good shot," Ollie bragged.

"You ever shot anybody, Gantry?" Mays asked.

Chancy was thinking of Missy and how he would dearly love to be sharing a drink with her at the saloon. "I'm no gun hand."

"He shot a snake once," Ollie said. "Best shot I ever saw."

"A snake?" Mays said, and snickered.

"There are snakes and there are snakes," Addy said. "The serpents we're up against have two legs and fangs that can shoot you full of lead. It could happen at any time, so don't let down your guard."

"Are you trying to scare us?" Ollie said.

"If you're not already, you should be," Addy replied. "Fear keeps us on edge when we need to be the most."

"All it makes me want to do is worry," Ollie said.

Addy raised his reins. "Well, we'd better get back to work. It's not wise to bunch up like this. Stout wouldn't like it."

"Be seeing you," Mays said.

Their silhouettes melted into the ink of the night.

"That was short," Ollie said.

"Addy is right," Chancy said. "We shouldn't all be in one spot. The owl-hoots can pick us off too easy."

They reined around and resumed their guard, the cattle

on their left, open prairie on the other side. The longhorns had long since bedded down. Only a few were moving about. Here and there one lowed or snorted.

"It's peaceable, the sounds cows make," Ollie said contentedly. "I sure do like this work. I can't think of anything I'd rather be than a cowboy."

"How about a rancher with your own herd and a spread as big as New Jersey?"

"New what?"

"It's a state back East."

"Oh. I never paid much attention to what they are called. Or to anything else east of the Mississippi River."

"Why not?"

"They live a whole different life than we do."

"People are people," Chancy said.

"Some are good and some are bad. Even I know that. And come tomorrow we'll be up against some of the worst." Ollie was silent for all of a minute, then said, "Do you reckon the trail boss is right and they'll hit us in the morning with their guns blazing?"

"Could be," Chancy said. "Pretty near fifty of those vultures and only fifteen of us. That's three to one. Remember to keep low and don't do anything reckless. I don't want to have to break in a new pard."

"I'll do my best to stay alive," Ollie said. "But I wasn't joshing about being worried. I'm scared, Chancy. More scared than I've ever been."

"That's normal."

"What kind of world is it where people are out to kill you over a bunch of cows?"

"They're out to kill us over the sixty thousand dollars they'll get for selling those cows," Chancy amended.

"Why can't folks get along? Me, I could go my whole life without hurting a soul and be happy as can be."

"You're a good man, Oliver Teal," Chancy said, and meant it.

"I suppose that counts for something," Ollie said. "But between you and me, what good does being good do if it gets you killed?"

“A parson would say that being good was its own reward.”

“I bet that parson never had outlaws out for his blood,” Ollie said. “All he has to fret about is the Devil.”

“There are human devils too,” Chancy said.

Chapter 35

Lucas Stout had everyone up and ready to head out before daybreak. His plan was to drive the herd to the north until the town was out of sight, then swing east to the main trail to Kansas.

Everyone was to check that their sidearms and rifles were loaded. Partners were to stick together. Since Finger was laid up in the chuck wagon, Jelly Varnes would ride with Stout. Ben Rigenaw and Lester Smith, along with Chancy and Ollie, were to bring up the rear and give warning if the outlaws streamed out of Prosperity to try to stop them from leaving.

Chancy thought it was a good plan. They had enough rifles that even though they were outnumbered, they might be able to drive the outlaws off.

"How come we're at the back?" Ollie asked anxiously. "We're not gun hands like Ben Rigenaw."

"Few of us are," Chancy said.

"Jelly should be back here. Not us."

"Stout wants a shooter at the front too."

Gnawing his lip, Ollie stared toward town. "They won't let us go. You know that, don't you?"

"Have a little confidence." Chancy sought to cheer him up.

No sooner had a golden arch crowned the horizon than they were under way. Usually the cattle were allowed to string out, but today the punchers kept the herd tightly bunched, the better to control them.

Chancy tried not to think of Missy Burke, and couldn't. Every step of his horse took him farther from her, and from any likelihood of the two of them getting to know each other better. That he hadn't been able to go back to see her was like a rock in the pit of his stomach.

He'd thought about asking Lucas Stout if they could take her along, but he knew what the answer would be. The trail boss would brand the notion preposterous. So would a lot of the others. A woman on a trail drive? And with a fight coming? They'd laugh him to scorn.

Chancy had no choice. He must leave with the rest and hope he would somehow see Missy again. Maybe if he got word to her, sent her a letter, she could come to Wichita. It was the only straw he had, and he clutched at the idea like a man caught in a flood clinging to a log.

Ollie kept twisting in his saddle to look back. After they had gone about a quarter of a mile, he smiled and said, "I reckon we were worried over nothing. There's no one after us."

He spoke too soon.

They hadn't gone another hundred yards when riders galloped out of town toward the herd.

"Get set, boys," Rigenaw called out, and fired a shot into the air to warn Lucas Stout, as Stout had instructed him to do before they started out.

Chancy counted ten outlaws. He wondered why the other thirty or so weren't with them, and speculated that maybe these ten were the best shots, or those with the most grit.

Ollie was wondering something similar because he said, "How do they figure to stop us with so few?"

"Ten is still a lot when there's only fifteen of us."

The flankers on the herd were watching the outlaws too. Drew Case raised his rifle, but the owl-hoots were too far off yet.

Soon Lucas Stout came riding back, Jelly Varnes at his side.

The pack of two-legged wolves had slowed well out of rifle range and were matching the herd's pace.

"What do you make of that, boss?" Ollie asked.

It was Jelly who answered. "They're afraid to tangle with us after yesterday. Bluff and bluster, the whole bunch."

"Or they could be up to something," Ben Rigenaw said.

Jelly reached down and patted his rifle in its scabbard. "Let them try. I'll drop two or three and the rest will tuck tail."

"I never have understood that," Ollie said. "People don't have tails. Dogs and cats and cows do, but not us. So how can we tuck them?"

Jelly looked at him. "Are you serious?"

"About what?" Ollie said.

"The saying is about our other tail," Chancy said.

"The ones on our horses?"

"Enough about tails," Lucas Stout said curtly. "Keep an eye on them and if they come any closer, send a holler up the line."

"Count on it," Rigenaw said.

Lucas Stout rode back. Jelly went to follow, then glanced at Ollie. "You shouldn't be let loose without a leash."

"How would that do me any good?" Ollie said.

Jelly snorted and trotted after Lucas Stout.

"Varnes is prickly today," Ollie commented.

Chancy reflected that all of them were on edge. With good cause. He developed a crick in his neck from looking back so much. To relieve the discomfort, he shifted in his saddle so he was half-turned, his hand on his Colt.

"Is that Ira Reid?" Ollie suddenly said.

Chancy squinted against the glare of the sun. "Damned if it isn't," he said. He saw no sign of Krine or Ives or the mayor, and mentioned as much.

"You'd think they would tag along, them being in charge, and all," Ollie observed. "Maybe Jelly was right and they're yellow."

Chancy doubted that was the case. Ives had impressed him as one of those men who didn't know the meaning of fear. Krine had a hardness about him that suggested he didn't either. Mayor Broom didn't strike him as particularly courageous, but there was no telling how brave someone was until he was put to the test. For all he knew, Broom was a hellion when he had to be.

"What's that?" Ollie said, and pointed to the northeast.

Not quite a mile off, a dust cloud was being raised by

a lot of riders. They were parallel with the herd but would soon be past it.

"It must be the other outlaws," Chancy realized.

"They get ahead of us, we'll have outlaws at the front and the back," Ollie said. "This is about to get bad, isn't it, pard?"

"Very bad," Chancy said.

Chapter 36

Lucas Stout must have thought so too. He called a halt, then had the flankers on the west move to the front of the herd while the flankers on the east reinforced the hands at the rear.

Every last cowboy unlimbered his rifle.

The outlaws following the herd drew rein. They had rifles too, and Ira Reid flourished his over his head and waved it as if it was some sort of challenge.

"He's awful eager for our blood," Ollie said.

"For mine, most likely," Chancy said. He would have to watch his back if shooting broke out.

All this while the dust cloud had circled to the northwest and would soon be directly in the herd's path.

"They'll have us hemmed," Ollie said worriedly.

"We have to trust Stout's judgment," Chancy said. "He'll know what to do." Or so he hoped. Trail bosses were accustomed to dealing with all kinds of problems, but battles with outlaws usually weren't one of them.

"Where's a tin star when you need one?" Ollie said.

"You know the answer to that," Chancy said. Lawmen in Indian Territory were scarce. Federal marshals, mostly. They were so few, and so overworked, that the territory had a reputation as no fit place for the law-abiding. Lawbreakers, on the other hand, had flocked in from all over to take advantage of being able to do as they pleased with little fear of ending up the guest of honor at a hemp social.

"What are they doing?" Ollie said.

Reid and his bunch were spreading out, forming into a curved line with each man about twenty yards apart.

"They're cutting off our retreat," Drew Case said. "They want to keep the herd here."

"Or us," Ben Rigenaw said.

Chancy's palms grew slick with sweat. He had an awful premonition that nothing could keep blood from being spilled. The outlaws would do whatever they had to in order to make the herd theirs.

Long Tom rose in the stirrups and peered over the cattle. "That other bunch is doing the same to the north of us."

"We're in for it," Drew Case said.

"They think they're smart, but they've made a mistake," Ben Rigenaw said.

"I'm listening," Case said.

"There are only ten of them back here. And six of us."

"The odds are still in their favor."

"Not as much as at the front of the herd," Rigenaw said. "We can scatter them if we do the last thing they'll expect." He smiled grimly. "We'll charge the bastards."

"Like the cavalry does?" Ollie said.

"Only without sabers," Rigenaw said.

Drew Case grinned and Long Tom laughed.

Chancy didn't find it funny. Riding into a hail of lead seemed to him to be certain suicide. "Why not let them come to us?"

"To rattle them," Rigenaw said. "They figure we'll stay put to protect the herd. Not take the fight to them."

"That's a good idea," Drew Case said. "It will shake them up.

"No matter which happens," Ollie said, "I'll be pretty shaken."

"It's just nerves," Long Tom said. "You can control them if you try real hard."

From off toward the front of the herd, angry shouts broke out. It sounded to Chancy as if Mayor Broom and Lucas Stout were yelling back and forth. He couldn't make out the words, but it was apparent that both sides were growing angrier the longer the shouting went on. Finally the moment that he dreaded came. Clear as a thunderclap, a volley of shots crackled like fireworks.

"Now, boys!" Ben Rigenaw cried, and spurred his bay.

Instantly Drew Case and Long Tom and Lester Smith followed suit, Lester whooping as if he was having a grand old time.

"Oh Lordy," Ollie exclaimed.

"Come on!" Chancy bawled, and worked his Winchester's lever on the fly. An image of Missy Burke standing over his grave filled his head, and he shook it to clear it. He needed to concentrate on the fight and nothing but the fight.

True to Ben Rigenaw's prediction, the outlaws were caught flat-footed. They were just raising their rifles when Rigenaw fired, and the instant he did, Drew and Long Tom and Lester cut loose.

An outlaw grabbed at his chest and fell. Another was nearly slammed off his horse and had to grab his saddle horn.

Chancy fixed a bead on Ira Reid. He held his rifle as steady as he could and banged off a shot. If his slug hit home, Reid didn't show it. Instead Reid fired at him.

Chancy heard the buzz of a lead hornet, worked his rifle's lever, and squeezed off another. To his surprise and delight, Reid's hat went flying and his head jerked to one side. But Reid stayed in the saddle, and the next moment he hauled on his reins and raced toward town.

Three of the outlaws were down. The others, including two who were wounded, decided Reid had the right idea, and fled.

Lester yipped in glee and would have gone after them except that Ben Rigenaw bellowed for him not to, and drew rein.

Chancy had no hankering to give chase. Lester seemed to forget the herd came first. He came to a stop with Ollie beside him. "You hurt, pard?"

"Not a scratch."

Long Tom hadn't been as lucky. He lay on his back, his arms outflung, a red hole smack in the bridge of his nose. The slug had gone clear through and spattered the ground with brains and hair.

Drew Case vaulted down and ran to him, but it was plain there was nothing he could do.

"Reload!" Rigenaw shouted. "Just in case."

Earlier Chancy had placed extra cartridges in his pocket. He fished some out and was inserting the first when the shots and the yelling at the front reached a crescendo.

"They're having a battle of their own," Ollie said.

"Should we go help?" Lester Smith asked.

Whether they should or they shouldn't was taken out of their hands by the next development. The longhorns at the front of the herd commenced to bawl in fear and mill about, and their fright spread like a contagion. In no time the entire herd was moving away from the gun battle and toward the rear.

Straight toward Chancy and his friends.

Chapter 37

"Oh hell," Lester Smith exclaimed.

"We have to calm them," Ollie hollered.

"Just us?" Drew Case said.

Chancy shared his skepticism. Fifteen hundred head were a lot of cattle. The five of them stood a snowball's chance in a furnace of stopping the flood. Still, it was part of the job, and no cowboy worth his salt would let it come to that, if he could help it. Shoving his Winchester into the scabbard, he resorted to his rope.

Without waiting for the others, he spurred toward the herd.

"Too late!" Rigenaw cried.

The longhorns were breaking into mass motion. Slowly at first, as the cattle on the south end were pressed by those to the north. With every few steps they went faster, until suddenly the herd gave way to panic.

"Stampede!" Ollie screamed.

Chancy reined around and brought his horse to a trot. A glance showed a phalanx of sinew and horns bearing down on him. The leading longhorns were only about seventy yards away, and closing.

"Ride for your lives!" Drew Case yelled.

Chancy passed Long Tom's body and tried not to think of the mangling it would take from all those hooves.

Ollie came up on his right, shouting, "What about Mr. Stout and the others?"

"We'll find out later," Chancy replied. The important thing now was to stay alive. He slapped his coiled rope against the dun.

Up ahead, Rigenaw, Lester Smith, and Drew Case were flying for their lives. Lester appeared terror-stricken but Rigenaw and Case were surprisingly calm.

Chancy wasn't. He slapped his rope harder but his horse was galloping full out. Behind him, thunder swelled, the pounding of six thousand legs. Even louder was the bawling from hundreds of bovine throats.

Chancy was so intent on not letting the cattle overtake him that he'd forgotten about a couple of others who were in danger.

"Old Charlie!" Ollie cried.

The chuck wagon had been lumbering like a canvas-topped turtle well behind the herd. The outlaws hadn't paid it any mind. They didn't rate Old Charlie much of a threat. And now the chuck wagon was directly in the stampede's path.

Ben Rigenaw reined over to it, held out his arm to Old Charlie, and motioned for the old man to swing on behind him. Old Charlie shook his head. The stubborn cuss wouldn't abandon his wagon.

"Jump on!" Chancy shouted.

Rigenaw tried to grab Old Charlie's arm but Charlie swatted his hand away and said something.

Chancy couldn't believe his eyes. The old fool would get himself killed. Worse, he'd get Finger Howard killed too. Reining over to the back of the wagon, Chancy bawled, "Finger! Wake up in there!" Not that he imagined Howard was asleep. "Hop on behind me or you're a goner!"

Finger's head poked out. His jaw was set, his teeth clenched. On his hands and knees he shouted, "A little closer!"

Chancy obliged.

Finger jumped, but he was still weak and would have missed had Chancy not gotten a hand around him and virtually pulled Finger on behind. Finger wrapped his arms tight.

"I'm on! Light a shuck."

The cattle weren't thirty yards from the chuck wagon.

Rigenaw was trying to pull Old Charlie out of the seat, but the old man was having none of it.

Chancy couldn't stay to help. With his mount bearing double, he needed a lead on the longhorns. He rode on, Ollie next to him.

Drew Case was well ahead by now, and so was Lester Smith. But Lester saw the hard time Old Charlie was giving his pard, and he slowed.

Chancy looked back.

Rigenaw had been able to clamp a hold on Old Charlie and was pulling him off the wagon. Incredibly the cook struggled to break free. Apparently deciding enough was enough, Rigenaw slugged him, then dumped the unconscious figure across his saddle and reined away. Not a second too soon.

The longhorns reached the chuck wagon. Their front ranks parted, sweeping to either side. The wagon might have been spared except that the frightened team reared and tried to turn, and in doing so brought about their own destruction. Longhorn after longhorn slammed into them and down they went. Their weight caused the chuck wagon to tilt. There was a resounding crash. Almost in slow motion the wagon canted and buckled and burst apart. Wood splintered as the horses voiced their death whinnies. Like a raging sea at high tide, the rest of the herd swept over everything.

"That would have been me," Finger gasped in Chancy's ear.

It still could be, Chancy was tempted to reply. He smacked his rope but it was useless. His horse couldn't go any faster. Ollie had pulled a little ahead, and Rigenaw was coming up fast with Old Charlie flopping and bouncing.

The lake came into sight, and the charred remains of their campfire.

Chancy's heart pounded in his chest. The longhorns were gaining, enough that he wasn't sure he could make it past the lake before the herd overhauled him and brought him and Finger down.

A desperate idea bloomed. Excited at the possibility, he shouted at the others and pointed at the lake. Their confused looks showed they didn't understand. The only way to remedy that was to do what Chancy did next. He reined toward it, and without letting his horse break stride, rode right into the water.

Chancy was taking a calculated gamble. All the stampedes he'd heard of, there were a few instances where cattle had plunged into a river or a stream and gone right across. But he'd never once heard of a herd stampeding into a lake. He was banking that if his hunch was right, the herd would stay away from the deep water, and anyone in it. The level rose to his boots and then his knees. Ollie and Rigenaw had followed but Drew Case and Lester Smith were still fleeing to the south.

"They should have done as I did," Chancy muttered, and then beheld a sight that turned the blood in his veins to ice.

The longhorns weren't staying shy of the water. They were plunging into it, too.

Chapter 38

Chancy sought to rein deeper into the lake. Turning a horse in water that high was slower than on land. For a few harrowing moments he feared the longhorns would reach them. But no. The ones that had plunged in were slowing, and those behind were turning to avoid the lake entirely.

Chancy rode out a little farther. Finger was slumped against him and breathing raggedly. "Are you all right?"

"Still not myself, but I didn't fall off."

Ollie and Rigenaw joined them. Old Charlie lay sprawled across the gun hand's saddle, part of his arms and his legs in the water.

For an eternity the herd thundered by, raising a choking cloud of dust. All fifteen hundred save for a few stragglers. To the south, beyond the seething river of horns, Lester Smith and Drew Case galloped hell-leather.

"Those critters will run a mile yet," Ollie said.

Rigenaw was staring after his pard. "Lester," he said, more to himself than to them. "Why'd you keep going?"

"They'll be all right if they stay ahead of the herd," Chancy said.

Old Charlie stirred and muttered and raised his head. He looked around and scowled. "Damn you anyhow, Ben Rigenaw. You had no cause to bring me against my will."

"Would you rather be busted to pieces like your wagon, you old goat?" Rigenaw replied.

"That wagon was all I had in this world," Old Charlie said. "I'd rather have died than be without it."

"Show some gratitude," Chancy said. "Ben risked his hide saving yours."

"I didn't ask him to," Old Charlie groused.

Ollie surprised all of them by saying, "Ben should dunk you in the lake, you ornery cuss."

Instead Rigenaw helped Old Charlie to sit up, then swung Charlie around behind him. "Your life comes first whether you like it or not."

Old Charlie made a "harrumph" sound.

"Some people," Ollie said.

The dust was in Chancy's nose and eyes. Coughing, he clucked to his horse. Once out of the lake, the dun shook itself.

A few straggling longhorns paid them no mind.

"I wonder how the others are doing," Ollie said.

"We'll soon find out," Finger said, and pointed to the north.

Addy and Mays were trotting their way, leading Lucas Stout's mount by the reins. Stout himself was doubled over in his saddle, his hand to his shoulder.

"That doesn't look good," Old Charlie said.

Caked with dust and looking frazzled, the two cowpokes drew rein. Lucas Stout stayed hunched over.

"Glad to see you gents are still breathing," Addy said.

"How bad?" Ben Rigenaw asked, nodding at their trail boss.

"He took one in the shoulder," Mays said. "It's still in there. We have to get it out before it becomes infected."

Chancy agreed. Blood poisoning from wounds killed more folks than being shot.

"We saw what little was left of the chuck wagon," Addy said.

"Hell," Old Charlie said, and spat.

"Forget the wagon," Rigenaw said. "What happened up there? Where are the rest of the hands?"

"Pretty near twenty of those outlaws got around in front of us—" Addy began.

"We saw that much," Ollie interrupted.

"Ives was with them, and that one called Krine, and the damn mayor," Addy went on. "The mayor hollered for us to turn back and Stout told him to get out of our way. The mayor yelled that if we didn't turn back, they'd take the herd as payment on the taxes and fees. Stout told them to come and try."

"Good for him," Finger said.

"The mayor gave us one last chance," Addy said. "He told us to throw down our hardware or there would be hell to pay. Stout shouted back that they'd take our herd over his dead body."

"That's when the shooting commenced, I reckon," Ollie said.

Addy nodded. "They charged us, all of them firing at once. Stout had formed us into a line, and we fired back. I saw some of the varmints drop but there were a lot more of them than there were of us. Parker went down, and Lafferty when he tried to help him. Webb was hit in the throat and screamed and was hit again."

"That's when the boss took a slug," Mays threw in, "and everything went to hell."

Addy nodded again. "We had to light a shuck or we'd all have bought the farm. The herd had stampeded, and the dust was so thick I figured the smart thing to do was follow after them and stay in the dust so the outlaws couldn't see us. I grabbed Stout's reins, and Mays and me lit out."

"What about Collins?" Ollie asked.

"And Jelly Varnes?" Chancy said.

"I don't know about Collins," Addy said, "but Jelly was a hellion. I never saw the like, the way he worked that Winchester. He shot three or four. I hollered for him when Mays and me took off. The last I saw, he was still shooting."

Chancy felt a swelling of pride. Evidently he wasn't the only one.

"Damn, that's grand," Ollie said softly.

"But not very smart, if it got himself killed," Ben Rigenaw said. "We need as many hands alive as we can if we're to reclaim the herd."

"That's right," Ollie said. "The outlaws will be after it, won't they?"

Lucas Stout picked that moment to straighten. He was slick with sweat and in terrible pain. "We can't sit here in the open like this," he said, taking command. "The dust will settle and they'll spot us." He nodded toward a strip of woods to the west of the lake. "Head for those trees yonder."

"We'll get that lead out and you can rest," Rigenaw said.

Stout stared after the herd. "Our outfit has been shot to ribbons, our chuck wagon is kindling, and we've lost I don't know how many good men."

"Too many," Addy said.

"Once those cattle tire and stop," Stout continued, "it will be easy for the outlaws to round them up. And you know what? We'll let them."

"Did that bullet rattle your brainpan, boss?" Ollie asked.

Stout gave a cold laugh. "Think, Ollie. We'll let those buzzards do our work for us. Once they've gathered up the cattle, we'll take the herd back." His mouth became a slit. "Or die trying."

Chapter 39

Luck favored them. They had no sooner reached the cover of the trees when hooves drummed out by the lake. Krine and Mayor Broom and the rest of the outlaws were hard after the herd and didn't give the woods a second glance.

"We just made it," Ollie said.

Ben Rigenaw swung Old Charlie down and lifted his reins. "The rest of you sit tight. I'm going after Lester and Drew."

"No," Lucas Stout said. He was slowly dismounting, using only his right arm.

"Les is my pard," Rigenaw said.

"You stay put," Stout said, "and that's an order."

Chancy could tell that Rigenaw wasn't happy about it, and Chancy didn't blame him. He'd feel the same if it were Ollie.

"Lester and Drew won't let themselves be caught," Lucas Stout assured the gun hand. Moving to a log, he sank down and winced. "If they don't show up after a while we'll all go after them ourselves, but right now I need this slug out. Who's going to do the digging?"

Chancy would if he was asked but fortunately Old Charlie pulled a clasp knife from his pocket and pried it open with a thumbnail.

"I reckon that would be my job. We need a fire, though, and water to clean the wound."

"No fire," Lucas Stout said. "Krine and his friends might spot the smoke and come back."

Old Charlie went over. "You're not thinking straight,

Lucas. Taking the bullet out ain't enough. Infection could set in. I have to clean it before and I have to clean it after, with hot water, or you can dig the thing out yourself."

"Damn it, Charlie."

"Do we have time to argue?" the cook said.

Lucas Stout was as tough an hombre as ever drew breath, but he was no fool. "Make it a small fire, and be quick. I don't aim to stay here any longer than we have to."

"Who wants to start it?" Old Charlie said to the rest of them. "And who has water in their canteen? I need a tin cup too, since all my pots and pans were with my wagon."

"You can have my canteen and my cup," Rigenaw said.

"Someone should keep watch," Lucas Stout said. "In case some of those sons of bitches stray back our way."

Chancy volunteered. Climbing down, he shucked his Winchester and moved to the edge of the trees. From his vantage he could see the entire lake and a dust cloud to the south, as well as the distant buildings to the east.

"I bet that I know who you're thinking of," Ollie said, stopping at a tree near his. "It's that pretty filly, ain't it?"

"It's not fair," Chancy said. "She and me just met, and we're broke apart."

"What are you fixing to do?"

"What can I?" Chancy rejoined.

"It's a cinch—you can't go see her," Ollie said. "Those owl-hoots will shoot you on sight."

"After dark I could slip in."

"Stout wouldn't let you."

"He doesn't have to know."

Ollie puckered his mouth as if he'd taken a bite out of a lemon. "You'd sneak off on your own? Desert your friends? Risk your hide over a gal you hardly know? With us in the middle of this war?"

Chancy stayed silent. His pard was right. But one way or the other he was determined to see Missy again. It could be—and his heart leaped at the notion—she would agree to come with him. And if Stout didn't like it, he'd up and quit and go on to Kansas with Missy.

Out of the blue Ollie remarked, "I think you creased

Ira Reid's noggin back there. I saw blood when his hat blew off."

"It's a shame I didn't blow his brains out."

"He'll be mad as anything at you," Ollie said. "I hope he doesn't take it out on Missy, her being your friend and all."

Chancy gave a start. He hadn't thought of that. He wouldn't put it past Reid to slap her around, or worse. All the more reason for him to go find her.

"This drive sure has gone to hell in a handbasket," Ollie said. "We don't even know how many of us are still alive."

Chancy tallied them in his head. If Lester and Drew were still among the living, that made nine. With the trail boss wounded, and Old Charlie of little use in a fight, they had seven who could fight. Hardly enough to take on all those outlaws.

"Someone's coming," Ollie said.

A lone rider was approaching from the north at a trot. It took a few seconds for his blond hair and the splash of ivory on his hip to jolt Chancy into exclaiming, "Why, it's Jelly! And he's in one piece."

"We have to stop him," Ollie said, stepping into the open and waving his arms.

Chancy did the same, but Jelly didn't spot them, so he hollered.

It worked. Jelly lost no time trotting over and drawing rein. He was as dusty as everyone else, and bore a bright red slash on his cheek from a nick. "Fellas!" he said happily as he halted. "I'm not the only one still breathing."

"Not by a long shot," Ollie said. "There's more of us in the trees. Old Charlie is taking lead out of Mr. Stout."

"Finger?" Jelly said.

"He's kicking still," Ollie said. "My pard got him off the chuck wagon in the nick of time."

"I'm in your debt, Gantry," Jelly said.

"Any of you would have done the same," Chancy said.

Jelly tiredly leaned on his saddle horn. "Parker and Webb and Lafferty and Collins are all dead."

"We'd heard about the others, but Collins too?" Ollie said.

"Shot in the face when he was reloading."

"You'll make ten of us now," Chancy said.

"That's more than I dared hope." Jelly glared in the direction of Prosperity. "This war ain't over by a long shot."

Chapter 40

The elation of the others over Jelly Varnes being alive was tempered by the goings-on at the fire.

Old Charlie had made Lucas Stout lie on his back, opened Stout's shirt, and managed to tug the trail boss's left arm out of its sleeve, exposing the wound. Now Charlie was gingerly probing with the thin blade of his folding knife. He paused whenever Stout looked to be in a lot of pain.

On hearing the hands converge, Old Charlie looked up. "It's in here somewhere. I figure it glanced off the collarbone."

"Don't take forever," Ben Rigenaw said.

Chancy should have returned to his lookout duty but he was as anxious as the rest to see how it turned out.

Old Charlie was surprisingly gentle. After a little more probing, he widened the entry wound, inserted his index finger, and probed with that instead.

"I'm feeling queasy," Ollie said.

"Don't watch," Chancy said.

"How can I not?"

"What's this?" Old Charlie said, and practically put his face to the cut. "I think I found it."

"You think?" Lucas Stout grunted.

Old Charlie gave a sharp twist of his wrist. Stout's mouth opened wide but he didn't utter a sound, and then Old Charlie was beaming and held up the bloody slug in his dripping fingers. "Slippery cuss but I got it."

Lucas Stout rose onto his right elbow. "About time. Now stitch me up so we can get on with things."

"I don't have anything to stitch you with," Old Charlie said.

"I have a sewing needle in my saddlebag," Ollie offered. "My ma gave it to me years ago but I hardly ever use it."

"That'll do," Old Charlie said. "Make me even happier and tell me you have some thread."

"Sorry," Ollie said.

Stout had his own suggestion. "Unravel the bottom of my shirt. That will give you enough to do the job." He glanced over at Chancy and Ollie. "Aren't you two supposed to be keeping a lookout? Those outlaws could sneak up on us and we'd be caught flat-footed."

"I knew we were forgetting something," Ollie said.

Chancy hurried out to the same tree and leaned against it, his Winchester cradled in his arms. Nothing had changed except that most of the dust in the vicinity of the lake had settled. Farther south, a lot still rose to the sky.

"How far do you reckon the herd will go?" Ollie said.

Chancy couldn't say. His stomach growled, reminding him he hadn't eaten since the evening before. Like a lot of the others, he'd skipped breakfast. He'd been too nervous over the impending clash to down more than a cup of coffee.

Ollie chuckled and said, "It must be our lucky day."

"Our herd was stampeded, our trail boss has been shot, and seven of us are dead," Chancy said in disbelief. "Where's the luck in all that?"

"Only five," Ollie said, and pointed.

A pair of riders had appeared out of the dust cloud. Their clothes marked them as cowboys, but it wasn't until they were closer that Chancy could put faces with the clothes. "It's Lester Smith and Drew Case."

"First Jelly and now them," Ollie said. "If that's not luck, I don't know what is."

Lester and Drew were looking all around and spied Chancy the instant he stepped from cover. One wave was all it took, and they spurred their lathered horses over.

"You're alive!" Ollie exclaimed.

"We wouldn't be sitting these saddles if we weren't,"

Drew Case said. "How many others have made it?" He peered into the woods. "And where are they?"

Chancy filled them in. Lester let out a squawk on hearing that Ben Rigenaw was unhurt and went to find him.

Drew wasn't in any hurry. His horse was tuckered, and he alighted. "You boys almost didn't see us again."

"We'd like to hear how it was," Ollie said.

Drew took off his hat and ran his hand over his hair, then placed his hat back on. "We stayed ahead of the herd, but it was nip and tuck. Twice the blamed longhorns almost overtook us but finally they slowed and we swung to the west to be shed of them. Once we were out of the dust, we headed back. Hadn't gone far when we spotted Broom and a lot of other outlaws. They were after the herd and didn't see us."

"By now they must have our cattle," Ollie said. "They'll be tickled, the buzzards."

"Not for long," Drew Case vowed. "Once our boss is on his feet, we'll take the fight to them."

"By attacking those owl-hoots when they have our cattle." Ollie repeated what Lucas Stout had proposed.

"There might be a better way," Drew said. "You don't kill a snake by chopping off its tail. You go for the head."

"Which snake head are we talking about?" Ollie said.

"They have three," Drew said. "Broom, Krine, and Ives. We snuff their wicks and the rest might fold and let us go our way."

"Might," Ollie said.

"You have a better brainstorm?" Drew snapped.

Chancy liked the notion, only there was a problem with it. "How will we get close enough to pick them off with all the others around?"

"Think for a minute," Drew said. "Once they have the herd, they'll likely drive our beeves to the lake and bed them down. A lot of the owl-hoots will stay with the longhorns to keep guard. But not the bigwigs, I suspect. They'll be in town where it's nice and cozy, and leave the work to those under them. And that's where we'll hit them."

"It's awful risky," Ollie said. "Mr. Stout might not go for it."

"What if we don't tell him?" Drew said. "What if the three of us sneak in and do the job ourselves?"

"Just us three?" Ollie said skeptically. He gestured at Chancy. "We're not gun hands. Tell him, pard."

Chancy was about to when it dawned on him that this might be his one and only chance to see Missy Burke again. "We should give it some thought," he hedged.

"Don't take too long," Drew said. "Stout will likely let everyone rest up tonight and then go try to retake the herd at daybreak. We have to do it before then." He looked at them. "We should sneak into town as soon as we can after it's dark."

"Your notion could get us killed," Ollie pointed out.

"What do you say, Gantry?" Drew said.

Chancy thought of Missy and knew what his answer would be.

Chapter 41

Things went as Drew predicted. Old Charlie sewed Lucas Stout up, and Stout called them together to say that they should try to catch some sleep because in the morning they were retaking their herd. Jelly Varnes wanted to head right out, but Stout brought up that their horses needed rest as much as they did, and once they reclaimed the longhorns, they'd need to move fast.

There was no sign of the outlaws until toward sunset. Addy and Mays were taking a turn keeping watch and Mays came to report that the herd was in sight. Everyone crept to the tree line.

With Krine and Ives in the lead, the outlaws brought the longhorns to the lake to let the cattle drink, then drove them to within a couple hundred yards of Prosperity to bed them down.

"Why did they move the cattle so close to town?" Ollie asked no one in particular.

"To make it harder for us," Lucas Stout said.

It would also make it harder for Chancy, Ollie, and Drew. With the herd that close, the outlaws needed fewer night guards. All it would take was a shout to bring the rest from their cabins or wherever.

Drew Case caught Chancy's eye and gave him a quizzical look.

Chancy nodded. He was going in, regardless. That his motive was Missy and not the three snake heads, as Ollie called them, was his little secret.

They were a quiet outfit that evening. The deaths of their friends had a somber effect. Their supper consisted mostly of jerky. Rigenaw and a few others had enough to share that each hand got at least one piece.

Chancy bit into his and chewed and debated the wisdom of the rash act he'd decided on. Was Missy Burke worth his life? The question was ridiculous. Yet he wanted to see her more than anything.

Lucas Stout insisted they turn in early.

Chancy contrived to spread his blankets close to a thicket. Ollie, without asking why, did the same.

Night fell. The hour after that was the longest of Chancy's life. Even though he was expecting it, he nearly jumped when Drew Case, having crawled over as quietly as a cat stalking a mouse, put a hand on his shoulder.

"It's time," Drew whispered.

They had already decided to leave their horses. A hoof fall in the quiet of the night carried a long way. Better to go on foot, they'd reasoned. All three of them had removed their spurs before turning in.

For once even Ollie was quiet. Not until the woods were behind them and they were moving toward the lake did he say, "It'll be a long walk, won't it?"

"Less than half a mile," Chancy said.

"That's more than I've walked at one time in a coon's age."

"You want us to carry you?" Drew Case sarcastically asked, and before Ollie could respond, he said sharply, "No more gum-flapping, Teal. I swear, you come across as a punk sometimes. From here on out, you only talk when you have to, and you keep your damn voice down. Savvy?"

"You don't need to be so mean about it," Ollie whispered.

"I'm not Gantry. I like salty pards, not paper-backed."

"Here, now," Chancy said, coming to Ollie's defense. "My pard's not yellow."

"He's not Ben Rigenaw either."

"Neither are you," Chancy said.

Drew Case wouldn't relent. "We're about to sneak on into a nest of sidewinders. Any blunder, even a small one, and we'll cash in our chips. Ollie here is a good man. I'll admit that. But he doesn't know when to shut up, and he's about as fierce as a puppy. So if I'm hard on him it's for his own good." He turned to Ollie. "You understand that?"

"I reckon," Ollie said.

They stalked on, Drew Case out in front.

Chancy smothered his anger at Case's treatment of his friend. Now wasn't the time for whittle-whanging. Not with, as Case rightly pointed out, their lives at stake. He would talk to Ollie later and reassure him that as far as pards went, Ollie was the best any puncher could have.

The night was cooler than had been the case recently, and more than a few clouds scuttled across the sky, blotting out swaths of stars. There was no moon, so for the most part they moved in near-black darkness.

They circled to the north to avoid the herd and the men riding guard. It took longer, but within an hour they were on their bellies less than a hundred feet from the north end of the single street.

"It sounds like they're celebrating," Ollie whispered. "If you don't mind my saying," he said to Drew Case.

Every window in the saloon glowed bright, and from it issued raucous laughter, loud voices, and the clink of bottles and glasses. Only one cabin showed a light. The rest of the town was dark.

"Makes it easier for us," Drew Case said. "All the chickens in one coop."

"Or all the ants in one hill," Ollie said. "Or all the coyotes in one den. Or all the—"

"Don't start," Drew growled.

"Sorry."

Chancy almost laughed. To distract Drew from Ollie, he whispered, "I don't see anyone patrolling the street."

"Why would they bother?" Drew said. "They think they've licked us. The herd is well guarded, and to them that's the important thing. I doubt Broom and Krine expect anyone to come after them."

"They're not as clever as they think they are," Ollie said.

"For once we agree," Drew said. "Most bad men think they're smarter than they are. It's why so many end up doing strangulation jigs or behind bars."

“My pa used to say I’d make a terrible outlaw because I’d be caught in no time,” Ollie whispered. “Once I took cookies from the cookie jar and he found me out right away. I asked him how and he pointed at the floor. I never knew cookies left so many crumbs.”

“You’re doing it again,” Drew Case said.

“Doing what?”

Drew sighed. “Are you set for this, Teal? Really and truly set?”

“I’m here, aren’t I?” Ollie said.

“And you, Gantry?”

“You can count on me,” Chancy said.

Rising into a crouch, Drew Case drew his six-shooter. “Then let’s get killing.”

Chapter 42

It seemed as if every time Chancy turned around lately, he had butterflies in his stomach. As he followed Drew Case around to the back of the buildings on the east side of the street, he almost wished he was anywhere but there. Then he thought of Missy and his butterflies died on the wing. Palming his Colt, he placed his thumb on the hammer.

Ollie had the good sense to stay quiet.

Drew Case hugged the rear walls. The few windows they came to, he ducked under. Doorways, he moved wide around and covered them as he went.

Chancy was impressed. Case didn't have the reputation that Ben Rigenaw and Jelly Varnes did, but he was obviously a gent you didn't want to trifle with. Chancy prayed he could hold up his end when the shooting commenced.

The saloon was midway down, the racket being raised more than enough to drown out the slight sounds they made. The back door was shut, and light gleamed along the bottom.

Drew motioned for them to wait while he tried the latch. Ever so slowly, he cracked the door enough to peer in. Suddenly he jerked upright, shut the door again, and motioned for them to back away. They retreated to the corner.

The back door opened and a man stepped out. He was humming to himself and smiling. His spurs jangling, he shut the door and moved toward the outhouses.

Chancy let out a breath of relief. It was short-lived. For without any forewarning, Drew Case darted toward the unsuspecting outlaw, drawing something from his left boot as he went. Chancy caught the glint of metal and remembered that Case carried an Arkansas toothpick in that boot. He'd seen Case use it to cut rope.

The outlaw was reaching for the outhouse door when Drew Case rammed the blade to the hilt into his back. The man stiffened, and Case drove the blade home again, higher up.

Like a puppet with its strings cut, the outlaw collapsed. Drew caught him and hauled the body behind the outhouses. He reappeared, wiping the blade on his pants.

Sliding the toothpick into his boot, he returned to the back door and beckoned.

"That was slick," Ollie whispered.

Chancy had been shocked by the brutality of the deed, but now that he thought about it, he realized it was necessary. They all needed to be brutal from here on out or they wouldn't live to see the morning sun. "We have to be just like him, pard," he whispered. "You can't be your usual nice self."

"I'll try," Ollie whispered.

Drew cracked the door, peered in, and quickly opened it wide enough to slip inside.

A hall led to the front, and a curtain. There was a door on the left and two on the right. Drew tried the first on the right, stuck his head in, and hastened them into what turned out to be a darkened storeroom filled with cases of liquor.

"Where did they get all this?" Ollie marveled.

From down near the curtain, a man said loudly, "I'll fetch the whiskey and be right back."

Drew Case gestured for them to move against the far wall and drew his Arkansas toothpick. He left the door partway open and slipped behind it, the knife held close to his chest.

George the bartender entered, pushing on the door. When it didn't open all the way, he stuck his head around to find out why.

With the speed of a striking rattler, Drew buried his blade in the barkeep's throat. He shoved it in and up with such force, George's head snapped back. George had no time to cry out, no time to dodge, no time for anything except an expression of astonishment, and then his legs buckled and he deflated like a punctured water skin.

Curled in a heap, he quivered, gasped, and was still.

"Two down," Drew said.

"What do you need us for?" Ollie whispered. "You're killing everybody."

"Your turns will come." Hunkering, Drew slowly pulled the toothpick out, careful not to get a lot of blood on him. He wiped it on the bartender's apron and stood.

"I never knew you were such a knife man," Ollie said.

"Some things a man doesn't talk about."

"If it was me, I would," Ollie said. "I'd be proud of it, and go around with a big knife like yours on my hip where everybody could see."

Drew stared at Chancy.

"Ollie," Chancy said. "Hush now."

"Well, I would," Ollie said.

Drew Case slid the toothpick into his boot sheath and checked the hall. "The coast is clear," he whispered. "From here on out stay close and be ready to sling lead."

"I'll sling as best I can," Ollie said.

They crept toward the curtain.

Chancy felt familiar butterflies. He tried to think of Missy, but the trick didn't work. The butterflies fluttered worse. He looked at the Colt in his hand as if he'd never seen it before. He was about to shoot other men. It didn't seem entirely real, despite the events of the day.

"Remember to aim," Drew Case whispered. "We want to be sure. Go for the leaders, like we talked about."

"Krine and Broom and Ives," Ollie said.

"And Ira Reid if you see him," Drew said. "I owe that bastard for Long Tom."

"It was Reid who shot him?" Chancy said.

Drew nodded.

A silhouette appeared on the other side of the curtain, and they froze. They saw a lucifer flare, and heard someone puff on a cigar, and the silhouette went away.

"I never have liked cigars," Ollie said. "They stink."

"Rein in that mouth of yours," Drew said. "Concentrate on the killing and nothing else."

"I've never done that before."

"There's a first time for everything." Drew paused at the curtain and thumbed back the hammer on his six-shooter. He did it slowly so the click wouldn't be as loud. "Ready?" he whispered.

Chancy swallowed and nodded.

"I have a question," Ollie said.

"Of course you do," Drew said.

"What do we do about them?" Ollie asked, pointing down the hall.

Chancy turned.

Della Neece and Margie had just come in the back way and were standing with their mouths agape.

Chapter 43

Chancy was worried one or the other would let out a yell and warn the men in the saloon, but they were rooted in surprise.

Drew Case didn't help matters by pointing his revolver at them. He put a finger to his lips to caution them to keep quiet.

The next moment the situation became infinitely worse, as far as Chancy was concerned.

Missy Burke walked in. She was smiling and focused on her friends and drew up in midstep when she spied Chancy and his. "What in the world?" she blurted, and covered her mouth with her hand.

"Don't you dare shoot her," Chancy warned Case.

Ollie smiled at the ladies and gave a little wave.

Then everything went to hell.

The curtain was jerked aside by Mayor Broom. He was looking over his shoulder and said, "I'll see what's keeping George. How long does it take to fetch a bottle anyhow?"

Broom faced them just as Drew Case shoved the muzzle of his long-barreled Colt at his face, and Della Neece let loose a shriek that would do justice to a panther.

A lot of outlaws were in the saloon. Most were at tables, relaxing with a drink of coffin varnish or beer after their day of blood and thunder. They all heard the shriek and turned toward the back.

Mayor Broom's eyes became the size of saucers. "No!"

"Yes," Drew Case said, and shot him.

Or tried to. Broom jerked aside at the absolute last

instant. Blood sprayed, and he cried out and pressed a hand to his temple while tottering to one side.

The outlaws galvanized into motion.

Drew Case fired while shouting, "Lend a hand, damn you two!"

Embarrassed that he had just stood there, Chancy extended his six-shooter and sent lead into a beefy outlaw taking aim at Case. Thumbing the hammer, he fired at another. Belatedly he realized Krine and Ives and Reid weren't in the saloon. Only Broom, of the big shots.

Ollie added his lead to theirs.

Several outlaws were down. Others were dropping flat or flipping tables over for cover. A man near the batwings fanned four shots that struck the curtain and made it jump.

"Light a shuck," Drew Case bawled. "We're sitting ducks in this hall." Whirling, he bolted.

Della Neece and Margie were backing out the rear door as fast as they could, and hauling Missy with them.

Chancy shoved Ollie. "Run!" he shouted, and fired as he retreated. He saw Mayor Broom scrambling toward a table and snapped a shot but missed.

Chancy wished that Jelly Varnes and Rigenaw were there. He fired at a head jutting out but he wasn't fast enough. That made two slugs he'd wasted. By his reckoning, he had only one cartridge left in the cylinder, and quickened his pace.

A glance showed that the women had made it outside. Drew Case was next to dart into the night, with Ollie close on his heels.

Chancy had delayed the outlaws as long as he could. Racing out, he stopped in consternation when he didn't see Drew and Ollie. They must have gone around the corner, he figured, and was about to hurtle after them when a hand fell on his shoulder. Tearing loose, he turned and trained his Colt—on Missy Burke.

"It's me!" she exclaimed. "Don't shoot."

Roars of fury rose from the saloon. Chancy turned, but none of the outlaws were reckless enough to show themselves in the hall. A warm hand gripped his, and he felt a tug.

"Come with me," Missy said. "I know where you might be safe."

The smart thing for Chancy to do was to find Ollie and Drew. The smart thing was to head for the woods, and the rest of the outfit. Instead he let Missy pull him in the opposite direction, past several buildings and into a gap between a couple of cabins. It was so dark he almost tripped over his own feet, but fortunately she knew where she was going and in short order they ducked into a dark cabin and she shut the door behind them.

Chancy could tell there was furniture, but not much else. "Where . . . ?"

"Della and me live here," Missy said. "Quick. I'll hide you. They're bound to come looking."

Chancy let her pull him. His shin bumped something hard and he stumbled.

"Sorry," Missy said. "That was a chair. I forgot it was there."

Chancy was about to say he forgave her when her hands were on his shoulders, pushing him down.

"Lie flat. Hurry."

Without hesitation, Chancy did. He trusted her. Completely. Given how short a time they'd known each other, some might brand that silly. But he flung himself onto his belly.

"Get under," Missy urged.

Only then did Chancy realize he was lying next to a bed. It was a tight fit, but he scrambled underneath just as shouts erupted out in the street. "I'm obliged," he said, but Missy wasn't there. She was rushing about, doing things. Why and what, he couldn't imagine, until a lamp flared with flame and revealed she had thrown a robe on over her dress and mussed her hair.

None too soon. The door shook to heavy pounding.

"Who's there?" Missy called out.

"Me. Open the hell up."

Chancy recognized Ira Reid's voice.

"Hold on. I'm not decent."

"I don't care," Reid replied.

The door opened, but all Chancy could see of Reid were

his boots and legs. He would dearly love to put lead into the coyote, but he didn't shoot. Other legs had appeared behind Reid's.

"What's going on?" Missy asked. "What's all the ruckus?"

"Why aren't you at the saloon?" Reid demanded. "You're supposed to be working."

"I wasn't feeling well. I intended to be there soon."

"You don't look sick to me."

"I'm not that kind of sick," Missy said.

"Then what the hell is wrong?"

"You know."

"If I did, you sow, I wouldn't be asking."

"It's my womanly complaint."

"Your . . . ," Reid said, and stopped. "Why didn't you say so sooner? You know I don't like to hear about those. It's disgusting."

"Women can't help how they're made."

"Don't remind me. Stay in here and bolt your door. You have the night off."

"I do?" Missy said, sounding amazed.

Reid and the other men turned to go.

"Wait," Missy said. "You haven't told me what all the fuss is about."

"Some of those cowboys snuck into town and killed three of ours at the saloon. We're hunting them down."

"Oh my. Who was killed?"

"I don't have time for this, you silly woman," Reid snapped.

All the boots clomped into the night.

Missy shut the door, threw the bolt, and laughed. "Pulled the wool over that so-and-so's eyes, didn't we?"

Chancy realized she was talking to him. "You were great."

"Come on out. No one can see in. We have drapes over the window."

Eager to be with her, Chancy slid his head and shoulders from under the bed and went to slide his legs clear. Then froze.

More knocks were shaking the door.

Chapter 44

A look of panic came over Missy Burke.

Chancy scrambled back under and cocked his Colt. He figured Reid had returned to search the cabin, and prepared to sell his life dearly.

"Ira? Is that you?" Missy asked, her voice quaking slightly.

"It's Della," was the reply.

Once more Chancy heard the latch rasp, then the rustle of Della's skirts.

"What are you doing here, girl?" the older woman demanded. "I lost sight of you in all the confusion, then just saw Reid leave."

"I was scared," Missy said.

"Who wasn't, with all that shooting?" Della moved to the table. "Why do you have your robe on?"

Afraid she might spot him, Chancy eased farther back.

"It's my time," Missy said.

"Say again?" Della said.

"What does Reid hate more than anything?"

"Oh," Della said. "That." She cackled merrily. "He should thank his lucky stars he was born male. He couldn't take being female."

"He told me to stay here."

Della put her hand on Missy's arm. "You do what he says, dearie. I'm going back to the saloon. And don't you worry. Me and the other girls will take care of things."

"Aren't you worried there might be more shooting?"

"I hope to heaven there is." Della stepped to the doorway. "Finally some excitement." She winked and skipped out.

Missy quickly closed and bolted the door. Leaning against it, she smiled. "You can come out now. Again."

Chancy was glad too. Unfurling, he arched his back to relieve a cramp, let down the hammer on his Remington, and slid it into his holster.

The cabin was comfortably furnished. In addition to two beds, in the center was the chair he'd bumped into, along with a table. Along a wall stood a chest of drawers. A small stand was by the other bed. A cupboard for dishes, and a stove, added to the hominess.

"Cozy," Chancy said.

Missy looked around. "It wasn't when Della and the other gals were first brought here. She told me there was a bed and a stove and nothing else. They hated it, and griped so much Reid gave in and let them brighten up the place."

Chancy smiled. Here he was alone with her, as he'd been yearning to be, and he was suddenly unsure of what to do. Coughing, he moved to a chair, pulled it out, and sat. "Thanks again for hauling me out of there."

Missy sat across from him. "What were you thinking, you and your friends? Just the three of you against the whole town."

"We were after the brains of the bunch," Chancy informed her. "Krine and Broom and Ives."

"All Ives is good for is killing," Missy said. "Krine is the one in charge. Broom is smart, in his way, but he's their mouthpiece more than anything."

"We almost had him."

"Too bad you didn't," Missy said. "As for the other two, I know for a fact that they're out with the herd. Krine figures you cowboys will try to take it back tonight."

"He figures right, but it will be in the morning."

Missy gazed at him expectantly, then shifted in her chair and ran her fingers back and forth across the edge of the table. "So," she said. "Want to tell me about the fight? When they came back, they bragged about how many of you they shot, and how easy it was to take your cattle."

Chancy thought of all his friends who had been killed. "I'd rather not."

"What would you like to talk about?"

Taking a deep breath, Chancy said, "You."

"Oh?"

"The real reason I came into town tonight had nothing to do with the outlaws," Chancy made bold to confess. "I wanted to see you."

"Oh?" Missy repeated herself.

Chancy looked deep into her eyes. "From the moment we met, I haven't stopped thinking about you. I couldn't hardly sleep. I couldn't hardly eat. And then this happened."

"I bet you've liked a lot of girls."

"You'd lose the bet."

"I'm flattered that you're so fond of me," Missy said, "but to be honest, that happens a lot. All a girl has to do is smile at a cowpoke and he thinks he's in love."

Now it was Chancy's turn to go "Oh."

"That's probably all it is."

"No."

"I beg your pardon?"

Chancy took another deep breath. "I've been thinking about it and thinking about it and I've made up my mind. I'd like to take you away from here. I'd like for you to come with me to Wichita, and once I'm paid for the drive, I'd like for you and me to become better acquainted."

"Oh, really?" Missy said. "Men offer me money to do that all the time."

Chancy felt himself blush from his toes to his hairline. "That's not how I meant it. We would live together."

Missy laughed.

"As husband and wife."

Missy stopped laughing.

"What do you say?" Chancy asked when she didn't respond.

"You're crazy."

"I've never been clearer about anything in my whole life," Chancy said. "Sure, we've only just met. But I feel for you like I've never felt for anyone." He mustered a grin. "And as folks like to say, I should strike while the iron is hot."

Missed bowed her head and said softly, "Chancy, Chancy, Chancy."

"What?"

"You don't know what you're saying."

"I sure as blazes do."

"I'm not for you."

"Says who?"

Missy looked up. "You hardly know anything about me. We might not be compatible. Could be if we moved in together, you'd toss me out on my ear inside of a week."

"Didn't you hear the part about husband and wife?"

"Some men don't take that any more seriously than they do sleeping together."

Chancy's ears burned fit to fall off. "I'm not one of them. If I say 'I do,' you have me forever."

Missy smiled with genuine warmth. "You're a romantic cuss. I'll say that for you."

"So, what do you say? Come with me when I go." Chancy added jokingly, "I'll make an honest woman of you."

Color bloomed in Missy's cheeks. "Are you suggesting I'm not now?"

"Never in a million years," Chancy assured her. "I'd stake my life you're as virtuous as any gal alive."

"I wouldn't go that far," Missy said, her color deepening.

"I don't care about any of that," Chancy said. "All I care about is you and me. I reckon what this boils down to is I'm asking you, Missy Burke, to be my wife. Not right this moment, you understand. But I'd like you to marry me, and I promise to do my best to make you proud."

"Oh, Chancy."

"I'd like an answer."

"You're crazy."

"You already said that."

"You're really crazy."

Chancy reached across the table and placed his hand on hers. She didn't draw back, and he took that as encouragement. "What do you say? Would you do me the honor of becoming Missy Gantry?"

"If I said yes, I'd have to be as crazy as you."

"Then we'd be two peas in a pod."

Missy laughed, but her face was troubled. "I honestly don't think you know what you're asking."

"I think I do."

"We're going to get married? Just like that?" Missy snapped her fingers.

"Well, I have to make it out of here alive, and we have to make it to Wichita, but after that, as sure as the sun rises and sets, I'll take you for my wife if you'll admit you're as loco as you claim I am."

"Oh God."

"Don't take the Lord's name in vain. Look in your heart and give me an answer."

"Right this second?"

"Those outlaws could bust in that door any minute and fill me with lead," Chancy said. "I'd like to die happy."

"Don't talk like that."

"Then what will it be?"

"You badger a person. Do you know that?"

"I'll badger you until doomsday if there's any chance you'll say yes. That's how serious I am."

Missy stared at him. *Really* stared, as if trying to see inside him. Abruptly rising, she came around the table, startled him by cupping his chin in both of her hands, and bent. "You want an answer? I'll give you an answer you'll never forget."

And she pressed her lips to his.

Chapter 45

Chancy Gantry thought he had died and gone to heaven. He woke well before dawn and lay in the dark with his eyes open staring at the ceiling and marveling at the miracle that had occurred.

Careful not to wake Missy, Chancy tilted his head to admire her profile. Her cheek was on his chest, her hand on his shoulder, exactly as she had fallen asleep after they talked and talked and talked about their future together. She still wore her robe over her dress, and had fallen asleep with her shoes on.

Chancy wanted to stroke her hair but refrained. He would let her sleep awhile yet. The day ahead promised to be fraught with peril, especially for him. Somehow he must sneak out of Prosperity and back to his outfit without being caught. At night it had been easy sneaking in, but broad daylight was another matter. Especially since Missy was going with him.

They had made up their minds. From here on out, they stuck together. He refused to leave her for any reason.

Chancy imagined Lucas Stout's reaction. The trail boss might fire him on the spot. But that was all right. He had a few dollars in his war bag, and Missy had more than a few socked away. They'd head north, be married by the first parson they came across, and start their new life together. They didn't need his pay from the cattle drive, although they could surely use the extra money.

Chancy thought of Ollie and frowned. His pard might take the news hard. He consoled himself with the notion that while Ollie might be a bit simpleminded, he was a grown man and would eventually come to accept Chancy's new status in life.

Missy stirred. She smacked her lips and made a soft cooing sound, and her hand drifted from his shoulder to his chest.

Chancy sensed that she was awake. To be on the safe side, he whispered, "Morning, beautiful."

"Morning yourself, handsome."

Chancy nearly burst with happiness.

"Have you come to your senses?" Missy asked.

"We're still getting hitched, if that's what you mean."

"Still loco, then," Missy said, and turning her face up to him, she smiled and kissed him on the chin.

"If this is a dream I hope it never ends."

"You should be so lucky," Missy said, and ran a finger along his cheek. "You proposed and I accepted, so now you're stuck with me whether you like it or not."

"I can't tell you how much I like it," Chancy said.

"What is it about you?" Missy said.

"Me how?"

"All the men I've met, all the gents who have bought me drinks, and you do what none of those others could."

Chancy scowled. "That's the last time we'll bring them up."

"Jealous, are you, Mr. Gantry?" Missy giggled and nuzzled her nose against his neck.

"Jealous as Hades," Chancy admitted.

"Don't be. Not one of them could hold a candle to you. From here on out it's you and only you."

Chancy hugged her and kissed the top of her head. "If I died right this second, I'd die at the best moment of my life."

"Do me a favor and don't," Missy said drily. "There are a lot more best moments to come." She suddenly raised her head and looked toward the front. "Say. I wonder where Della got to. She stayed out the whole night."

"Maybe she took up with one of the outlaws," Chancy said.

"Could be. She does that from time to time. When she has the itch, as she likes to say."

"That's the last time we'll bring up itches too."

"Not if you're married to me, it isn't."

"You're downright scandalous, Mrs. Gantry," Chancy teased.

"And proud of it."

They embraced and kissed. After a while Missy disentangled herself, sat up, and patted him. "That's enough. We carry this any further, we'll get carried away. And you were the one who insisted we wait."

"It seems right," Chancy said.

"My perfect gentleman," Missy said tenderly.

"My ma would laugh herself silly to hear you say that. She used to say I had the manners of a goat."

"How old were you when she said that?"

"Eight or nine."

"You've grown since then." Missy slid off the bed and went to the stove. "Give me ten minutes and I'll have coffee perking. How do you like yours?"

"Usually black, but today with sugar and milk if you've any to spare."

Placing his hands behind his head, Chancy closed his eyes and listened to her patter about. The cupboard opened and closed, and then the door to the stove squeaked.

"I have to go out and fetch some firewood," Missy informed him. "The pile is right around the side. I'll be right back."

"Take your time," Chancy said. He wasn't in any hurry. He aimed to stay there half the morning, at least. Grinning, he sighed with absolute contentment.

The latch rasped and the door hinges creaked. A gust of cool breeze filled the cabin, and Chancy broke out in gooseflesh. He was so at peace he started to drift off.

It was only with an effort that he jerked himself out of the deep well of sleep. He listened for Missy and thought he heard her at the side of the cabin.

A minute or two went by.

Chancy yawned and perked his ears. He wondered what

was keeping her, and went to call out but thought better of it. Someone else might hear. Figuring he'd better go see, he opened his eyes and found himself staring up into the muzzle of a cocked six-shooter.

"Morning," Ira Reid said.

Chapter 46

Chancy's reaction was to sit bolt upright and tense to stab for his Remington. He saw others in the cabin, saw a man who had hold of Missy around the waist and his other hand clamped over her mouth, and he turned to stone.

"Shucks," Reid said. "I was hoping you'd do something dumb." Smirking, he relieved Chancy of the Remington and took a couple of steps back. "Rise and shine, cowboy. The last day of your life is about to commence."

Filled with fear for Missy, Chancy slowly swung his boots to the floor and sat up. "Don't you harm her, damn you.'

"The little dove?" Reid said, and laughed. "Hell, I'll slap her silly later. Right now it's you we're going to have fun with."

Chancy's mouth had gone so dry that he had to moisten it in order to say, "How did you catch on that I was here?"

"You have Della to thank," Reid said. "Everyone at the saloon was talking about you cowboys and she mentioned how scared she'd been when Margie and her showed up and saw the three of you near that curtain."

"How did that give me away?" Chancy asked when the gunman stopped.

"I'm not there yet," Reid said. "Then she let drop how Missy had come walking in, and she was scared the three of them might take a stray slug."

"I still don't—" Chancy said, and stopped.

"Figured it out, have you?" Reid said. "When I was here last night, little Missy there led me to believe she hadn't been to the saloon. That she'd been here the whole time because of her womanly complaint. It got me to thinking.

Why would she lie to me?" Reid's mouth curled in a vicious grin. "Guess I have my answer."

Chancy couldn't stand seeing Missy manhandled. "Tell that lout to let her go. He shouldn't be pawing her like that."

"You have a high opinion of doves," Reid said, but he motioned with his Smith & Wesson. "Release her, Simmons."

The moment she was free, Missy darted past Ira Reid and threw herself into Chancy's arms.

"Isn't this sweet?" Reid said, and snorted.

"I'm sorry," Missy whispered in Chancy's ear. "They were waiting outside. I didn't have a chance to warn you."

"Enough of that," Reid said. "On your feet, girl."

Missy turned in Chancy's lap. "No."

"Are you hankering to be pistol-whipped?"

Thrusting her chin out defiantly, Missy replied, "Do what you will with me. I'm his now, and whatever you do to him, you have to do to me."

"Missy, no," Chancy said.

"You're his?" Reid said in puzzlement.

"He asked me to marry him and I accepted."

Reid snorted, then said to the men behind him, "Lord help us, boys. What we have here are two jackasses in love."

Some of them laughed.

"Stop treating her like she's a no-account," Chancy said, bristling.

"She is what she is," Reid said, and shook his head. "I've known women to pull stupid stunts, but this takes the cake."

"People fall in love all the time," Missy said.

"Get off him and step aside."

"I will not," Missy said, and wrapped her arms around Chancy.

"Enough of this," Reid said. "Simmons, you and Ackerman haul her off him, and if she resists, club her."

The two men moved toward the bed.

Swinging Missy behind him, Chancy prepared to protect her as best he was able. "They're not to touch her, you hear?" Unarmed, he couldn't do much, but he might get in a few licks.

The pair was grinning like wolves about to pounce on prey when several newcomers filed through the doorway. The other outlaws were quick to make room.

"What do we have here?" Artemis Krine asked. He was flanked by Mayor Broom and Ives.

Reid didn't appear happy about the intrusion. "I caught one of the cowboys. This sow was hiding him."

"Is that a fact?" Krine said. He flicked a finger, and Simmons and Ackerman hastily got out of his way. "What do you have to say for yourself, girl?"

"She's in love," Reid said.

"I didn't ask you," Krine said.

"What are you mad at me for?" Reid said.

Krine faced him. "We hear tell you learned about the cowboy a while ago. Yet you didn't get word to us."

"We don't like being kept in the dark, Ira," Mayor Broom said.

"No," Krine said. "We don't." He placed his hand on his Starr revolver.

"Whoever told you got it wrong," Reid said. "I wasn't sure for certain anyone besides the girl was in here until a little before you got here. Ask the others."

Simmons and Ackerman and another man nodded.

"I didn't bust in sooner because I figured you'd want him alive," Reid explained hastily, "so I took him by surprise."

Krine took his hand off the Starr. "You did right fine." He turned toward the bed. "As for you two, I don't kill women. That's not to say I won't let Reid teach you a lesson, girl." He paused. "Your boyfriend is another matter. I can use him as a bargaining chip."

"A what?" Missy said.

"Ever played poker?" Krine said. "Those cowboys might be out to cause more trouble." He wagged his thumb at Chancy. "With his help, I believe I can persuade them to change their minds."

"I'll never help you," Chancy declared.

"That's where you're wrong, boy," Krine said. "You see, I don't need you to cooperate. All I need is your body."

Chapter 47

Reid gleefully pointed his six-shooter at Chancy's head. "Let me blow out his wick."

"No," Krine said.

"But you just told us—"

"I know what I said."

Mayor Broom held out his hand to Missy. His head had been bandaged, and he wasn't wearing his bowler. "Come on, Miss Burke. It'll be daylight soon and we have things to do before the sun is up."

"I'm staying right here," Missy declared.

"You know me, Miss Burke," Broom said. "I don't hurt ladies. I'm always polite. Always considerate. I only have your best interest at heart. Come quietly and I give you my word no harm will come to your young cowboy friend."

"He's my betrothed."

Broom glanced at Chancy and snickered. "My word."

"Well, he is," Missy said.

"He'll be your dead betrothed if you don't stop being so stubborn. There's only so much pigheadedness Krine will abide. Do you and your young man a favor by getting up and coming with us and convincing him to do the same."

"I don't know," Missy said.

"Otherwise," Mayor Broom continued, "these gentlemen behind me will beat him to a pulp and carry him out. So you see? One way or the other he's coming with us. How damaged he is, that's up to you."

Chancy wouldn't have let go of her for the world, but Missy reluctantly unwrapped her arms and rose.

"I have your word?" she said to Broom.

Broom glanced at Krine, and Krine nodded. "You do," Broom said. "His and mine. Mr. Reid will holster his hardware now to demonstrate our good intentions."

"I don't believe this," Reid said angrily. He shoved his Smith & Wesson into his holster so hard it was a wonder he didn't tear the holster off.

Not trusting any of them, Chancy warily rose and held his hands in the air. He'd go along for now, but only for Missy's sake.

"No need for that, boy," Mayor Broom said. "You can lower your arms."

"Why so reasonable?" Chancy said.

Krine answered with "You'll find out soon enough. Let's head for the saloon. And don't try anything, boy."

"Stop calling me that."

Surrounded by outlaws, Chancy was ushered out. He was tempted to try to grab a six-shooter, but he'd be dead before he got off a shot. There were too many of them and they watched him like hawks.

In the east a glimmer was slowly brightening the horizon. The sun would be up in less than an hour. The town lay quiet. To the west, the longhorns had yet to stir. Other outlaws were riding herd.

"Nice morning," Mayor Broom remarked.

Chancy couldn't think of a worse one. He was their captive, completely at their mercy. So far, Krine wanted him alive, but that could change at any minute.

In the saloon, an outlaw had fallen asleep slumped over a table. Another was nursing a drink at the bar.

Krine chose the table by the window. He picked a chair and shoved another out with his boot. "Sit there, boy."

Not that Chancy had a choice. Simmons and Ackerman shoved him into it and held him down when he tried to rise.

"Don't be dumb," Krine said.

Without being told, Missy pulled out the chair next to Chancy's. "Whatever you have to say to him, I want to hear."

"You take a lot on yourself, girl," Krine said. He rested his elbow on the table. "It's like this. Those cowboys aren't going to give up. They've lost men and we've lost men, but all they care about are the cattle. They'll do anything to get those cows back. Unless I give them a good reason not to."

"That's where Chancy comes in?" Missy said uncertainly.

"My bargaining chip, yes. Because he's going to tell you where to find them and you're going to ride out and give them a message for me." Krine cocked his head. "You can ride, can't you?"

"I was raised on a farm. Every farm girl can ride."

"Good. Then you'll ride out and tell them that unless they tuck their tails and light a shuck, I'm going to hang your betrothed from a beam in the stable."

"You wouldn't!" Missy gasped.

"Oh, he most certainly would," Mayor Broom said.

Missy was so upset that Chancy was compelled to say, "Don't worry. I won't betray my friends. You won't have to deliver his message."

"That's where you're mistaken," Krine said. He slowly drew his Starr revolver and just as slowly pointed it at Missy. "Either you tell me what I want to know or you'll be marrying a corpse."

"He's bluffing," Missy said.

Chancy knew better. But he still balked. "If I tell you where they are, you'll send your men to wipe them out."

"And lose more of my own?" Krine shook his head. "I've lost too many as it is. All I want is for your trail boss to admit he's beaten and let us have the herd."

"Lucas Stout hasn't ever been beaten in his life," Chancy said proudly.

"Say good-bye to your sweetheart, then." Krine thumbed back the hammer on his revolver. "I'll make it quick and shoot her between the eyes."

Missy recoiled, her hand flying to her throat. "Please, no."

"It's not up to me, girl," Krine said. "It's your husband-to-be who doesn't care whether you live or die."

Chancy was in a quandary. His insides felt as if they were being torn apart. No matter what he did, people he cared for would die. The question was, who did he care for more? The answer was right beside him. He opened his mouth to tell Krine what he wanted to know and saw Krine look past him and stiffen. Not knowing what to expect, Chancy half turned. To say he was astonished was an understatement.

Ollie had just walked in.

Chapter 48

For all of five seconds the outlaws were transfixed with surprise.

Ollie smiled and called out, "Howdy, pard! I saw them bring you in and figured I'd come see if you're all right."

"Another cowboy!" an outlaw bawled.

Revolvers were jerked from holsters as over half the men in the saloon drew and pointed their weapons. Strangely Ives was one of those who didn't. His thumbs hooked in his gun belt, as was his habit, he sauntered up to Ollie and looked him up and down.

"I remember you. The simpleton."

"I remember you," Ollie said. "The gun hand."

Ives smiled thinly. "How about you and me step outside and go to it?"

"Go to what?" Ollie said.

Chancy was beside himself with fear. "Don't!" he said. "He's harmless."

"I agree," Ives said, "but I'm still going to gun him."

Krine rose out of his chair and holstered his Starr. "Don't be so hasty." He beckoned to Ollie. "Join us, cowpoke. I believe you might come in handy. You can help me solve a problem I'm having with your pard."

"Don't mind if I do," Ollie said, and grinning, he started to go around Ives. His grin widened when the man in black plucked his six-shooter from his holster. "Gosh, you're quick."

Ives made as if to bash Ollie with the revolver but lowered it. "Do you know what I hate more than stupid?"

"Brussels sprouts?" Ollie said.

"What?"

"I hated them growing up," Ollie said. "My pa liked them, so my ma was always cooking them, but I never could stand the taste. They're too dang bitter. And you have to chew them forever before you can swallow, which only made it worse."

Several outlaws laughed.

Ives smacked his left palm with Ollie's pistol a couple of times, then said, "Turn sideways."

"How's that?" Ollie said.

Grabbing Ollie by the arm, Ives turned him partway around, then put his eye to Ollie's ear.

"What are you doing?" Ollie asked in bewilderment.

"Looking to see if there's anything in there."

More laughter filled the saloon.

Chancy was relieved to his core when Ives shoved Ollie toward their table. He pushed a chair out. "Sit here, next to me."

"Gladly," Ollie said. Sinking down, he nodded at Mayor Broom and then at Krine. "Nice to see you again, gents."

"Is this clod the real article?" Krine said to Broom.

"Real what?" Ollie asked.

The mayor chuckled. "I believe his last name is Teal. I met them when they rode in with their friend, the one Dodger operated on. And yes, Mr. Teal is the real article. He is, as they say, as innocent as a newborn babe. And also, as they say, slow in the head."

"I'm no baby," Ollie said, offended. "I'm a grown man."

"You should be wearing a diaper, you half-wit," Ives said. He had come up behind Ollie's chair and looked fit to bean Ollie.

"I'll handle this," Krine said, and raised his voice. "Someone bring a glass for Mr. Teal. And a bottle of our best whiskey."

"That's awful nice of you," Ollie said.

Chancy could hardly think, he was so worried. "Why aren't you back at the outfit with Drew Case? What have you been doing?"

Ollie crossed his arms. "Shucks. I couldn't run out on you. Last night when these owl-hoots started shooting and

Drew lit out, I turned around and you weren't there. I ran off a ways and fell into a little ditch, and hid there while they were looking for us. No one even came close, though. When things quieted down, I snuck between a couple of the buildings. That's where I was when I saw them bring you to the saloon, and here I am." Ollie beamed.

"What did I tell you?" Mayor Broom said to Krine.

"He'll do perfect," Krine said.

"You wouldn't hurt a sweet soul like him, would you?" Missy asked in horror.

"I would," Ives said.

"I decide who gets hurt and who doesn't," Krine said. "And the half-wit stays alive."

The glass and bottle were brought. Krine personally filled the glass and slid it across to Ollie. "You must be thirsty after all that skulking about you did."

"Is that what you call it?" Ollie said. "Back at home we call it sneaking." He took a sip and sighed happily. "I'm obliged, mister. You're a lot nicer than I figured you'd be."

"How would you like to do something nice for me in return?"

"If I can," Ollie said.

Krine sat back. "It's like this, Mr. Teal. I asked your pard's girl to deliver a message for me to your trail boss and he won't let her."

"He won't?" Ollie looking questioningly at Chancy.

In a flash of insight, Chancy had an inkling of what Krine was about to do. And there was nothing he could do to stop it.

"You can see he hasn't been harmed," Krine said. "But that will change if I don't get my way."

"I don't quite savvy," Ollie said.

Krine spoke as if to a five-year-old. "I'll spell it out for you. I want you to go to your trail boss and tell him the herd is now mine, and that every last one of you cowboys is to leave and never come back."

"Oh," Ollie said. "I don't know as I can do that. Mr. Stout won't like it much."

"He might once he hears about your pard."

"Huh?"

"I'll have men on the rooftops, watching," Krine said. "If they don't see your outfit heading north by, say, noon, I'm going to let Ives use your pard as a target to practice his quick draw."

"Don't listen to him," Chancy said.

"How can I not?" Ollie said.

"Will you deliver the message?" Krine said.

"No, he won't," Chancy said.

"I won't let them shoot you," Ollie said.

"You're a good man, Mr. Teal," Krine said. "Thanks to you, your pard will go on breathing."

"I'd better go now, then," Ollie said. "I need to let Mr. Stout know before the sun is up. He's fixing to try to take the cattle back along about dawn."

"You don't say?"

"I just did," Ollie said.

Krine chuckled. "Ives, you heard our new friend. Send some extra men to watch the herd. Mr. Teal, you can go ahead and leave right this minute."

Ollie stood, then caught himself. "I don't have a horse, so it will take a while. And I'd like my six-shooter back."

Krine snapped his fingers. "Simmons, you'll see he gets a horse from the stable. Ives, let him have his smoke wagon." Smiling, he stood and came around the table and offered his hand to Ollie. "I wish you'd shown up sooner. You're not nearly as stubborn as your friend."

"Hold on," Ollie said. "If Mr. Stout does as you want, will you let Chancy go?"

"You have my word," Krine said. "Now go with Simmons there, and he'll help you on your way."

Chancy was powerless to prevent them from ushering Ollie out. At the batwings Ollie looked back.

"Don't worry, pard. Everything will be fine."

Mayor Broom smothered a laugh. As the batwings closed, he nudged Krine and said, "That was slick as anything."

"Slicker than you think." Krine turned to Ives. "Send two men to trail him. They're not to let him spot them. That shouldn't be hard, as witless as he is. Have them report back as soon as they find out where the rest of those damn cowboys are hiding."

"And then we wipe them out?" Ives said.

"And then we do," Krine said.

Chapter 49

Chancy Gantry slumped in his chair, appalled at the turn events had taken. Things had gone to hell and it was largely his fault. He shouldn't have come into town with Drew Case. His hunger to see Missy had brought this on. His pard and the rest of the outfit might lose their lives on his account.

"Why so glum, cowboy?" Mayor Broom said. "You're still breathing, aren't you?"

"Not for long," Ives said, and dropped his left hand to the revolver on his hip.

"No," Krine said. "We might need him yet."

"For what?" Ives asked skeptically.

"To hold over their heads if they don't light a shuck." Krine's face hardened. "And since when do you question my decisions?"

"I was only wondering," Ives said.

Chancy wondered what it was about Krine that he held such sway over killers like Ives and the others. The man must truly be lightning in a bottle. Or maybe it was just that he was one of those rare curly wolves others of the breed naturally feared.

Ira Reid had been quiet awhile, but now he jabbed a thumb at Missy Burke. "What about the girl?"

"Take her to her cabin and post a guard."

Reid made a fist and smacked it into his other palm. "Want I should beat her first to teach her a lesson?"

Chancy poised to spring up. He would be damned if he'd let that happen.

"You're not to lay a finger on her," Krine said.

"Damn it," Reid muttered.

"You're worse than Ives," Krine said. "Try to pay attention. We hold the cowboy here over his outfit's heads to keep them in line. We hold her over his head to keep him in line. Savvy?"

"I suppose that makes sense," Reid said grudgingly.

Krine looked at Broom and sighed. "Do you see what I have to put up with? Why can't they all be as intelligent as you?"

"Some are born with brains and some are born with other skills," Broom said, clearly pleased by the praise.

"Here, now," Ives said.

Reid stepped up behind Missy and grabbed her by the arm. "On your feet, woman. You heard the man. I'm taking you back."

Chancy had no real reason to do what he did next. Reid wasn't going to harm her. But the sight of Reid touching her caused something in him to snap. He was out of his chair before anyone could blink and rammed his fist into Reid's cheek, knocking Reid sideways. Someone bellowed, and fingers clutched at his shirt. He barely heard or felt either. Fists pumping, he tore into Ira Reid like a furious bobcat into a rival. He caught Reid with four or five solid punches before his arms were seized and he was slammed to the floor and pinned by Ackerman and the others.

Reid was on his knees, his fingers splayed to his bloody face. "What the hell?" he roared. "What the hell?"

"You shouldn't ought to have done that, boy," Mayor Broom said.

"He's not to lay a hand on her," Chancy practically shouted, beside himself with rage. "He's not to so much as touch her."

Reid heaved to his feet, red rivulets running down his cheek and neck. "You buzzard. No one does that to me twice and gets away with it."

"Reid, don't," Broom said.

Ira Reid went for his Smith & Wesson.

And Chancy saw it. He saw why the others feared Krine so much. If he had blinked, he would have missed it.

In a blur, Krine was up out of his chair. His six-shooter

seemed to fill his hand as if by arcane magic and he fanned the hammer two times so fast the explosions of sound were as one. The impact of the heavy slugs jolted Reid onto his bootheels. But Krine wasn't done. He fanned the hammer a third time, and Reid crashed onto his back, taking a chair at a nearby table down with him.

In the silence that followed, Chancy's ears rang. Some of the outlaws looked to be in shock. Interestingly Ives was one of them.

"Damn him." Mayor Broom broke the quiet. "He never did know how to do as he's told."

"Now we're one less," someone said.

Krine came around the table and glared at all of them. "Anyone else have something to say?"

No one did.

"We do things my way," Krine said, his voice cracking like a whip. "That's how it's always been. Reid knew that. You know that. You do as I tell you, when I tell you. If you can't live with that, light a shuck. Because if you don't do as I say, you'll end up like him."

"It's just that we might have needed him against the cowboys," an outlaw by the bar said.

"There's still twice as many of us as there is of them," Krine said. "And I didn't just hear you imply I did wrong, did I?"

"Not on your life," the man replied, vigorously shaking his head.

"Anyone else have a gripe?" Krine demanded, and when no one spoke, he nodded. "Good. Broom, have the body drug out and buried. We don't want him stinking up the place. Ackerman, you and Franklyn take three men and put the girl in her cabin and her boyfriend in another. Post men to keep watch. Then I want everyone else back here. We have to be ready when those I sent get back with word of where the cowboys are so we can end this once and for all."

In the bustle that ensued, Chancy let himself be yanked to his feet and didn't resist when outlaws hauled him out the batwings. He was behind Missy, and could have kissed her when she looked back and gave him a warm smile of encouragement.

The outlaws didn't pay any attention. They were discussing something else.

"Did you see that?" Ackerman said.

"I was right there," Franklyn said. He was paunchy and sallow and had yellow teeth. A Remington was strapped to his waist.

"I never saw anyone so fast in my life," Ackerman said. "No wonder even Ives goes easy around him."

"Krine is the real article, that's for sure," Franklyn said. "I wouldn't buck him for all the gold in the Rockies."

"Reid learned that the hard way," a fourth man said.

"Reid wasn't thinking straight," Ackerman said. "Not after being pounded on." He gave Chancy a hard look.

"I'm just glad it wasn't me," Franklyn said.

At Missy's cabin, Ackerman opened the door and stepped aside. She gave Chancy another smile as she went in, her eyes lingering on his. Then Ackerman slammed the door and told one of the others to stay put.

Chancy was taken across the street to a smaller cabin. The door was flung open and he was roughly shoved inside. The place had a musty smell, and dust motes hung in the air.

"Behave yourself, boy," Ackerman growled, "and you'll live a little longer."

"I'm not no damn boy," Chancy said.

The door closed, and Chancy was alone in the dark interior. He moved to the only window, which was covered by a piece of burlap, and peered out. The outlaw called Franklyn was right outside the door. The rest were making for the saloon.

Dejected, Chancy turned and leaned his own back against the wall. He sagged and said to the empty air, "What do I do now?" He waited, hoping for a brainstorm, but nothing came to him.

Nothing at all.

Chapter 50

Voices outside brought Chancy out of himself. He had slumped to the floor and been mired in gloom for he knew not how long when Franklyn said something and was answered by someone else. He recognized the second voice and, curious, he pushed upright and swiped at the dust on the window.

Laverne Dodger was hobbling toward the cabin. He was carrying a sack, and a canteen hung from his right shoulder.

Chancy strained to hear.

". . . doing here, Doc?" Franklyn was asking.

"Food and water for the cowpoke," Dodger replied.

"Who cares if he goes hungry?" Franklyn said.

"Krine, apparently, since he told me to bring them," Dodger said.

"Why feed a dead man?" Franklyn said. But he shrugged and opened the door. "Go on in. Be careful. He's a scrapper."

"He won't hurt me. I saved his friend," Dodger said as he thunked into the cabin. "Wait outside."

"What for?" Franklyn said.

"I need to talk to him. Krine wants to know how many cowboys are left, and he thinks Gantry might open up to me, the favor I did them."

Franklyn shrugged a second time and shut the cabin door. The moment he did, Laverne Dodger quickly hobbled over to Chancy and thrust the sack at him. "Take these. And don't let on."

Puzzled, Chancy accepted the sack. It was heavier than

he thought it would be and he nearly dropped it. He discovered why it was so heavy when he peered inside. "A Colt!"

"Yell it louder, why don't you?" Dodger said, with an anxious glance at the door. "Keep your damn voice down."

"What . . .?" Chancy said in confusion.

Dodger slid the canteen's strap off his shoulder and held it out. "This too. It's the best I can do."

"Why are you helping me?" Chancy whispered. "I thought you were on their side."

Dodger leaned in close. "I told you before. I never got to know any of the other outfits Krine and his bunch rubbed out. But I've gotten to know some of you and it's made a difference."

"You're saying you're not one of them anymore?"

"Look at me," Dodger said. He touched his empty sleeve and pointed at his peg. "I'm next to worthless except for my doctoring. It's the only reason they keep me around." He went on in a rush. "I'm not half the man I used to be. Not just my body, but inside too. I used to believe in things. In my country. In my fellow man. It's why I enlisted. That all changed the day I was almost blown to bits. I lost more than my arm and my leg and part of my face. I lost my faith. I lost any good qualities I had. I turned sour, and tried to drink myself to death. I was lost in a bottle when Krine and Broom heard about me and offered me a share if I'd tend their wounds and treat them when they were sick."

Chancy didn't interrupt. He had a sense that it was important for Dodger to get whatever was bothering him off his chest.

"I went along because I had nothing else. I was at the bottom of a barrel with nowhere to go. I told myself it didn't matter if I rode with them. Sure, they're vicious and vile. But no one else wanted anything to do with me. People would look the other way when they saw me come down a street, or go out of their way to avoid me. I was shunned, the same as the outlaws."

"There's a difference," Chancy got out.

Laverne Dodger frowned. "I know that now. Maybe I knew it all along but refused to admit it."

"Don't be so hard on yourself."

"You see?" Dodger said, brightening slightly. "That's why I can't let them kill you. You're a good person, Chancy Gantry, like I used to be. So I snuck you that revolver. The rest is up to you."

"I'm obliged."

"Do me a favor and wait awhile before you make your break," Dodger whispered. "I don't want it obvious I lent a hand."

"What will they do if they figure out you did?"

"What do you think?" Dodger rejoined. He started toward the door.

"Wait," Chancy said. "Have you heard anything about my outfit? When are the outlaws planning to attack?"

"The men who followed your pard aren't back yet," Dodger said. "Krine expects them anytime, and all his gun sharks are ready to ride."

Chancy realized he couldn't wait long to escape. He must warn Lucas Stout and the others.

Dodger limped out, closing the door behind him.

Hefting the sack, Chancy moved to a small table and set it and the canteen down. He slid out a chair and sat. Five minutes. That was all he'd give Dodger to get clear. Then he would bust out, jump on the first horse he saw, and fan the breeze to the woods near the lake.

The door opened again, framing Franklyn in the doorway. "What did he bring you?"

Unable to hide his surprise, Chancy blurted, "Bring me?"

"The food, you lunkhead," Franklyn snapped. "What's in the sack? I'm half-starved and could use a bite myself."

"He brought it for me, not you," Chancy said, stalling.

"I want some anyway," Franklyn said. "Now, what the hell is in there?"

"Jerky and beans, is all," Chancy lied.

"That will do. Give me some jerky."

Chancy was tempted to scoop open the sack and jerk the revolver out, but he played it smart. "You want some, help yourself."

Franklyn showed his yellow teeth in a sneer. "You've got gall, boy. I'll give you that." He rested his hand on his six-gun. "Bring me some. I won't tell you twice."

"You won't shoot me," Chancy bluffed. "Krine wants me alive."

"There's always your sweetheart," Franklyn said.

"What?"

"Forgot about her, did you?" Franklyn said. "Make me mad, and tomorrow or the next day I'll pay her a visit and beat on her until she's black and blue. Krine won't care once we've wiped out you cowboys." He laughed at the prospect.

For Chancy, it was do or die. Or have Missy suffer. "Fine," he said. "You want some jerky? You can have it." Gripping the sack, he slid his hand in and molded his fingers to the Colt.

Chapter 51

"What are you waiting for?" Franklyn said when Chancy just sat there. "Bring it here."

"Want me to feed you too?" Rising, Chancy went over, his hand still in the sack, his thumb on the Colt's hammer.

"You've got a mouth on you, cowboy," Franklyn said. "When it comes time to buck you out in gore, I think I'll ask Krine if I can do the honors."

"If I had a pistol you wouldn't be saying that," Chancy said.

"Hell, boy," Franklyn scoffed. "You're about as fearsome as a kitten. Just give me the damn jerky and shut the hell up."

"I'll give it to you all right," Chancy said. By then he was close enough. He lunged, jammed the Colt's muzzle as far as he could into the pit of Franklyn's gut while simultaneously gripping the outlaw's shoulder to hold him close, and squeezed the trigger. He was afraid the blast would be so loud they'd hear it over to the saloon. But the sack, and the fact that the barrel was buried in Franklyn's paunch, muffled the shot considerably.

Franklyn jerked at his own six-shooter. He had it half out when blood spurted from his mouth, and he staggered. He would have fallen except for Chancy's grip on his shoulder. "You bastard!" he gasped, and doubled over.

Chancy tripped him. He hooked a boot behind the outlaw's, and Franklyn came down hard on both knees. "Beat on my sweetheart, will you?" Chancy said, and pulling the Colt out, he struck Franklyn across the temple, not once but again and again and again. When he stopped, Franklyn lay still on the floor.

Chancy checked for a pulse. There wasn't any. "Serves you right," he said. Helping himself to Franklyn's Remington, he rose with a revolver in each hand.

Moving to the doorway, Chancy scanned the street. No one was in sight except for the man standing guard at Missy's cabin. He had his arms folded and his shoulder to the wall and appeared to be dozing on his feet.

"Good," Chancy said. All the rest of them, he figured, were at the saloon. All he needed now was a horse. Conveniently enough, the hitch rails in front of the saloon and the general store were lined with animals. Several others were at another. The general store's was the closest, but the outlaw guarding Missy would see him.

Missy. Her image rooted Chancy in place. There was no predicting what the outlaws would do to her if he escaped. They might punish her. Beat her, as Franklyn wanted to do, or worse.

Chancy couldn't leave without her. But how to effect her rescue with the guard yonder? On an impulse, he dashed out and around to the side. No outcries broke the stillness. He ran to the rear and began to work his way from cabin to cabin until he reached the stable. From there, he sprinted to the rear of the buildings on the other side of the street and along them until he was behind Missy's cabin.

Once again, luck was with him.

Pausing to catch his breath, Chancy gazed skyward and did something he hadn't done in a coon's age. He prayed.

Cat-footing to the front, he risked a quick glimpse. The guard hadn't moved.

About to step out, Chancy ducked back. A figure had appeared at the batwings. He couldn't be sure, but he thought it might be Krine. He stood stock-still, his heart thudding in his chest; no alarm was given. He let a minute or so go by, then peeked out. The figure was gone. The guard had shifted position and had his back to him.

Another glance at the batwings, and Chancy made his move. He was behind the guard in three bounds. The man heard him and began to straighten. Chancy slammed Franklyn's Remington against the guard's head, then the Colt, then the Remington again. Somehow the outlaw stayed on his feet and clawed at his own hardware. "Fall, damn you," Chancy hissed, and swung the Colt with all his might. The *crack* of metal on bone was too loud for comfort. The outlaw melted at his feet.

Backing to the door, his eyes on the saloon, Chancy slid the Colt under his belt and lightly knocked. When Missy didn't answer, he tried the latch. She had bolted the door. He knocked again, whispering, "Missy?"

There was no answer. Chancy reckoned she hadn't heard him, so he said her name a little louder. Her continued silence worried him. He imagined her unconscious, or worse. Krine had said she was to be kept alive but outlaws were notorious for not keeping their word.

Chancy shook the door until it rattled. "Missy?" he called softly. "It's me! Let me in before they catch me."

Muffled sounds reached him. The next moment the bolt rasped, the door was pulled wide, and Missy's arms were around his neck and her face buried in his throat.

"Chancy! Oh, Chancy!"

"Shh," Chancy cautioned, pulling her in after him.

Missy drew back, her eyes glistening with tears of happiness. "I dozed off. I was so sad I cried and I cried, and then I—"

Chancy kissed her full on the lips. The urge just came over him, and he did it. He was as astonished as Missy, who put a hand to her mouth, her eyes widening.

"Oh my. What was that for?"

"What do you think?" Chancy said, and since he'd been so bold once, he saw no harm in being bold a second time. Only he let the kiss linger a little, until sounds from the vicinity of the saloon reminded him they were in the middle of a nest of vipers and not at a church social.

"You kiss real nice."

Chancy coughed and turned. "We have to go. Stay close. I'll help you on a horse and I'll climb on another and we won't stop for anyone or anything until we reach the lake and my friends."

"You came for me," Missy said softly.

"Did you hear what I just said?"

"You could have gotten clean away and you came for me."

"What sort of man would I be if I didn't?" Chancy said. He tugged on her hand, but she didn't move.

"I've never had anyone do something like this. It's scary."

"Missy, *please*."

"If I had any doubts, I don't anymore."

Nearly beside himself with worry, Chancy pulled harder. "Now isn't the time. We're going, you hear me?"

"Whatever you say, Chancy."

Intent on her, Chancy didn't hear the approaching footsteps until they were almost to the cabin door.

Chapter 52

Chancy swung toward the door, drawing the Colt as he turned so that both pistols were level and cocked when Laverne Dodger limped up and put his only hand on his hip. "What in hell do you think you're doing?" he demanded, and didn't give Chancy a chance to answer. "I told you to light out. Instead you sneak over here. I saw you club Amos. And then you just left him lying there in the open for anyone to see."

"Chancy came for me," Missy said.

"That's no excuse for being stupid," Dodger said.

"Don't talk about him like that," Missy said.

"Lady, harsh words are the least of your worries." Dodger pointed at the bleeding Amos. "Drag him in here or all of us will be in hot water."

Chancy finally got a word in. "I couldn't leave without her. I'm sorry."

"Amos, damn you," Dodger said, glancing toward the saloon. "Any moment, someone could see him."

Giving his pistols to Missy, Chancy slipped past Dodger, grabbed hold of both of Amos's ankles, and dragged him into the cabin. He used the outlaw's belt to bind his ankles. For the wrists, he tore a strip from the blanket on Missy's bed. He was almost done when Laverne Dodger swore and shook his head.

"Why did you waste time with that? Get the hell gone while you still can."

"You sound afraid," Missy said.

"Girl, if you'd seen some of the things Krine has done

to those who displease him, you'd be afraid too. So afraid you'd wet yourself."

"You're awfully crude," Missy said.

Dodger appealed to Chancy. "Get her out of here before it's too late. I was willing to help you, but I don't hanker to die on your account."

Chancy took the pistols back and slipped the Colt under his belt once more so he had a hand free to clasp Missy's. "Let's go," he said, and was pleased when Missy came without an argument. He paused in the doorway long enough to make certain the street was still empty.

Off to the west, visible between buildings on the other side, was the herd, an outlaw riding a circuit.

Breaking into a run, Chancy made for the hitch rail in front of the general store. Missy matched him stride for stride, as lithe and graceful as an antelope. They were halfway there when a shrill shout came from the saloon.

Chancy glanced at the batwings, spied a figure about to push out, and snapped a shot to discourage him.

They ran faster.

Chancy deliberately let Missy gain on him so he was between her and the saloon and could shield her with his body. A shot boomed and lead nearly sizzled his ear. He returned fire without taking aim and heard glass crash and tinkle; he'd accidentally shot out the front window.

An inner blare of warning spurred Chancy into seizing Missy and propelling her bodily toward the nearest mount, a sorrel that was fidgeting and straining at its reins because of the gunfire. They reached it just as a ragged volley erupted from the saloon. The next horse down whinnied in pain. Hornets buzzed right and left. Heedless of the danger, Chancy virtually threw Missy into the saddle. "Stay low!" he bawled as he undid the reins. More lead sought him. His left shoulder flared hot as he turned the sorrel toward the south end of the street and gave it a solid smack on the rump.

"Chancy!" Missy screamed.

Several outlaws were barreling from the saloon, firing as they came.

Dashing to a bay, Chancy banged off two shots and the

outlaws dropped flat to keep from being hit. It took him harrowing seconds to free the reins. Hooking his boot in the stirrup, Chancy was only half on when he wheeled the bay after the sorrel and fired on the fly. He didn't expect to hit anything, yet an outlaw cried out and thrashed in the dust.

"Stop him!" another roared.

Missy was almost to the stable but she had slowed to wait for him. "Keep going!" Chancy hollered, forking his leg up and over. He swiftly caught up and side by side they swept around the stable and off across the prairie.

"We did it!" Missy yelled in elation.

Chancy hated to disabuse her, but the outlaws would be after them in no time, a pack of bloodthirsty wolves who wouldn't let anything stop them this side of the grave.

"Ride," he hollered, and buckled down to covering as much distance as they could before pursuit materialized.

Chancy's aim was to swing wide of the herd and reach the woods.

Her hair streaming in the wind, Missy was grinning with excitement. She glanced over and laughed.

Chancy could have hugged her and never let go. She was wonderful, this girl who had come out of nowhere and staked a claim on his heart. When they got to Kansas he'd have the first parson they came across hitch them, and forever after she'd be his. Visions of their life played across his mind, of the house they'd live in, and the kids they'd have, and how in their waning years they'd rock side by side on their porch and be as happy as anything.

Long minutes passed, and he became so lost in his wonderful daydream that he didn't realize Missy was hollering his name.

She pointed behind them.

Chancy looked but saw nothing to be concerned about. No one was after them. Yet how could that be? He hauled on the reins to bring the bay to a halt and Missy did likewise with her sorrel.

"Why aren't they chasing us?"

"I don't know," Chancy admitted. He would have staked every cent in his poke that the outlaws would be hell bent to catch them.

"They should be, shouldn't they? You shot one of them and beat another senseless."

"I shot two," Chancy said, remembering Franklyn.

"Even more cause." Missy swept her arm at the empty prairie. "But they let us go as easy as pie."

"I wouldn't call that easy," Chancy said. But she had a point.

"What's more important to them than us?" Missy asked absently.

"The herd!"

"Excuse me?"

"All that matters to Krine is the herd. He didn't come after us because he's not in town. Only a few of them were. The rest must have left to attack my friends."

"They're in great danger." Missy stated the obvious.

Chancy swung toward the distant woods. "Krine must be closing in on them even as we speak. We have to get to them first. We have to warn them."

"If we're not too late already," Missy said.

Chapter 53

Chancy and Missy rode as if possessed. In Chancy's case, he was: possessed by a gnawing fear that he wouldn't be in time, that the outlaws would surround his friends and slaughter them before he could get there.

Missy impressed him with her riding ability. So did the grim set to her face. She fully appreciated what was at stake.

Chancy tried not to think of the new danger he was putting her in. He thought of Ollie and Jelly and Rigenaw, and all the others. *Please let me be in time,* he prayed, and lashed the reins.

To the northwest the blue of the lake glistened in the sun. To the north the longhorns were bunched under the watchful eye of four or five outlaws. One of the cutthroats spotted Chancy and Missy but stayed where he was. Apparently Krine had given orders that the herd guards weren't to leave the herd for any reason.

It puzzled Chancy, though, that he didn't spot the main body of outlaws. He should be able to if they were making a beeline from town. Maybe they weren't. Maybe they were circling around to come at the woods from the west instead of the east and take the Flying V hands by surprise.

Rising in the stirrups, Chancy scoured the woodland. It seemed peaceful, but he was too far off yet to tell much.

"Chancy!" Missy yelled, jabbing a finger.

Chancy was mystified until he made out stick figures to the west of the woods. They were on foot, a line of them, the sunlight glinting off metal in their hands. He had been right. The outlaws were coming at his friends from a direction they wouldn't expect. And he was much too far away to warn them.

In despair Chancy tried to push the bay harder. His frustration was boundless.

The rest of the ride was the longest of his life.

They came to the south end of the lake and started around just as gunfire crackled in the woods. Men yelled and screamed, their cries punctuated by the bang of revolvers and the louder boom of rifles. The battle rose to a frenzy.

In desperation, Chancy swore and jabbed his spurs so hard it was a wonder he didn't draw blood. The bay, though, was lathered with sweat and flagging. So was Missy's mount.

Chancy was so frantic to reach his friends that he would have recklessly plunged into the trees if not for her. He came to his senses just in time, and slowed as they drew near. At the tree line he stopped and swung down. Several long strides brought him to a broad trunk, and he squatted and palmed both six-shooters.

Missy wasted no time in joining him. "What do we do?" she asked breathlessly. "There has to be something."

Judging by the din, the Flying V hands were putting up a fierce fight.

Chancy couldn't just hunker there while his outfit fought for their lives. "Stay here," he said, and went to move around the oak into the underbrush.

"Not on your life," Missy said, gliding close to his side.

Chancy shook his head. "Please. I can't fight and protect you both." A scream from deeper in made him want to run to the aid of his friends.

"How can you leave me alone?" Missy said incredulously. "What if Krine or his men find me?"

Chancy deemed that unlikely but he was wasting precious time. "All right," he said, reluctantly giving in. "But you keep behind me and don't stray."

"Like glue," Missy promised.

Hurrying, Chancy stayed alert for movement. It was a trick his pa had taught him when he was a boy and his pa took him hunting for the first time. Often a hunter would become aware of movement before he saw the actual animal.

Chancy nearly jumped when Missy placed her hands on his back. He was going to tell her not to, but changed his mind. He liked the feel of them, liked the warmth. They reminded him there was more at stake than a herd of longhorns. Human lives were in the balance, hers included.

He caught a flash of motion.

Chancy stopped so abruptly that Missy bumped into him. She had the presence of mind not to blurt anything and peered over his shoulder, her cheek nearly brushing his ear.

Up ahead, a man was slinking through the trees, a revolver in his left hand. He was focused on the middle of the woods, where the cowboys were making their stand, and hadn't noticed Chancy and Missy.

"It's one of them," Missy whispered. "His name is Larkin."

Chancy vaguely recollected seeing him in Prosperity.

"What are you waiting for?" Missy said. "Shoot him."

Chancy smiled. He had found a gem of a woman. Taking careful aim, he thumbed back the hammer, steadied his arm, and sent a slug into Larkin's torso. The slug appeared to catch the outlaw low in the ribs, jarring him. Larkin staggered and looked wildly about, unsure where the shot came from.

Chancy shot him again.

As the man crumpled, Missy touched Chancy on the neck and said softly, "Nicely done, handsome."

Chancy couldn't reply for the constriction in his throat. He moved on, glad he had the two revolvers. The Colt was strange to his hand but the Remington was the same model as his own.

"Another one!" Missy whispered.

Chancy drew up short. He saw an outlaw, and then one more, and yet a third, creeping from tree to tree and brush to brush. The second outlaw had a rifle. It was Ackerman.

"Drop them dead," Missy whispered.

Chancy hesitated. He wasn't Wild Bill Hickok. He couldn't down all three just like that. They'd return fire, and Missy might be hit. "Hunt cover," he said.

"I'm behind you," Missy said. "I'm perfectly safe."

"No, you're not," Chancy said. It was common knowledge that slugs sometimes tore clean through the person shot at and hit bystanders. He bobbed his chin at a tree about six feet away. "Over there will do."

"I don't want to leave you."

"Consarn it all," Chancy said. He was still watching the outlaws, which proved fortunate.

Ackerman glanced over and saw them.

Chapter 54

Surprise rooted Ackerman for the heartbeats it took Chancy to point the Remington and fire. He didn't aim. He just shot. Which made it all the more rewarding when Ackerman's head snapped back and he took a couple of disjointed steps, then did a slow twirl to the ground with a bright scarlet hole in his forehead.

Missy clapped and squealed in delight.

Reaching behind him, Chancy gripped her wrist and pulled her toward the tree. They'd only taken a couple of steps when the other two outlaws got off shots. Missy cried out and fell against him. In terror for her life, he wrapped his arm around her waist and threw them both behind the trunk. Lead pockmarked the bark but they made it around and he dropped to his knees, pulling her with him.

Missy doubled over and clutched her left shoulder.

"How bad?" Chancy said, fearing the worst.

Grimacing in pain, Missy removed her hand.

The bullet had creased her, ripping through her dress and her flesh and leaving a bloody furrow a quarter inch deep.

Rage seized Chancy. A fury so potent a red haze filled his vision and his blood boiled in his veins. He wasn't even aware that he had stood and stepped from behind the tree until he had done it.

In the act of rushing them, the two outlaws were caught off guard.

Chancy shot the one on the right and then the one on the left. They returned fire and he took a step and shot the one on the left, twice. Something seared his side. Swiveling, he shot the outlaw on the right, again and yet again. Only when he realized the hammer was clicking on an expended cartridge did he stop thumbing and squeezing.

The outlaws were down, the one on the right gurgling loudly, with crimson spurting every which way.

"What were you thinking? You could have been killed."

Chancy turned. Missy had come around the tree and was right beside him. "You never listen when I say you should stay put."

"I couldn't."

"Why not?" Chancy asked without taking his eyes off the fallen outlaws. None were moving, but he wasn't taking any chances.

"I care too much."

Chancy grew warm inside. He made certain the outlaws were dead and noticed a black-handled Remington on the ground near the outstretched fingers of the last one to fall. Chancy dropped the Colt he'd been using and helped himself to the Remington. Now he had two. He liked this new one. Black handles like these were rare. They weren't wood. Or pearl. Or ivory. He didn't know what they were. But they fit his hand nicely. His grip was solid. He helped himself to cartridges from the outlaw's gun belt too.

Deeper in, the battle was winding down. There were fewer shots, fewer yells and screams.

Missy had torn a strip from the hem of her dress, folded it, and was pressing it to her wound to stanch the blood. "Who do you reckon won?" she whispered.

"Impossible to say." Chancy suppressed an urge to call out to Ollie and the rest. He'd only draw lead.

"Give me a gun."

"No." Chancy would do whatever shooting was needed.

"I'm serious."

Chancy looked at her.

"It shouldn't all be on you."

"You're a dove, not a gun hand."

"And you're a cowboy. So what?"

"No."

"Give me one good reason."

"They see you with a pistol," Chancy said, "they'll shoot you."

Missy indicated her makeshift bandage. "They already have. At least let me defend myself."

"Consarn you."

"You're saying that a lot today," Missy remarked with a smile. "Don't be so stubborn. Your friends might need us."

Chancy hated the idea, but he picked up the Colt he had discarded and handed it to her. "Happy now?"

"Very much so." Missy held it in both hands, pointed it at an imaginary enemy, and said, "Bang."

"It's not that easy."

"Nothing ever is."

Chancy led the way. They didn't see a soul but they did come across a body, an outlaw with half his face blasted away.

Missy giggled.

"What?" Chancy whispered.

"He looks funny that way."

Hideous, was how Chancy would describe the gaping hole rimmed by strips of flesh. The handiwork of a large-caliber rifle slug, unless he was mistaken.

Around them, the woods were unnaturally still. Not so much as a single bird chirped or a single insect stirred.

"Where did they all get to?" Missy whispered.

"Don't start taking after Ollie."

"What?" she said. Then, "Oh."

More bodies appeared. A couple of outlaws, and Addison. The older puncher had taken several rounds to the chest and was sprawled with his limbs, and his mouth, wide apart.

"Damn," Chancy whispered.

They went a little farther and there lay Mays. The young hand had been hit in the middle of his back. The shot had undoubtedly shattered his spine, yet he had managed to crawl four or five yards before someone had come up and shot him in the head.

"Another of yours, isn't he?" Missy whispered.

Chancy nodded.

"I wonder if there are any left."

"Let's find out," Chancy said.

Chapter 55

By Chancy's reckoning, eight of the Flying V outfit were unaccounted for: Lucas Stout, Old Charlie, Ben Rigenaw, Jelly Varnes, Lester Smith, Drew Case, Finger Howard, and his pard, Ollie.

A tangle of dead brush barred their way, and as they skirted it, Chancy subtracted one more from the total.

Finger Howard had survived his appendix only to lose his life to a hail of lead. It appeared he had been shot six or seven times. His left eye was an empty socket, his mouth twisted in a silent scream.

"Wasn't he the one . . .?" Missy whispered.

Chancy nodded.

They neared the clearing. More bodies littered the ground. Some were outlaws. Some weren't. There was Lester Smith with a hole in his gut, and Old Charlie, who'd caught one in the head.

Chancy stopped.

"What's wrong?"

"So many of them dead." Chancy was afraid to go on, afraid of finding more.

"We have to know," Missy said, giving his arm a reassuring squeeze. "I won't leave your side."

Swallowing hard, Chancy crept on. The last of the vegetation parted and before them spread the clearing. It was empty. No bodies, no horses, nothing.

"Where did they get to?" Missy said.

She went to move past him, but Chancy stopped her and put a finger to his lips. He thought he'd heard something. As quietly as they could, they circled the clearing.

They were north of it when he saw a pair of boots, toes up, sticking out of high grass. The boots were shaking as if the wearer had palsy, and someone groaned. Dreading who he would find, Chancy pointed the black-handled Remington.

Lucas Stout was on his back, his dark shirt speckled with wet spots, his whole body twitching. His hat was half under him. His eyes were open, a haunted aspect to his features. He must have heard them or sensed them, because his eyes swiveled and he gasped out, "Can't move."

Chancy scanned the woods. "The outlaws?"

"They're gone," Stout said. "Went after those of us as were left."

"What can I do?" Chancy hunkered. "Dig the slugs out?"

"I'm a goner," Lucas Stout said.

"Don't talk like that," Missy said. "People have survived worse."

Stout didn't respond.

"How many are still alive?" Chancy was keen to learn.

"Rigenaw," Stout said. "But he was hurt. Drew Case is wounded too. Jelly isn't dead yet, I don't think. Now, there's a hellion. He killed four of them his own self."

Chancy had to wet his mouth to ask, "What about Ollie?"

"He went back to town as soon as he gave us their message." Stout coughed, and drops of blood trickled from a corner of his mouth. "I told him not to, but damned if he'd listen. He was worried about you."

Missy placed her hand on the trail boss's arm. "Is there anything we can do for you? Anything at all?"

"No, ma'am," Stout said. "I've played out my hand and lost. It's the hereafter for me."

"Don't be so hard on yourself," Missy said.

Lucas Stout closed his eyes and shuddered. "If not me, then who? I lost the herd I was entrusted with. I lost most of my hands. I have proven next to worthless and I have got what I deserved."

"That's ridiculous," Missy said.

"It's not over yet." Chancy sought to give the man hope. "There are still five of us who can shoot."

With an obvious effort, Lucas Stout reached up and gripped Chancy's wrist. Beads of sweat popped out on his brow and he licked his lips. "Listen to me, Gantry. I'll only have time to say this once."

"You should rest," Missy interrupted.

"Quiet, miss," Stout said. His fingers tightened on Chancy. "Find my horse and my saddlebags. In them are the papers on the herd, and where to get hold of the owners. Take over for me. You're the new trail boss. Get the herd to the railhead."

"Me?" Chancy said in amazement.

"Why not?"

"Ben Rigenaw is a better hand than I'll ever be," Chancy said. "And there's Jelly, and Drew Case. They're all older. I'll have one of them take over."

"I want you."

"You're delirious," Chancy said. "You don't know what you're saying."

Growling deep in his throat, Lucas Stout raised his head. "Damn you, boy. Listen. Rigenaw has never wanted the responsibility, and I won't force it on him. Jelly is too reckless. Case doesn't always do as he's told, and that's bad in a boss. Your pard would be worthless. He was born slow in the head. That leaves you. And as this gal is my witness, I'm giving you the job of getting the herd to Wichita. You're the new trail boss whether you like it or not."

Chancy didn't like it, not even a little bit. The notion was preposterous.

Stout let out a groan and sank down, his arm falling limp at his side. "Never reckoned on it being like this. Gored by a longhorn, maybe. Shot over cards. Maybe even have lived to old age and died peacefully in bed. But not this." He shook more violently. "We never know when it's our time, do we?"

"How about I find you some water?" Chancy said.

"Where? From the lake? And bring it in your hands?" Stout dabbed the tip of his tongue at the blood leaking from his mouth. "This will do."

"That's not funny," Missy said.

"Not meant to be, ma'am."

Chancy thought of an important question. "Did the others get away on horseback or on foot?"

"Horses. They headed north," Stout said. "The outlaws had left their own animals somewhere and snuck in on foot and couldn't give chase." He paused. "I had a man up a tree. He saw the two who were trailing Ollie. I had a suspicion what Krine and that so-called mayor were up to. That's why we were ready for them. They surrounded the clearing but we weren't in it, and they didn't catch on to their mistake until too late." He scowled. "It wasn't the slaughter they'd hoped it would be. But it didn't work out for us either. We weren't able to kill as many of them as we needed to when we opened fire."

Chancy mustered his courage. It took a lot to buck Stout, even now. "Mr. Stout, I'd like to ask you to reconsider. I'm too young to be trail boss. I'd be no good at it. I don't want the job. Let me give it to Ben Rigenaw, if no one else. What do you say?"

"He won't be saying anything ever again," Missy said sadly.

Lucas Stout's face had taken on a waxy aspect. His eyes were open, but vacant, and his chest had stopped rising and falling.

"Lord, no," Chancy said.

"What will you do?" Missy said.

"I don't know."

"You're the trail boss now."

"Saying I am doesn't make it so," Chancy said. "I can't do it, I tell you."

"You have to try."

"Why?"

"For his sake," Missy said, nodding at Lucas Stout. "And for me. I'd lose a lot of respect for you if you didn't."

"Do you have any idea what you're asking?"

"Yes."

"There will be more killing."

"A lot more, I suspect," Missy said.

"That doesn't upset you?"

"Not nearly as much as being in love with a man who won't do what's right when he has it to do."

Chancy had no answer to that.

"Just don't die on me," Missy added.

Chapter 56

The sun was an arch of fire on the western horizon when Chancy spotted wisps of smoke. They had spent all afternoon in the saddle, and he was tired and sore all over.

"Is that them?" Missy asked. A stray bang hung over one eye, and her dress was rumpled and speckled with dust.

"Reckon so."

"You don't sound very happy about it. Are you still worried about Ollie?"

"I should have gone after him first," Chancy said. Guilt had been eating at him since they left the woods.

"Into town by yourself? That would have been dumb, and now that you're trail boss, you have to be smart about things."

"Maybe you should be trail boss," Chancy said, only half in jest.

"What I know about cows wouldn't fill a thimble. I know men, though, and I have complete confidence you're up to the job, whether you believe you are or not."

Chancy was learning that arguing with her was pointless. She won nearly every time. "Fine," he said, and rode toward the smoke.

"You're adorable when your dander is up."

"Men aren't adorable. Babies are."

"My ma used to say that men are a lot like babies in that a lot of them never grow up."

Chancy let that one be.

A low hill rose ahead. The smoke was behind it. Tracks led up and over. Chancy was almost to the crest when a man with a Winchester reared from behind a boulder.

"Well, look who it is," Drew Case said. "And with your saloon gal, no less." His right arm bore a crude bandage, as did his left thigh. "You missed the fight, Gantry."

To Chancy's amusement, Missy came to his defense.

"Like blazes he did. He killed two of those buzzards in town and four more in the woods. And he was with your trail boss when he died. The only one of you who was," she added meaningfully.

"Stout is dead?" Drew said. "We lost sight of him in all the confusion."

"Take me to the others," Chancy said.

"I'm keeping watch for the outlaws," Drew informed him. "Rigenaw and Jelly are just over the hill."

"The outlaws aren't after you," Chancy said. "And I have something to say to all of you. Lucas Stout's own words."

"In that case," Drew said, and shouldered the Winchester. He waited until they reached the boulder, then fell into step alongside the bay. "Did you see any sign of Addy?"

"Dead."

"Mays?"

"The same."

"Damn. They tried to sneak around behind the outlaws so we'd have them in a cross fire. This just gets worse and worse."

Ben Rigenaw and Jelly Varnes were on opposite sides of a small fire. The former was propped on his saddle, strips from a blanket wrapped tight around his chest. Jelly was sipping coffee. Both came to their feet, Rigenaw more slowly than was his wont.

"Look at who I found," Drew Case exclaimed. He related Missy's information, ending with "He says he has words from Stout."

"Lucas is gone, then?" Rigenaw said sorrowfully. "As good a man as ever lived. I knew him a lot of years."

"We're all that's left out of the whole outfit?" Jelly said.
"Ollie might be alive," Chancy said.
"Fat lot of good he'll do us," Drew muttered.
Climbing down, Chancy stepped to the sorrel and assisted Missy. She didn't need his help, but he did it anyway.
"Have some coffee, ma'am," Jelly said. "There's plenty."
"I'll wait until you hear my man out," Missy said.
"Your man?" Jelly said.
Chancy cleared his throat. "Mr. Stout had a lot to say before he died. About how bad he felt at losing the herd. About how he put it all on him, even though he shouldn't have. And how there should be a new trail boss to take his place. So he picked one."
"Ben Rigenaw here," Jelly guessed, nodding. "That makes sense."
"Fine by me," Drew said.
Rigenaw was giving Chancy a strange look. "No, it wouldn't be me. Lucas knew I'd been offered the job with another outfit and turned it down."
"Why, I bet he picked me!" Jelly said, and grinned. "I've always cottoned to the idea. I can give orders as well as anyone."
"It wouldn't be you," Rigenaw said.
"Me?" Drew said, touching his chest. "I'm as cow savvy as the next puncher, but I'm not sure I'm ready for the job."
"Not you either," Rigenaw said, and he was smiling.
"Then who?"
Both Drew and Jelly Varnes looked at Chancy, and Jelly's eyebrows tried to climb into his hair.
"You're joshing," Jelly said.
"Him?" Drew said in disbelief.
"I was there," Missy declared. "Mr. Stout said I was to be his witness. He picked my Chancy. Told him he was to be trail boss whether he liked it or not."
"Well, hell," Drew said.
"Just when you reckon you've heard everything," Jelly said.

"I can't hardly believe it myself," Chancy said. "But I'm trail boss. At least until we get the herd to Wichita. And my first order is that we're going to get our cattle back from those buzzards, come hell or high water. We'll rest until midnight and then head for Prosperity. By this time tomorrow the herd will be ours again or all of us will be dead."

"Listen to you," Drew said, and laughed.

"I like what I hear," Jelly Varnes said. "Go on, boy."

"It's 'boss' now," Ben Rigenaw said.

"The herd is only half of it," Chancy continued. "Those outlaws have to pay. Krine. That mayor. Ives. We can't leave them alive to do this to anyone else."

"Now I *really* like what I hear," Jelly said.

"Just the five of us?" Drew said, "Provided your pard is still breathing," he added.

"Six," Missy said.

"Worse and worse and worse," Drew said.

"Are you in or are you out?" Chancy demanded to know.

Drew glanced at each of them, threw back his head and laughed. "I must be as loco as all of you. Count me in."

"Do you have a plan?" Jelly asked.

To Chancy's surprise, he did; it burst full-blown into his head. "As a matter of fact, I do. I'll tell you about it after my lady and I have eaten and rested a bit and I've given it more thought. The thing to keep in mind is that from here on out, it's them or us. We don't leave any of them alive if we can help it."

"Shouldn't the herd come first?" Ben Rigenaw said.

"Nothing else but," Chancy said. "But those owl-hoots have our cows under guard and won't give them up without a fight. So I say we give them that fight first, and take our cattle after."

"There are more of them left than there are of us," Drew Case said.

"So what? There won't be any left if we do it right. We're going to rub out every last outlaw."

"Oh my," Jelly Varnes said. "Aren't you a surprise? If you were any more bloodthirsty, you would be me."

"Are all of you in?" Chancy pressed the issue. "Do we give them back the hell they brought down on us?"

Ben Rigenaw nodded grimly.

"You bet," Drew Case said.

As for Jelly, he grinned and said, "We give them hell in spades, boss."

Chapter 57

Chancy always liked riding herd at night. He liked riding at night, period. The sparkle of the stars, the bright moon on occasion, the wind, and the general quiet were a tonic. They relaxed him. Made him think that all was right with the world.

Not this night.

As they neared Prosperity's mostly dark buildings, Chancy was a bundle of nerves. He had made a decision that might cost others their lives, and the possible consequences weighed on his shoulders with all the weight of the world.

On his right were Jelly and Drew Case. To his other side, Missy and Ben Rigenaw. He'd wanted to leave Missy behind, but she wouldn't hear of it. They'd argued for nearly half an hour, until he gave up in frustration.

Chancy was also worried about Rigenaw. Ben had been uncommonly reticent all night. Chancy figured that the wound was bothering him. He'd quietly suggested to Missy that she should take a look at it and see how bad it was, but Rigenaw refused to let her. Twice, earlier, Chancy saw Rigenaw put a hand to his side and wince as if in great pain. It was doubly troubling that the strips wrapped around Rigenaw's chest showed fresh splotches of blood.

Drew Case had been unusually quiet too. Maybe because, as he had made plain, he thought Chancy's idea would land all of them in early graves.

Jelly Varnes was the only one in merry spirits. As they slowed from a trot to a walk, he chuckled and said, "Look out, bastards, here we come." He glanced over past Chancy at Missy. "My apologies for the language, ma'am."

"I've heard worse."

"It's just that there's nothing I like more than bucking out a bad man," Jelly said. "When I was fourteen, the local tough made the mistake of making my pa dance to his bullets, and then slapped him around. So I took my pa's old revolver, looked that tough up, and added a new nostril."

"Boast, why don't you?" Drew Case said.

"I want the lady to understand," Jelly said.

"She's my lady," Chancy said, "and the only one she needs to understand is me. Spare us your exploits."

Drew chuckled.

"Exploits?" Jelly said. "You become trail boss and suddenly you're using big words."

"You men," Missy said.

By then they were close enough that everyone fell quiet. When Chancy drew rein, so did the rest. They were about three hundred yards north of town. To the southwest, about twice the distance, the herd was a dark blotch of shapes against the backdrop of night. The only light in Prosperity came from the saloon.

"We've been all through what to do," Chancy said. "Any last questions before we get to it?"

"I don't have a question, but I do have something to say," Ben Rigenaw said. "I'm older than the rest of you, so pay attention." He turned slightly in his saddle. "We're never to say a word about what happens here tonight. Take the secret with you to your grave."

"How come?" Drew Case said. "It's not as if we're breaking the law. We have the right to get our herd back."

"And to kill these buzzards for killing our pards," Jelly said.

"The law might not see it that way," Rigenaw said. "And no good ever came from bragging about a killing."

"Says you," Jelly said.

"No," Chancy said. "We'll do as Ben says. I want your word, from each of you, that you'll never talk about this night your whole life long."

"Well, hell," Jelly said.

"You have my word," Drew said.

"Mine too," Rigenaw said.

"I have better things to talk about than bloodshed," Missy said.

"Jelly?" Chancy said.

Jelly sat there.

"Are your ears broke?"

"Dang it, Gantry."

"I'm waiting."

"You ask me, it's a hell of a note when a man can't shoot somebody and brag about it. What else is bragging for?"

"Jelly."

"Damn it. All right. I give my word. But Lucas Stout wouldn't make us give a stupid promise like this."

"Yes," Ben Rigenaw said, "he would."

"It's settled," Chancy said. "Let's get to it."

They dismounted and gave their reins to Missy, who was gnawing on her bottom lip. Chancy was the last to do so, and as he went to turn away, she leaned in and pecked him on the cheek.

"For luck."

"Thank you."

"I wish I had someone to give me luck," Jelly said.

"Behave," Rigenaw said.

"All of you," Missy said, "please take care. Enough have already died. We don't want to lose any of you."

"Amen to that, lady," Drew said.

"Check your six-shooters," Ben Rigenaw advised, and drew one of his.

"Mine is always loaded and clean and ready to shoot," Jelly said.

"Check it anyway."

"Who's the boss here?" Jelly said. "You or Chancy?"

"Check your six-shooter," Chancy said.

"Well, hell."

Chancy made sure there were six pills in the wheel, and shoved the black-handled Remington into his holster.

They had delayed long enough. With a parting look at Missy, and a yearning such as no other, he stalked toward Prosperity.

"Let the killing commence," Jelly Varnes said, and laughed.

Chapter 58

The town was deceptively still. The only sound was the tinkle of a bottle or glass in the saloon.

Chancy didn't know how many outlaws were left. He reckoned at least a dozen. Krine and Ives were the gun hands of the bunch, the ones to worry about the most.

He reached the first building and crouched along the dark wall. "You know what to do. Do you have your lucifers?"

Jelly patted a pocket. "Right here."

"Start them, and we'll meet back at the saloon," Chancy said.

"We've already been through this five times," Drew said. "We know what to do." He threw in a "boss."

"Then go."

They melted away.

Chancy crept toward the general store.

Low voices came from the saloon. Broken glass from the window lay scattered about, and shadows moved inside.

He had to be careful they didn't spot him. Easing onto his belly, he snaked the last thirty feet.

The store was directly across from the saloon. Through the busted window, Chancy saw Ives and Simmons and a couple of others at the bar. Mayor Broom was at a table, playing cards.

Chancy wondered if they had been up all night or had risen early. It occurred to him that Krine might start the herd north as soon as possible, maybe even that very day. They were in for a surprise, Chancy reflected, and smiled.

He figured the front door would be locked, but he was wrong. The latch moved easily; the door didn't squeak.

Once he had slithered in, he quietly shut the door behind him, rose, and moved down an aisle to the collection of used clothes. He thought it fitting that the apparel taken from dead cowpokes would help bring the outlaw operation to ruin.

Chancy couldn't say exactly when the notion came to him that wiping out the outlaws wasn't enough. He aimed to wipe out the town itself. Every last building. Only when this den of evil was removed from the face of the earth would future outfits that passed by be safe.

Chancy's dander was up as it had never been up before. He'd always been a peaceable sort. He wasn't like Jelly, always looking for trouble, or to be more exact, the excitement that came from trouble. He'd be happy to go the rest of his life and not have to shoot another human being.

Striking a lucifer, Chancy applied it to a shirt, but the shirt didn't catch. He tried a second with the same result. Stymied, he roamed about and discovered a lantern on a hook. The tank was half-full. With almost perverse glee, he emptied it over the clothes and prepared to strike another lucifer.

Loud, harsh laughter from the saloon gave Chancy pause. Straightening, he peered out the front window, curious about the fuss. What he beheld sent an icy spike rippling down his spine clear to his toes. He hadn't noticed before because Ives and them were in the way.

Ollie was hanging from the back wall. Literally hanging, his arms and legs spread-eagle, his head drooping. Splashes of scarlet around his wrists and ankles filled Chancy with horror. *The outlaws had nailed Ollie up as if he were a tapestry.* And one of them—Simmons—had just thrown a drink in Ollie's face. That was why they were laughing. They thought it was hilarious.

Chancy started for the door, and caught himself. He couldn't do anything for Ollie just yet. Not alone. He must stick to his plan, and soon he and the others would get Ollie out of there.

"You miserable bastards," Chancy said under his breath, so choked with emotion he could scarcely breathe. Tears formed in his eyes and he blinked them away. Ollie was the kindest, gentlest man he knew, and the outlaws had done *that* to him. Chancy couldn't wait to commence squeezing the trigger.

But first, the store.

Squatting, Chancy struck the lucifer. This time the clothes caught right away. Small fingers of flame sprouted and grew larger as more garments ignited. Smoke rose, the acrid smell filling his nose and his mouth. He swatted at it, and coughed.

Chancy returned to the front. He opened the door wide enough to crawl out. The horses at the hitch rail showed little interest. Most were dozing. He crawled around them, and stopped.

Up the street, flames were visible in the stable. A cabin had a flickering light in a window, and smoke poured from an open door.

Chancy smiled. The others were doing their part, starting fires of their own.

More coarse laughter from the saloon. Simmons was poking Ollie with a whiskey bottle. Ollie raised his head. There was blood on his cheek and his chin, and the left side of his face appeared to be swollen.

Rage gripped Chancy. That was his pard. His saddle mate. His best friend.

Heaving to his feet, Chancy drew his Remington and started across. He should wait for the others. The plan was to attack the saloon together. To set the saloon on fire and shoot the outlaws as they came out.

Chancy couldn't wait. That was Ollie in there. He walked up to the broken window, took aim, and shot Simmons square between the shoulder blades.

At the blast, everyone inside froze. All except Ives, who spun and whipped out his revolvers and cut loose with ambidextrous skill.

Chancy jerked aside, pressing his back to the wall. Yells sounded, and boots thudded. An outlaw shouldered through the batwings and Chancy shot him in the face.

Inside, Mayor Broom hollered, "Out the back! Out the back! They're waiting for us out front!"

More boots drummed. Lead clipped the edge of the window and whistled into the night.

Shouts broke out both up and down the street. So did shots.

Chancy swore he heard Jelly Varnes let out a whoop of delight.

Outlaws were running down the hall toward the back door. One snapped a shot at Chancy. The rear door slammed open, and the moment the last of them piled out, he vaulted up and over the windowsill.

Ollie was looking at him and smiling. "Pard," he croaked happily.

Chancy ran over. He had been right about the nails. The outlaws had driven them through Ollie's wrists and ankles. "Almighty."

"I hurt, pard," Ollie said weakly. "I hurt something awful."

"Don't talk," Chancy said.

"I came back to town for you, but you had gotten away and they were mad, so they did this."

Chancy put a hand on Ollie's chest. He had to force his vocal cords to work. "I'll have you down in two shakes."

"The hammer is behind the bar," Ollie said.

Chancy turned and nearly walked into the twin barrels of a shotgun.

Chapter 59

Mayor Broom was holding it. His eyes twinkling, he thumbed back a hammer and said, "Try something. I dare you."

Chancy turned to stone. There was a saying on the frontier to the effect that buckshot meant burying. At that range, he'd be blown in half.

"Smart cowpoke," Mayor Broom said, and chuckled. "I suspected it was you, come for your friend. When the others bolted, I snuck back in. Clever of me, no? And here we are."

"Mayors shouldn't point weapons," Ollie said.

Broom glanced at him and rolled his eyes. "Honestly, Gantry. For the life of me, I don't know how you put up with that simpleton. Having him for a partner would irritate me no end."

"Was it you nailed him to the wall?" Chancy wanted to know. Out in the street, yells and shots were spreading like a prairie fire.

"I can't claim credit, no," Mayor Broom said. "It was Krine's idea, but Simmons did the actual nailing." He looked at the body of the culprit, not two feet away. "And you nailed him, so to speak."

"And now it's my turn." Chancy braced for the blast sure to come. He was sorry he had failed the others. Sorry too that he would never indulge his dream of living to a fine old age with Missy for his missus.

"How many are with you?" Mayor Broom asked.

Chancy didn't respond.

Broom thumbed back the other hammer. "I won't ask you again."

"Blow my head off and you still won't get your answer," Chancy blustered.

"It can't be that many," Broom said. "There aren't enough of you left to cause us much trouble."

"That's what you think."

The mayor surprised Chancy by taking a couple of steps back and leaning against the wall. "We'll wait for Krine. He'll likely want to talk to you personally. Unbuckle your gun belt and let your smoke wagon hit the floor."

"What can I say that he'd possibly want to hear?"

"Who your outfit was selling the herd to, for starters," Mayor Broom said. "When we take it north, we'll sell to the same folks."

"Don't you reckon they'll find that a little bit suspicious?"

"Not at all. Krine will pass himself off as Lucas Stout. Everything should go smoothly. It's worked with other outfits." Broom wagged the shotgun. "That gun belt, if you please, and even if you don't."

Chancy slowly moved his hand to the buckle and pried. From the ruckus outside, a gun battle was raging.

"That will be my friends and associates wiping out the last of you cowboys," Mayor Broom said. "And I must say. The Flying V has given us more trouble than all the other outfits we rubbed out put together."

"Glad to hear that."

"Don't be petty, boy," Mayor Broom said. "I could have killed you the moment I stepped in here."

You should have, Chancy almost said. He slid the end of the belt from the loop that held it.

"You're taking too long," Broom said impatiently. "Take that thing off or I'll let you have a dose of buckshot here and now, Krine or no Krine."

"Got to say," Chancy said, stalling, "you put on a good act of pretending to be top dog at first. But you lick Krine's boots, the same as the rest of them."

"We're partners, him and me, like you and the oaf there."

"Is that what you call it when one tells the other what to do? I bet he helps himself to a bigger share of the money too."

"Stop prattling and take off that damn belt."

Up on the wall, Ollie groaned and said barely above a whisper, "I could use some water."

"Shut up, you," Mayor Broom barked.

"I'm awful parched, pard," Ollie said to Chancy. "They wouldn't let me have so much as a drop except for the liquor they threw on me."

"Tough hombres," Chancy said scornfully.

"Tougher than you, boy," Mayor Broom said.

"Water, please," Ollie said.

Broom glanced up again, scowling. "If you don't shut up, I will shut you up. This shotgun has two barrels, so I have one to spare."

"You were so nice to us when we met you," Ollie said. "You helped Finger and everything."

"What an idiot," Broom said.

"You shouldn't ought to be mean to folks," Ollie said. "My ma always said that being mean is wrong."

Mayor Broom jerked his shotgun to his shoulder and trained it on Ollie. "I have listened to all I'm going to."

It was the moment Chancy had been waiting for, the mistake he'd hoped Broom would make. He drew as quick as he was capable, cocking the Remington as it cleared leather. Broom caught the movement and tried to swing the shotgun in his direction. Chancy fired, thumbed the hammer, fired again.

The slugs smashed Mayor Broom back. His arms flailing, the portly mayor stumbled against the bar and clutched at it to keep from falling. He looked down at the holes in his chest and gasped, "No! It can't be."

"You've been shot," Ollie said.

The mayor gave him the strangest look. Then his legs gave, and he hit the floor with a fleshy thud, rolled onto his big belly, and was still.

"Serves him right for being so mean."

Chancy wasted no time darting behind the bar. The hammer was on a shelf in plain sight. Going back around, he slowed at a shriek in the street.

"Who was that, you reckon?" Ollie said.

"Will you stop talking?" Chancy said as he ran to a chair

and dragged it to the wall. "You're in no condition to do anything."

"My mouth isn't nailed to the wall. It works fine."

"Consarn you, Ollie."

"Why are you so upset with me?"

"It's not you," Chancy said. "It's what these vultures did to you." A feeling of urgency ripping at his vitals, he holstered the Remington and set to prying the nails out. To do so, he had to hook the hammer's claws under the head of the nail, gouging Ollie's wrist in the process.

"Ouch," Ollie said, and gritted his teeth.

"I'm trying to be gentle," Chancy said.

"Don't worry. I can take it. Do what you have to. I'm mighty sick of hanging here."

For two bits, Chancy would have climbed down from the chair, taken the hammer, and beaten Simmons's head to a pulp. He managed to hook the first nail and swiveled the hammer to loosen it. Fresh blood flowed, and Ollie gasped.

"I've never hurt so much in my life."

"I bet."

"People shouldn't do this to other people."

Chancy pulled with all his strength, but the nail resisted his efforts.

That was when the batwings crashed open.

Chapter 60

Chancy whirled so fast he lost his balance and fell off the chair. He tried to land on his feet but tripped and sprawled to his hands and knees. The hammer went skittering. Fearing an outlaw would shoot him before he could rise, he fumbled at his holster and got the Remington out, only to realize it was a friend, not a foe.

Drew Case reeled as if drunk, his gun hand level but his other arm hanging as if broken. Scarlet ran from a hole near his elbow and another high on his shoulder. He also had a crease in his temple that was bleeding badly. "Gantry!" he gasped.

Pushing up, Chancy ran to help. He was looking at Case and not at the batwings and almost didn't spot the revolver barrel that blossomed above them. "Get down!" he shouted, and snapped a shot to discourage the shooter. It worked. The revolver was yanked back.

Drew Case turned and fired at the batwings, but he was much too slow to hit whoever was out there. Backpedaling, he said, "That buzzard shot me from an alley. He's been after me since."

"Hunt cover," Chancy said, watching the entrance and the window both. He was thinking of Ollie, helpless on the wall behind them, and how a stray slug might hit him instead of them.

"It's a war out there," Drew said through clenched teeth. "I lost sight of Ben and Jelly." He glanced toward the rear wall, and stiffened. "What have they done to Ollie?"

"Nailed me up," Ollie said.

"I have to get him down," Chancy said, stating the obvious. "Can you watch out for them while I do?"

"Go," Drew said. He sank into a chair facing the front. "I'll shoot anyone who shows his face."

Time seemed to slow down. Retrieving the hammer, Chancy pried and pried and finally got the first nail out. Ollie didn't complain once. Quickly moving the chair, Chancy was about to pry at the nail in Ollie's other wrist when he realized the mistake he was making. He should do the ankles first so Ollie could stand on a chair while he did the wrists. Leaping down, he hauled a second chair over.

If he thought the nail in the wrist had been difficult, it was nothing compared to the nail in the ankle. The bone was a lot thicker. It was like trying to pull the nail out of rock.

"Hurry," Drew urged.

Chancy bit off a sharp retort. He was doing the best he could. He tried scraping the claws deeper, and Ollie groaned. "Sorry, pard."

"Do what you have to."

Chancy clenched his jaw. Ollie was right. He must get the nails out, the pain and the blood be hanged. He renewed his attempt.

"Oh Lordy," Ollie said.

The boom of a shot made Chancy jump.

"Missed!" Drew exclaimed.

Without warning, the nail came loose, causing Chancy to stumble back a few steps. He stared at the bloody nail dripping red, then cast it down in disgust and moved to the other leg.

"I won't be able to walk for a spell, will I?" Ollie said weakly.

Chancy hadn't thought of that. "Probably not. But don't you worry. You've got my shoulder to lean on."

"How can you shoot with me leaning on you?"

"Let me worry about that."

The second ankle nail was as stubborn as the first. Chancy sweated buckets trying to get it out. When it loosened, he nearly yipped for joy. Grabbing the other chair, he placed it under Ollie.

"Do you have to sit and rest?" Ollie asked.

"It's for you, you silly goose," Chancy said. "When I get this nail out, try to put both feet on the chair. It will hold you up long enough for me to take out the last nail."

"I'll try, pard."

"You're doing fine."

"I don't feel fine."

Another shot rocked the saloon.

"Show yourself again!" Drew hollered. "I dare you, you no-account polecat."

"Drew sounds real mad," Ollie said.

"Aren't you?" Chancy said, his sole attention on the nail.

"Not that I know of, no."

"They nailed you to this wall."

"What good does it do to be mad at a wall?" Ollie said. "And you called me a silly goose?"

Chancy figured the torment and the loss of blood had made his friend more addlepated than usual. He accidentally scraped bone and felt Ollie quiver. "Sorry."

"It's a good thing wood can't feel like we do. It would hurt a board something awful to be nailed up."

"Where do you come up with this stuff?"

"What stuff?"

A loud crackling caused Chancy to look toward the street. The general store was fully engulfed in flames, the light from the fire so bright the street between the store and the saloon was lit up as if it were the middle of the day.

"Ain't that pretty?" Ollie said.

With a sickening sound reminiscent of a fingernail on a blackboard, the nail came out. Instantly Chancy clamped his arm around Ollie's legs to steady him and helped guide his feet to the chair. "Can you stand or not? I have to know."

"I think I can."

Maybe it was the fact that he was acutely conscious that they were running out of time, or maybe the fact that he had done it three times, but Chancy extracted the last nail in less than a minute. Throwing the hammer aside, he supported Ollie, helping him down from the chair. "I've got you."

Ollie collapsed against him. "I feel so puny," he apologized. "You should leave me and go before more of those owl-hoots come."

"Not going to happen," Chancy said.

"You're my pard. I don't want you hurt."

"Right back at you."

Ollie, astoundingly, chuckled. "That was a good one. I'll have to remember it."

Draping Ollie's arm across his shoulders, Chancy hooked his left around Ollie's waist to hold him up. "We're going out the back. Can you make it?"

"Watch me."

Chancy turned. "Drew!" he called. "Let's get while the getting is good."

Grimacing, Drew rose. "Fine by me."

It was then that the outlaw who had been lurking out front charged through the batwings with his pistol blazing.

Chapter 61

Drew Case was caught with his back to the shooter. He swiveled toward the entrance just as the outlaw fired. The impact of the slug jolted him. He banged off a shot and it was the outlaw's turn to be jolted, but the curly wolf fired again, and once more. Drew started to melt.

Chancy grabbed for his Remington. But with his arm around Ollie, he couldn't get it out fast enough. Fortunately for them, the outlaw was melting too, falling in slow motion with a look of bewilderment on his face.

Both men sprawled flat. Drew's wide, unblinking eyes told Chancy that there was no hope for him.

In the streets boots thumped and shadows moved.

Chancy had to get them out of there. He hustled Ollie toward the hall, saying, "Sorry, pard," when Ollie moaned. He kept expecting to be shot at, but they made it to the rear door and out into the night.

It was obvious Chancy couldn't fight and hang on to Ollie at the same time. He headed north, moving as quickly as Ollie's weight allowed. Once past the last of the buildings, he angled toward where they had left Missy and their mounts.

Prosperity was an inferno. Flames twenty feet high soared up out of the general store. The stable was ablaze, and so were a couple of cabins. Figures ran about and yelled back and forth.

Chancy grunted in satisfaction. The outlaws couldn't possibly save their town. By noon much of it would be cinders. He heard more shots and a scream. Ben Rigenaw and Jelly were still alive and taking a toll on their enemies. He needed to get back, needed to help.

"Who's there?" a voice said out of the dark.

"Me," Chancy said. "I've got Ollie."

Missy came to help. She took one look and said in horror, "What did they do to him?"

"Nailed him to a wall."

"How could they—"

Chancy cut her off. "I don't have time for a chat. Can you take him?"

"Sure," Missy said, and slipped her shoulder under Ollie's arm on the other side. "You're going back?"

"It's not over."

"Be careful, you hear me?" Missy touched his arm. "I don't want to lose you."

"As Ollie might say," Chancy said, and grinned, "I don't want to lose me either."

He caressed her cheek, then broke into a run. It was hard leaving her. He imagined that with time it would get even harder. His ma always said that love was like a flower. The more you watered it, the deeper its roots went.

Much of the street was now awash in light. The crackling flames threw writhing shadows everywhere. The outlaws were nowhere to be seen. Nor were Chancy's friends.

Chancy ran to the first cabin on the same side of the street as the general store. Hunkering, he cocked his Remington.

There was still no sign of thc outlaws. Evidently they had hunted for cover. Then Chancy stiffened. Down at the far end, close to the burning stable, Krine and Ives briefly appeared. They were there and they were gone, swallowed by smoke.

That smoke posed a problem, Chancy realized. It was spreading like fog. If he wasn't careful, an outlaw could be right on top of him before he knew the man was there.

Slipping around to the back, Chancy went past the next building and into a narrow gap that brought him to the street. Cautious not to show himself, he edged forward until he could see out.

It saved his life.

An outlaw materialized out of nowhere not more than two steps away. They saw each other at the same instant. Both were so surprised that there was a delay of two or three seconds before the outlaw brought his revolver into play.

Chancy shot him smack in the sternum. He thumbed the hammer, fired once more, and retreated as the man crumbled. Once clear of the building, he sprinted a dozen yards out into the prairie and turned to the south.

Off to his right a ways, the herd was growing restless. Some of the cattle were moving about and lowing. The flames, the acrid smell, and the thunder of gunfire were agitating them. Chancy prayed they didn't stampede. He doubted the outlaws riding herd were up to the task of stopping them. It took special skill that only came from long experience. Experience only cowboys had.

The loss hit him like a blow to the gut. All the cowboys, all his friends, who had fallen. Men he had worked with for years. Finger and Addy, Mays and Long Tom, and that crusty wizard with an oven, Old Charlie. Drew Case. And the others. There was only Ben Rigenaw and Jelly and Ollie and himself. But his pard was in no shape to ride herd or anything else and wouldn't be for a good long spell.

Shaking his head to dispel a wave of grief, Chancy moved on. There would be a better time and place to let his emotions out. For now, he must focus on the here and now. On exterminating the vermin who had decimated their outfit.

The thud of hooves brought Chancy up short a second time. Crouching, he sought the source.

A rider was approaching from town, heading in the direction of the herd. A silhouette took shape, the man and the animal as one. The rider was looking back at Prosperity. He was holding the reins and nothing else.

Chancy had never shot an unarmed man. But this was a bad man, one of those responsible for the killing of his friends. All he had to do was shoot. Instead he stood and called out, "You there!"

The outlaw's reaction was predictable. He drew sharp rein and cursed and stabbed for his six-gun.

Chancy blasted him out of the saddle. Crouching again, he waited to see if the man would rise. The horse, oddly enough, just stood there, unfazed by the noise. Half a minute went by and nothing happened. Slinking over, Chancy discovered the rider on his back, his hands empty, and still alive.

The man saw him. "You've done killed me, cowboy," he said barely above a whisper. "You bastard."

"You would have done the same to me." Chancy felt no sympathy whatsoever. "You got what you had coming."

The man did an astounding thing, given the circumstances. He chuckled. "I reckon I have, at that. I always knew I'd be shot or wind up gurgling at the end of a rope. But you won't hear me whine."

"Good for you."

Sucking in a breath, the outlaw got out, "I lived my life how I pleased. From the day I was fourteen and shot a farmer and took his poke. And you know what? I liked it, cowboy. Liked it more than anything."

"Robbing and killing," Chancy said in disgust.

"Go ahead. Judge me. But what do you know?"

"I know I'm not your judge," Chancy said, and gestured at the firmament. "Someone else is."

"I don't believe in that bunk."

"Which makes you doubly worthless." Chancy pointed his Remington.

"Wait. What are you doing?"

"Finishing you off. Putting you out of your misery. Sending you straight to hell. Take your pick."

"There's no need. I'm fading. I can feel it."

"Good for you," Chancy said again, and squeezed the trigger.

Chapter 62

The crackling and roaring of the flames had grown so loud the din of destruction drowned out everything else. As Chancy came up on the stable from the rear, a rafter gave way with a tremendous crash, bringing part of a wall down with it. Apparently the horses in the corral had panicked and broken through the rails. He crept through the opening they had made and squatted in the dancing shadows.

There hadn't been any yells in a while. No shots either. Chancy hoped it didn't mean Ben Rigenaw and Jelly Varnes had been bucked out in lead. As for himself, he'd lost count of how many men he'd shot since the whole business started what seemed like an eternity ago. He'd never thought of himself as a gun hand, yet here he was, six-gun in hand, tackling a pack of curly wolves.

Chancy dropped lower. A couple of men were slinking along the corral from the other side, one of them moving as if hurt, the other's corn-colored hair spilling from under his tilted hat.

"Jelly! Ben! Over here!" Chancy said as loudly as he dared.

Jelly Varnes was smiling, as happy as could be, but Ben Rigenaw was somber as death.

"We saw you sneak up," Jelly said.

"Have you seen any sign of Drew?" Ben Rigenaw asked. His face was etched in pain.

"He went down fighting," Chancy said. "I found Ollie and got him out. He's hurt real bad."

"Case is dead?" Jelly said. "One more we owe them for."

Rigenaw eased onto his heels and leaned back against

the rails. "There can't be many left. No more than seven or eight, I calculate."

"Don't forget those with the herd," Chancy said.

"The more to kill, the better," Jelly declared, and laughed.

"How can you be so happy?" Chancy marveled.

"Why, trail boss," Jelly replied with mock gravity, "how can I not? I'm doing what I like best."

"I thought you like being a cowboy more than anything else."

"I work with cows to fill my belly and so I won't have to go around bare-assed naked," Jelly said. "And to buy the bullets I need to do what I really love. Which is filling polecats with lead."

"You're a mite peculiar."

"No one should *like* to kill," Ben Rigenaw said.

"Says the gent who bucked out three of those owl-hoots so quick, they were dead before they knew they'd been shot," Jelly said.

Rigenaw looked at the Remingtons in his hands. "I don't do it because I like it. I do it only when I have to."

"The same as me," Jelly said, "only I *do* like it."

"My pa used to say there's such a thing as a natural-born killer," Chancy remarked. "Maybe you're one of them."

"Why, thank you, trail boss," Jelly said. "I'd like to think I'm a natural at something."

"Enough about him," Ben Rigenaw said. "It will be daybreak soon and this is far from over. Once the sun is up, their numbers will give them an edge."

"Then we whittle them down," Jelly said, and added teasingly, "If it's all right with our new trail boss, that is."

"Keep it up," Chancy said.

"I aim to please," Jelly said.

Ben Rigenaw groaned, but whether from his wounds or because of Jelly's antics, Chancy couldn't say. "We need to get the leaders," Rigenaw said. "Krine and that mayor and Ives."

"You can scratch His Honor," Chancy said. "I did him in the saloon."

"Damnation, boss," Jelly said. "Stick with us long enough and we'll turn you into the next Wild Bill."

"Will you stop?" Rigenaw said.

"What did I do?"

Chancy kept them on track with "What about the other two? Krine and Ives? I only saw them once, a while ago."

"I haven't seen hide nor hair of either," Jelly said.

"That's strange," Ben Rigenaw said. "You'd think they would be in the thick of it, looking to snuff our wicks. They're the best gunnies in the gang."

"Who can predict outlaws?" Chancy said.

"Who can predict anybody?" Jelly threw in.

"You sound just like Ollie," Chancy said. "I'm commencing to suspect the two of you are kin."

"I almost forgot about him," Jelly said. "You say he was hurt bad? What did they do to him?"

Chancy related the ordeal Ollie had been through. "He's safe with Missy at the moment."

Jelly had lost his smile while listening. "They nailed Ollie Teal to a dang wall? A calf like him, who hasn't ever harmed a fly?" He started to rise. "Let's hunt the scum down."

"Hold on," Ben Rigenaw said. "We have to do this smart."

"You're not the boss," Jelly said.

"I am," Chancy said. "And Ben is right. We have to figure out what their next move will be."

"What's to figure?" Jelly said. "They're hunting for us like we should be hunting for them."

"It's too quiet," Rigenaw said. "We haven't seen hide nor hair of any of them in half an hour or more."

"They must be up to something," Jelly said. "Planning to lay a trap for us, I bet."

"Or maybe they're lying low because they're scared. We've killed a heap of the buzzards, and their town is burning down around their ears."

"Krine and Ives aren't yellow-backed," Rigenaw said.

Jelly gazed at the burning stable. "Doesn't matter. Pretty soon they won't have anything left."

"They still have our herd," Chancy reminded him.

Ben Rigenaw glanced to the west. "That must be it. Consarn us for idiots anyhow. Why didn't we see it sooner?"

"See what?" Jelly said.

"The reason we haven't seen them. They're with the herd, getting set to take it north at first light."

"That doesn't give us much time to stop them," Jelly said.

"No," Chancy said. "It doesn't."

Chapter 63

They hurried to reach their mounts, moving along the back of the buildings on the east side of the street.

Chancy was in the lead. He spied a cluster of figures ahead and stopped. He took them for outlaws until he heard low voices.

"Why, it's a bunch of females," Jelly whispered.

Even so, Chancy advanced warily. It wasn't uncommon for doves to be armed, usually with a knife but sometimes a derringer or a pocket pistol. He recognized one of the voices and called out, "Della Neece? Is that you?"

"Who's there?" came the frightened reply.

"Chancy Gantry, ma'am, with some friends."

"Thank heavens!"

The next Chancy knew, four women descended on him in a rush, all talking at once.

"We're so happy to see you!"

"We didn't know what to do!"

"How could they do this to us?"

"Quiet down!" Chancy said. "One at a time, please." Besides Della, he recognized Margie and the older dove, Cora. One other was with them. "What are you doing out here?"

"Where else would we be with the town burning down around us?" Della Neece said.

"And lead flying every which way," Margie said.

Della continued. "When the fuss started, I asked Mr. Krine to protect us. And do you know what he did?"

"He told us to shoo," Margie said.

"Can you believe it?" Della said. "They went to all the

trouble to hire us, to bring us all the way down from Kansas, and then they ran out on us when we needed their help."

"You can't trust men," Margie declared. "Not ever."

"Ain't that the truth, honey?" Cora said.

Chancy wanted to get a word in, but he was too slow.

"Now you have to help us," Della said, gripping the front of his shirt. "You just have to!"

"We won't last long on our own," Margie said.

"We're not redskins," Cora said. "We can't live off the land like they do, and that's what it might come to."

The fourth woman finally had something to say. "We should go back into the saloon and grab as much liquor as we can carry before it burns down. Things go better with liquor."

"Don't listen to Sadie," Della Neece said. "Shc goes around booze-blind half the time."

"Like Hades I do," Sadie said indignantly.

"Ladies—" Chancy said.

"Just because I take a nip now and then doesn't give you call to insult me," Sadie said to Della.

"Sister, if whiskey was water, your boiler would be rusted out."

Margie and Cora laughed.

"I resent that," Sadie said, placing her hands on her hips. "Keep it up and I will sock you."

"Not if you know what's good for you, you won't."

"Ladies—" Chancy tried again.

Della Neece poked Sadie in the chest. "Do you know what your problem is, you silly woman? You look in the mirror and don't see your own nose paint. You think you're still the sweet little gal you were five years ago when what you really are is a walking whiskey vat."

"Why, you . . . ," Sadie said, and cocked a fist.

Ben Rigenaw stepped past Chancy, his growl cracking like a whip. "*Enough!* You stand here squabbling like biddy hens while your outlaw friends are set to steal our herd. Not another peep out of any of you or we'll do what they did and leave you on your own."

Della opened her mouth to speak but evidently thought better of it.

"I'm obliged," Chancy said.

"Nothing riles me more than a female who doesn't know when to shut up," Rigenaw said.

"You must not plan to get married, then," Jelly snickered.

Rigenaw looked at him. "Or a fella either."

"Do you mean me?" Jelly said.

Chancy had an accusation of his own to level at Della. "You haven't once asked about Missy."

"Oh goodness. I'm sorry. It's just that with all that's been happening, my head isn't working as it should. Is she all right? I helped her, you know. I covered for her at the saloon so she could stay the night at the cabin with you."

"I'm obliged," Chancy said. "And yes, she's fine. We'll take you to her right now."

"What then, trail boss?" Jelly said. "These gals don't have horses of their own, and they sure as hell can't walk clear to Wichita."

"We'll find horses somewhere," Chancy said. "Take them from the outlaws, maybe."

"If we can find Laverne Dodger, you wouldn't need to," Della Neece said.

Chancy wanted to kick himself. He'd forgotten about the sawbones—and after the man had been so helpful. "What can Dodger do?"

"I saw him," Della said. "When the stable caught on fire, Laverne got the horses out and led them off this way. I figured he wouldn't have gone far, and we were looking for him when you found us. I'm sure he'd let us use some."

From out of the night came a chuckle. "You thought right, sugarplum." Laverne Dodger limped into view, leading a lot of horses by their reins and several ropes.

"Laverne!" Della squealed, and running over, she threw her arms around his neck, almost knocking him off balance.

"First these whores and now a cripple," Jelly Varnes said. "We keep this up, pretty soon we'll have our own army."

"Every little bit helps," Ben Rigenaw said.

Chancy agreed. He was elated, in that now Dodger could tend to Ollie, and Missy would have the other women for company. He could leave her knowing she'd be safe, and go after the outlaws.

He would get the herd back or die trying.

Chapter 64

The longhorns had been on the move since before dawn. They were strung out over half a mile, and the outlaws riding herd didn't seem to care. They let the cattle mosey as the animals pleased and did nothing about the stragglers. Things no real cowboy would do. Krine and Ives were on point, the rest were flankers. Not one outlaw rode drag. The dust was too much for them.

Atop a hill to the northeast of the herd, Chancy Gantry lay on his belly and watched with keen interest.

"You should have let us hit them before they headed out," Jelly Varnes complained. "Why let those coyotes get so far?"

"We pick the right time and the right place," Chancy said.

"What was wrong with back near their town?" Jelly persisted.

"It was dark and we didn't know how many we were up against," Chancy said. "And we had to tend to the women."

"Dang skirts," Jelly grumbled.

"Our new boss did exactly right," Ben Rigenaw said.

"You're taking his side a lot," Jelly huffed.

"We can't all be bulls in a china shop," Rigenaw said.

Chancy grinned. His chin was on his crossed forearms, and he was grateful to be resting. They'd ridden hard to get ahead of the herd, and had stayed ahead once they were. He reasoned that Krine would figure they were trailing behind, not out in front.

"I count nine owl-hoots," Rigenaw mentioned. "More than I reckoned there would be."

"They don't worry me none," Jelly said.

"They should," Rigenaw said. "Krine and Ives aren't amateurs. Krine, in particular, might be faster on the shoot than you or me."

"Let me at him and we'll see if he is."

"Not yet," Chancy said. "Not until I'm good and ready."

"When will that be?" Jelly said. "When they reach Wichita?"

"Quit picking on him," Rigenaw said.

"Are you his ma now?"

Chancy sighed. There was only so much of Jelly Varnes he could take. When Jelly wasn't crowing, he was carping. "Enough of that. We should show each other some respect."

"Respect is one thing," Jelly said. "Licking boots is another."

Now it was Ben Rigenaw who sighed.

"How about we use our rifles and pick them off when they come closer?" Jelly suggested.

"We couldn't drop them all," Chancy said, "and the cattle might stampede."

"So?"

"So no on the rifles."

Jelly swore. "I wouldn't have believed it, but you're almost as hard-nosed as Lucas Stout."

"That's high praise," Chancy said. He glanced at Ben Rigenaw, who grinned and shook his head despite being as pale as paper and slick with sweat. "You should have let Laverne Dodger take a look at you."

"No need," Rigenaw replied.

"You still haven't told me how bad you were hit," Chancy said.

"Look yonder," Jelly Varnes interrupted.

Krine and Ives had drawn rein. Krine raised an arm and waved it, the signal for the entire herd to halt. Presently several outlaws rode up the line and held a palaver, with the result that two of the curly wolves were sent on ahead.

"What do you suppose those polecats are up to?" Jelly said.

"Could be they're scouting the lay of the land," Chancy speculated. "Looking for water and graze."

"It puzzles me, them not taking the main trail," Jelly said. "That's what we would have done."

"On the trail they'd run into other herds," Ben Rigenaw said. "Could be Krine wants to avoid that."

The same notion had occurred to Chancy. "He's afraid someone familiar with the Flying V might spot our brand and wonder."

"That hombre doesn't take risks if he can help it," Rigenaw said.

Jelly was staring after the departing riders. "That's two less for the time being. We should hit them before their scouts come back."

"Seven to three," Rigenaw said.

"Since when do those kinds of odds bother you?" Jelly said. "And a couple of them are hurt. See that tall one with the white on his arm? That must be a bandage. The same with that skinny polecat wearing a brown hat, only it's his leg that looks to have been tended to."

"It's not the odds, it's the daylight," Chancy said. He'd already worked out how they were going to do it. "We'll wait for them to bed down for the night, then slip in, kill as many as we can, and hope the rest turn tail."

Just then Krine rose in his stirrups and waved his arm, and the outlaws set the herd into motion.

"I just had a thought," Jelly said.

"You?" Rigenaw said.

"I'm serious," Jelly said. "Let's say we drive the owlhoots off and take the herd back. There's only the three of us. How in thunder will we handle fifteen hundred head? Those critters will drift all over the place."

"What's that old saying?" Chancy said. "We'll cross that bridge when we come to it."

"The women can help," Rigenaw suggested. "They can't rope but they can ride. And Dodger too."

Jelly Varnes laughed. "A passel of ladies driving a herd into Wichita. That would be something to see. The locals will laugh us silly."

"Just so long as we get there," Chancy said.

"I bet the ladies would do it if you paid them," Rigenaw

went on. "They lost everything in the fire, and hardly have a cent to their names."

"Doves and cows," Jelly said. "Don't this beat all?"

"We're getting ahead of ourselves," Chancy said. "First we have to take our herd back."

Jelly patted his ivory-handled Colt. "Just give us the word, trail boss, and the killing will commence."

Chapter 65

Krine and his company of cutthroats made camp for the night well out on a flat stretch of prairie. They had the good sense to bunch the cattle. Three men rode herd while the rest settled around a fire.

Shortly before dark, the two scouts returned.

"Wish we could hear what they're saying," Jelly Varnes said.

Chancy had sought cover in a gully deep enough to hide their horses. He was on his belly near the top, only his head showing. Unfortunately the gully was so far from the outlaw camp he couldn't make much out.

Jelly was beside him.

Ben Rigenaw, though, had roosted at the bottom with his back to a boulder. He hadn't said much all afternoon.

Twice, earlier, Chancy saw Rigenaw place his hands on his twin Remingtons and look down at them as if he was contemplating something. Chancy couldn't imagine what.

Unexpectedly Rigenaw broke his silence. "You two should make your suppers. You want to be rested and ready when the fight comes."

"Who can rest?" Jelly said. "I'm itching to tangle with those vermin."

"Ben has a point," Chancy said. He *was* tuckered out, and some coffee would do wonders. They had enough water in their canteens.

"I can keep watch while you do the honors, boss," Jelly said with another of his mocking grins.

"You just don't like to cook," Chancy said.

"There's that," Jelly said.

Sliding down far enough that he wouldn't be exposed when he stood, Chancy rose and descended. He got the coffeepot, and with his canteen hanging by its strap from his arm, he moved to a convenient spot for the fire. There was plenty of dry brush. He gathered enough to last a spell, and broke some of the bigger pieces. As he worked, he studied Rigenaw out of the corner of his eye. The man looked worse than ever. Deciding enough was enough, he went over.

Ben looked up. His face was as pasty as clay and large drops of sweat dripped from his chin.

"I have a right to know how bad it is," Chancy said.

"Do you?"

"As you keep reminding Jelly, I'm trail boss now. You practically shoved the job at me, so you have yourself to thank if I'm too bossy."

"I'll last long enough."

"Let me be the judge." Chancy squatted and nodded at Rigenaw's bandage. "More fresh blood? You're still bleeding after all this time?"

"I've always been a bleeder," Rigenaw said. "When I was little, the doctor told my folks that I had to be extra careful not to be cut. That it's a condition some have."

"I think I've heard of it," Chancy vaguely recollected. "Most that have it spend most of their days indoors where it's safe."

"That wouldn't do for me. I never could stand to be cooped up."

"So you picked the safest profession you could think of," Chancy said. "Cowboying?"

"I could bleed all day from a paper cut as well as being gored. Why hide from it?"

"And you became a gun hand because that's even safer than working with cattle with seven-foot horns?"

Rigenaw laughed and said, "If you're trying to cheer me up, you're doing a fine job."

"I'm trying to savvy whatever is going on in that head of yours."

"The answer is simple," Rigenaw said. "If there's one thing I've learned, life is for living."

"That doesn't tell me much," Chancy said.

Rigenaw gazed off down the gully as if gazing into his past. "My folks tried to keep me safe. They wanted me to stay indoors most of the time, and wouldn't let me do any chores where I might be cut or nicked. My pa wouldn't even let me use the pitchfork in the barn, or the ax for chopping wood."

"You resented that?"

"I sure didn't like it any. All the other boys were running around having fun and doing all the things boys do. But not me. Not sickly Ben. Finally when I was twelve I couldn't stand it anymore and told my pa and ma that from then on, I'd do as I saw fit. And I saw fit to live like everybody else."

"How come this is the first I've heard of it?"

"What business is it of yours or anyone else's? It's my problem." Rigenaw touched the bandage. "Only a jackass tells everybody everything there is to know about himself."

"I grant you that," Chancy said. "But still."

"As to your questions, I went to work at a nearby ranch. That's how I got into the cattle trade." Rigenaw lowered his hands to his Remingtons. "As for the guns, I couldn't very well let myself be shot, now, could I? So much as a scratch, and I might bleed out. So I practiced and I practiced to where if I got in a scrape, I'd be the one who shot first and maybe end it before I took a slug."

"I'll be damned," Chancy said.

"Now you know all you need to."

"Not quite." Chancy indicated Rigenaw's side. "I'd like for you to unwrap that so I can see for myself."

"I'd rather not."

"What if I insist?"

"No."

Chancy gave it to him straight. "Ben, you look like death warmed over. I need to know I can count on you in the fight."

"Don't fret on that score."

"Be reasonable. What if I remove the bandage so I can examine you? Would you let me?"

"Being trail boss doesn't give you the right to prod,"

Rigenaw said. "Not about this, it doesn't." He paused, and his features softened. "Listen, Chancy. I appreciate your concern. I truly do. You'll have to take my word that I won't let you down. In fact, I might do better than you expect."

"What does that mean?"

Rigenaw smiled but wouldn't elaborate.

Reluctantly Chancy went back to kindling the fire. It was plain Rigenaw was up to something, but what?

He figured he'd find out soon enough.

Chapter 66

Their meal consisted of jerky and coffee and a few biscuits Old Charlie had made a few days ago and Jelly had stashed in his saddlebags to nibble on while riding herd.

Chancy kept the fire small so its glow wouldn't alert the outlaws. "We'll rest until midnight," he announced between bites. "Then we move in."

"And do what, exactly?" Jelly said. "March up to their fire, say 'How do you do?' and blaze away?"

"No." Chancy had given it a lot of thought. "We'll take the night riders first. Quietly. That will leave those who hopefully are sound asleep."

"It'll be a massacre," Jelly said gleefully.

"I wouldn't count on it being easy," Ben Rigenaw warned. "Not with Krine and Ives to deal with."

"You keep bringing them up like they're special," Jelly said.

"They are."

"Shucks. They have to sleep, the same as everybody," Jelly said. "We'll catch them under their blankets."

"Some gun sharks wake up quick," Rigenaw said.

"Then let's shoot them first," Jelly said, "and the others will be candy."

"You have an answer to everything, don't you?"

"I try."

"I admire a gent with confidence," Rigenaw said drily.

"Then you should admire the hell out of me," Jelly said.

Chancy sipped and said, "I had no idea you two could be so entertaining." But a massacre would suit him right fine, given all the good men they'd lost, and what the outlaws had done to Ollie. He couldn't wait to wipe out every last badman.

"Me neither," Jelly said.

Chancy realized he had said it out loud. "They deserve it, all the outfits they've exterminated."

"I bet they were all small outfits like ours," Ben Rigenaw said.

"What makes you say that?" Chancy asked.

"Word would get around if a big outfit up and disappeared," Rigenaw replied. "If it was a Chisholm herd, say, he'd have men scouring the prairie from Texas to Kansas and back again."

"Yellow-belly outlaws," Jelly spat. "Only jumping outfits they think they can whip."

"Smart of them," Chancy said. Whatever else could be said about Krine, the man was no dunderhead.

"You're playing it just as smart," Ben Rigenaw complimented him. "Smarter than Lucas Stout did."

The assertion shocked Chancy.

It must have surprised Jelly Varnes too, because he remarked, "That was harsh. I thought you and him were friends."

"The best," Rigenaw said.

"What did he do that he shouldn't have?" Jelly said. "He was cautious as cautious could be."

"Not cautious enough. He took that polecat mayor at his word, and left the main trail. The water and grass were too much to resist. It made him forget one of the most important rules of life."

"Which is?" Jelly prompted.

"When something seems too good to be true, it usually is."

"He was only thinking of the cattle," Jelly said. "And of Finger."

"Even so," Rigenaw said, and he gave Chancy a pointed look. "A gent in his position can't afford to be too trusting."

"I can't fault Stout for doing what he thought best," Chancy said. "I'd probably have done the same in his boots."

"And be just as dead."

Chancy pondered on that now as he lay on his back with his hands behind his head to try to catch forty winks. It seemed to him Rigenaw was being unfair. A person made the best decisions he or she could. Sure, some were wrong. Everyone made mistakes. But how were they to know? No one could see into the future. It was only when you looked back that you saw where you had gone astray.

Closing his eyes, Chancy made a blank slate of his mind and waited to drift off. A nap would refresh him for what was to come.

Half an hour later he admitted sleep was a lost cause. He was too worked up. There would be more killing soon, with no guarantee he'd survive the night. That weighed heavily, as did the knowledge that his decisions had brought them to this point. What if his decisions, like Lucas Stout's, were wrong? But what else was he to do? Let the outlaws get away? Let them sell the herd and profit from their slaughter of his friends? Not so long as he drew breath.

Jelly Varnes was snoring lightly but Rigenaw was by the fire, sipping coffee.

"You should try to get some sleep, Ben," Chancy suggested as he refilled his tin cup.

"Couldn't if I tried," Rigenaw said. "I never can when I know there's to be shooting. It's not a thing to take lightly."

They both looked over when Jelly let out with a particularly loud snore.

"He seems to be able to," Chancy said.

"Jelly is a marvel," Rigenaw said, not unkindly.

"I wish I had his nerves," Chancy confessed. "Varnes never lets anything bother him."

"You're doing fine, Gantry."

Chancy swallowed some coffee. They didn't have sugar, which was a shame. He liked his coffee sweet.

"Are you open to some advice?" Rigenaw said.

"From you, anytime."

"When we get to it, you take the small fry. Leave Krine and Ives to Jelly and me."

Rigenaw held up a hand when Chancy went to speak. "Not meaning no insult. We have more experience, is all."

"I'll take them as they come, thank you very much." Chancy resented the implication that they needed to protect him.

"I was afraid you'd say that."

"Would you do any less if you were me?" Chancy demanded.

"I surely would not," Rigenaw admitted. "Which is why I won't hold it against you. You have to do what you have to do. The same for Jelly." He paused. "And the same for me."

"I don't know as I like the sound of that. You're not to do anything that will get you killed, you hear me?"

"In a gunfight?" Ben Rigenaw said, and he did what anyone would do; he laughed.

Chapter 67

Midnight arrived on the legs of a turtle. Each minute was an eternity, or so it felt to Chancy. He woke Jelly Varnes about half an hour before they were to head out. The instant he touched Jelly's arm, the blond gun hand sat bolt upright with his hand on his Colt.

"Oh. It's only you."

"You must be part cat," Chancy said.

Chuckling, Jelly stretched and studied the sky. "It's almost time. Did you and Ben get any rest?"

"No."

"If you're going to be trail boss, you have to learn the trick. Stout could fall asleep as soon as he laid his head down."

Curious, Chancy said, "There's a trick to it? No one ever told me. What's the secret?"

"Empty your head. Just stop thinking. Wipe all your thoughts away like you're wiping a blackboard clean."

"I tried that," Chancy said.

Ben Rigenaw had overhead. "It's easier for some than it is for others. They have emptier heads to begin with."

Jelly Varnes took the rib good-naturedly. "I admit I'm not much for thinking. Waste of time, if you ask me. I'm more of a doer. I go and I do, and that's that."

"The things you learn about the fellas you work with," Chancy said.

Pushing to his feet, Jelly stepped to the fire. He tucked at the knees several times, then windmilled his arms. "Limbering up," he said.

Chancy didn't see the need. No amount of limb waving

would do away with the tension that clawed at his innards. To take his mind off it, he said, "We have to take the night guards without using our pistols. Any ideas?"

"We can bean them with rocks," Jelly said.

"I'm not much good at rock chucking," Rigenaw said. "Even if we can find some to chuck."

"Sneak up close and rope them, then," Jelly said.

"They'll have time to squawk and alert the rest," Chancy said. "We want them dead before they hit the ground."

"I've got my boot knife," Jelly said. "I hardly ever use it, but it will cut a man's heartstrings as quick as anything."

"I have a knife too," Rigenaw said.

"I've got a folding knife in my saddlebags," Chancy remembered. "But it's a mite small for throat slitting."

"How about this?" Jelly said. "You two grab a guard and keep him from hollering, and I'll do him in with my blade."

"Works for me," Chancy said. "Ben, are you up to it? You've been moving a little slow."

"I'll do what I have to."

Chancy climbed to the rim for a look-see. There was no moon, not so much as a sliver. They'd only have the pale starlight to work by. Which was both good and bad. Good, in that it would be harder for the outlaws to spot them. Bad, in that it was easier to blunder in the dark.

Ben Rigenaw and Jelly Varnes came up on either side.

"Ready when you are, trail boss," Jelly said.

Chancy glided up out of the gully. Staying low, he stalked toward the cattle. His hand was on the Remington.

Jelly loped at his side as effortlessly as a panther on the prowl, his teeth white in the night in that perpetual smile of his. The stories told about him were true; he did smile when he killed.

Ben Rigenaw appeared to struggle to keep up. Twice he stumbled, if only slightly, and caught himself.

"Are you sure you're all right?" Chancy whispered.

"If I wasn't, you'd know."

It upset Chancy, Rigenaw being so evasive, but what could he do other than let the man come along and hope for the best?

The low of a longhorn brought them to a stop. When Jelly slicked his Colt, Chancy did the same with his Remington. Ben Rigenaw, oddly, left his six-shooters in their holsters.

The longhorns had long since settled in for the night. Many were lying down. Horns glinted, and a big steer roved restlessly.

A night guard came into view, the outlaw hunched in his saddle, his horse moving at a slow walk.

"He looks half-asleep," Jelly whispered. "This will be easy as pie."

Chancy wished he could be as confident, but too many things could go wrong. He motioned for Jelly to swing to the left and for Rigenaw to go right while he crept directly toward their quarry. Either he or Ben would get a hand over the man's mouth as they pulled him from his mount, and Jelly would strike.

The last ten feet were a nightmare of apprehension. He thought for sure the outlaw would hear him, and turn, but the man did indeed appear to have dozed off. It wasn't unheard-of to sleep in the saddle, but should a Flying V hand be caught at it, he'd be lucky to keep his job.

On soundless soles, Chancy slipped in behind the horse. Jelly crept up from one side, and nodded. Chancy looked for Ben Rigenaw to do likewise, but there was no sign of him. Puzzled, he slowed and peered into the darkness. All he saw was prairie. He glanced at Jelly, who was also looking, and Jelly shrugged to signify he had no idea either where Rigenaw had gotten to.

Chancy figured the wound had taken its delayed toll, and Ben had collapsed and was too weak to help. He had a choice to make. Carry on or go look. With the night guard mere yards away, the answer was obvious.

Chancy nodded at Jelly and pointed, and Jelly nodded in return. They moved faster, Chancy coiling for the leap he must make. He was so close he could touch the animal's tail when the rider did the last thing they wanted.

He straightened and shifted in the saddle.

Chapter 68

Chancy reacted without thinking. He took two long bounds and sprang. The outlaw opened his mouth to shout, but Chancy struck him on it even as he hooked his other arm around the man's shoulder and neck. He let their combined weight and gravity do the rest, punching again and again as they toppled. They struck hard. By a fluke, Chancy was on top, and rammed his fist into the man's throat. Cursing vehemently, the outlaw clawed for his six-shooter.

Chancy was sure they were making so much noise the other two night guards would come at a gallop. He drew back his fist to hit the man again, and steel flashed out of nowhere. Jelly's knife, driven to the hilt, went clear through the man's neck. With a powerful wrench, Jelly sliced the knife up and out, in effect half severing the man's neck from his body. Chancy threw himself back as blood sprayed every which way. Some spattered his shirt and his pants, but it couldn't be helped. Scrambling to his knees, he drew the Remington.

The outlaw was already fading. His mouth opened and closed as he tried to gulp in breath like a fish out of water. He broke into convulsions, his back arched into a bow, and he uttered a long, low hiss. His eyes locked in fear on Chancy, and he was gone.

"Damn, that was slick," Jelly Varnes said, and laughed.

The humor was lost on Chancy. He started to swipe at the blood on his clothes but stopped. He'd only smear it worse. "We were lucky."

"Luck, hell. You were punching him so hard he didn't have a chance to yell for help." Jelly wiped his knife on the man's shirt. "I keep this as sharp as my razor. Never know when a blade might come in handy."

"I would have taken you for guns only," Chancy said.

"I'd rather shoot than stab, but either will do when the need calls for it."

Chancy looked around. "Where did Ben get to? He should have helped."

"Maybe he got lost."

"This is no time for you to try to be funny."

"Try?"

The outlaw's horse had gone a short way and stopped. Apparently the smell of blood didn't disturb it, because it stood there looking at them as if it was bored.

Chancy walked in a circle. "I don't see him."

"Could be he's dead."

"You're a big help."

"That slug is still in him, or didn't you know? It's been sloshing around in his vitals, and that can't be good."

"Sloshing?"

"Whatever a bullet does when it's inside you. He should have let the sawbones take a look at him. The man has too much pride."

Chancy could have said that Jelly was a fine one to talk, but didn't. "Let's find him. We'll spread out."

"You're not thinking straight, trail boss," Jelly said. "The outlaws are more important. The other two might wonder where their pard got to and give a holler, and we'll have all of them on our heads. Do you want that to happen?"

No, Chancy didn't. "Good point. We'll take care of the other two first."

"You're the boss."

Chancy almost punched him. Instead he started around the herd, staying close to the cattle so his silhouette would blend into theirs. Jelly padded in his wake.

Troubled by Ben Rigenaw's absence, Chancy struggled to concentrate. He nearly collided with a cow that stepped into his path. Rather than smack it on the rump, he moved wide. He didn't go much farther when a hand fell on his shoulder, bringing him to a stop.

"Yonder," Jelly Varnes whispered.

It was the second night guard, moving away from them. He was wide-awake, and turning his head from side to side. On the scrawny side, he didn't look all that tough, but looks could be deceiving.

Chancy commenced a silent stalk. He froze whenever he thought the outlaw might be about to look back. Before long he was as close to the man's horse as he had been to the other one. He matched his steps to those of the horse so that all the man heard was the animal.

Jelly, at his elbow, motioned for him to get to it.

When he was good and ready, Chancy told himself. They couldn't afford a mistake. He crept past the horse's tail, its thigh, its flank. Only a stride behind the saddle, he saw his chance when the outlaw let his arm dangle. Lunging, Chancy grabbed the man's wrist, dug in his bootheels, and pulled.

The outlaw let out a yip as he was unhorsed. Chancy swung at his throat to smother the outcry, and missed; he clipped the man's shoulder. As the outlaw fell, he jerked his pistol. Chancy heard the click of the hammer and swooped his hand over the cylinder. Instinctively he slid his forefinger between the hammer and the frame so the hammer couldn't strike the cartridge. The outlaw stroked the trigger and pain flared from Chancy's hand to his elbow. He fought an urge to pull loose. The hammer might rip his finger open.

Out of the night flew Jelly Varnes. Legs bent, his knife held aloft in both hands, he slammed his knees onto the outlaw's chest while simultaneously plunging his knife into the man's chest. The scrawny cutthroat went to yell, and Jelly clamped a hand over his mouth.

Like a bucking bronco, the outlaw heaved and thrashed. Tenacious of life, he sought to throw them off. Gradually he weakened, until, with a gurgling grunt, he went as limp as a wet towel.

"Tough hombre," Jelly whispered.

Chancy removed his hand from the man's revolver and regained his feet. Two night guards down, one to go. He continued on around the herd but didn't see the third guard.

The campfire came into sight. Chancy figured most of the other outlaws would be asleep, but he was wrong. Three were still up, seated around the fire: Krine, Ives, and one other.

Chancy flattened before they saw him.

Jelly dropped next to him, bumping his arm. "Let's shoot the buzzards."

"Not yet." To Chancy, it was wiser to deal with the last guard first, but it could be the man was on the far side of the herd.

"Tell that to him," Jelly whispered.

"Eh?" Chancy looked up.

Ben Rigenaw, his thumbs hooked in his gun belt, was casually strolling toward the outlaw camp.

Chapter 69

"What's he doing?" Chancy blurted.

"Hogging the big apples for himself," Jelly Varnes said, and went to go past Chancy toward the fire.

Thrusting an arm out to stop him, Chancy said, "Hold on. We go barreling over, they're liable to see us."

"So what?"

"So they'll give a yell and all the others will be on their feet and Ben's right there among them."

"It's where he wants to be. He waltzed on over by his lonesome, didn't he? Must reckon he can take Krine and Ives both."

"This isn't about hogging," Chancy said.

"Then what is it?"

Chancy remembered how Rigenaw had been favoring his side and wouldn't let him examine the wound, and how pasty he was, and how much he sweated, and an awful truth became crystal clear. "Oh no."

"What?"

"He's doing it for us."

"What are you babbling about?" Jelly said in confusion.

"You've seen how poorly he looks. He's dead on his feet. He doesn't have much time left, so he's going to try to blow out the wicks of the deadliest of them so we don't have to face them."

"The hell you say."

"Come on." Chancy stalked forward. The outlaws had possessed the good sense not to make their fire too close to the herd, and it was a good twenty-five yards away.

Krine and Ives and the third outlaw had put down

their tin cups and were on their feet. By their expressions, they were surprised by Ben's Rigenaw's brazen act.

"We'd best hurry like hell," Jelly said, "or we won't get there in time to help."

"They'll hear us," Chancy said. But he burst into a sprint anyway, pumping his legs for all he was worth.

Ives had taken a step so that he faced Rigenaw square-on. His hands were at his sides, brushing his holsters. He was sneering, and said something that made the third outlaw chortle.

Ben Rigenaw hadn't moved. His thumbs were still in his belt.

With a sinking feeling in the pit of his stomach, Chancy realized he and Jelly wouldn't get there in time. A fourth outlaw, woken by the talking, had sat up in his blankets. Soon they would all be awake.

And then several things happened at once.

Ives's hands flashed. So did Ben Rigenaw's. Flashed so fast they were blurs. Six-gun explosions rocked the night. Before Chancy could tell who was hit, hooves pounded to their rear, and Jelly Varnes bellowed.

"Behind us! The last night guard!"

Chancy spun. Beside him Jelly's Colt boomed. So did a six-gun the night guard was pointing at them. A hornet buzzed past Chancy's ear as he returned fire. Jelly grunted.

The outlaw was almost on top of them when Chancy thumbed the hammer and fired again. Suddenly Jelly took half a step to one side and fanned his Colt three times, as quick as could be.

As if smashed by a club, the outlaw was flung from his saddle and tumbled boots over head. His horse galloped on by and kept going into the dark.

Jelly immediately commenced to reload.

Fearing the worst, Chancy whirled toward the fire.

Ives was on his knees, looking down at himself, incredulous at the holes in his chest.

Ben Rigenaw had a six-shooter in each hand, and was swaying.

For some reason neither Krine nor any of the others had resorted to their hardware, but now the others did.

Chancy hurtled forward, yelling, "Ben! Get out of there!"

Revolvers boomed like thunder. Outlaws fell. Ben Rigenaw pitched to his knees. Still game, he shot right and left.

Krine, amazingly, hadn't drawn his six-gun. Suddenly it appeared in his hand as if out of thin air, and spat lead once.

Ben Rigenaw was slammed onto his back.

"No!" Chancy raged. He fired even though he wasn't close enough to be sure.

All the outlaws were up and those still alive turned toward him, their own revolvers banging.

Chancy shot, saw a man stagger, shot again. He would have gone on firing but his right boot came down on a rock that moved under him, and he stumbled. It might have saved his life. Lead plucked at his sleeve, at his hat. He fell onto a knee, saw outlaws rushing toward him.

Then Jelly was there, his Colt low at his waist. He fanned, shifted, fanned, shifted, fanned twice more.

The abrupt quiet was more thunderous than the gunfire.

Chancy's ears were brass bands. He shook his head, but the ringing persisted. He rose and took a step and pain shot up his leg. Gritting his teeth, he tested it. He had twisted his ankle, bad.

Jelly had been shot in the thigh. The glow of the firelight revealed a spreading stain on his pant leg.

Bodies lay scattered. Dark pools were spreading. One man gasped and gulped and shook.

"We did it," Chancy said in breathless wonder.

"Don't count your chickens yet," Jelly said. He was reloading once more.

"Ben," Chancy said, and made to go to their fallen friend.

"We check the owl-hoots first," Jelly said. "Unless you want to be shot in the back while you're bending over Rigenaw."

"They don't look to have any fight left in them," Chancy remarked.

As if to prove him a liar, an outlaw rose onto his elbows, his pistol gripped in both hands, and pointed it at them.

Chapter 70

Chancy took aim, but compared to Jelly Varnes, he was molasses. Jelly's smoke wagon cracked twice and the outlaw's face exploded in a shower of blood and flesh.

The man was dead before his head smacked the earth.

"Told you," Jelly said.

They went from body to body, both of them limping, but Jelly limped worse. His bleeding had apparently stopped, though.

The outlaw who was gasping and gulping looked up. Blood ran from his nose and dribbled from both sides of his mouth. Every breath was ragged. His six-shooter lay well out of his reach.

"Lung-shot," Jelly said.

"I'll put him out of his misery," Chancy said.

"Like hell you will. Him and his friends did in our friends. Let the buzzard suffer."

Chancy wasn't disposed to argue. He kicked the six-shooter farther away and they moved on to the next man. Hooking his boot under the outlaw's shoulder, Chancy rolled him over. An eye had been shot out.

"One of mine," Jelly said. "I usually go for the face."

They were almost to the last outlaw when hooves pounded. In unison they swung around, their six-guns leveled, but the horse was moving away.

"Who. . . ?" Jelly said.

Chancy glanced all around and felt a stab of bafflement. "Where's Krine's body?"

Jelly swiveled from side to side and swore a blue

streak. "That must have been him. The bastard is getting away."

"Not if we can help it," Chancy vowed, and bobbed his chin at the string of outlaw mounts, theirs for the taking.

Jelly grinned and took a couple of strides and almost collapsed when his leg gave out. Clutching his thigh, he gritted his teeth and hissed through his nose. "Damn. It's seizing up on me."

Chancy was about to suggest they should take a look at it when a low groan caused them to spin yet again. But it wasn't an outlaw.

It was Ben Rigenaw.

Quickly they hobbled over. Chancy dropped to his knees and felt for a pulse. There was one, but oh so weak. "Ben?" he said. "Ben, can you hear me?"

Jelly couldn't seem to bend his wounded leg. He gave up trying, and simply tucked at the waist. "Rigenaw? Don't you die on us, you ornery so-and-so."

Ben Rigenaw's eyelids fluttered open. As if pulling himself back from a great inner void, he focused on Chancy and then on Jelly, and his lips quirked. "Dang," he said. "I was hoping for angels."

Jelly laughed.

Not Chancy. He gripped Rigenaw's arm. "Is there anything we can do?" He knew full well there wasn't.

"Did we get them all?"

"Krine lit a shuck," Jelly said. "But his days of murdering cowpokes are over. I'll hunt him down if it's the last thing I do."

Rigenaw smiled. "You got the herd back, trail boss. Congratulations."

"As much your doing as ours," Chancy said. "You shouldn't have braced them alone."

"Had it to do," Rigenaw said. "I reckon you can guess why."

"You should have told us how bad off you were," Chancy said. "There might have been something we could do."

"Or that sawbones," Jelly said. "He saved Finger."

"No time for that," Rigenaw said. "The herd came first." He grimaced, and quaked, and dug his fingers into the dirt.

"Ben?" Chancy said.

"Sawbones couldn't have done much anyway," Rigenaw said. "Had two slugs in me."

"Two!" Chancy shook his head in awe at the iron will it must have taken for Rigenaw to last as long as he did.

"You've got more grit than any hombre I've ever known," Jelly said. "I hope when my time comes, I go out half as glorious."

Rigenaw closed his eyes. "You two should light a shuck after Krine. If he gets away, this was all for nothing."

"We're not leaving you," Chancy said.

"You're the trail boss now," Rigenaw said. "You have to do what's best for the outfit, not for one man."

"What outfit?" Jelly said. "There's us, and Ollie, and that's it."

"Go after him," Ben Rigenaw insisted. "Don't worry about me. Do what you have to."

"Not yet." Chancy would be damned if he'd leave him to die alone.

"I'd like to lie here in peace and quiet," Rigenaw said. "Or is that too much to ask?"

"You're not fooling anyone," Chancy said.

"And you're too softhearted. A good trail boss has to be hard inside to do what needs doing."

"Stop with that," Chancy said. "Lucas Stout cared about his hands as much as the herd. Look at the trouble he went to for Finger."

"And look at what that cost him."

"Why are you making such a fuss?" Jelly broke in. "You lived like a man, now die like one and quit your bellyaching."

"Jelly," Chancy said.

"That's all right," Ben Rigenaw said weakly. "I'm about done in. If you can find the time later, bury me. I hate to think I'd be food for the coyotes."

"Count on it," Chancy promised.

"You're a good man, Chancy Gantry," Rigenaw said, and died with a smile on his lips.

"Finally," Jelly said.

Chancy felt a surge of anger. "Must you?"

Jelly hitched at his gun belt. "Time to go after the high and mighty Krine and end this once and for all."

Chapter 71

They weren't halfway to the string when Jelly Varnes bleated in pain, and staggered. His hands splayed to his thigh, he came to a stop. "Just what I need at a time like this."

Chancy had been thinking. Rigenaw was right about the herd coming first. And if both he and Jelly lit out after Krine, there'd be no one to look after the cattle. Granted, one man couldn't do much, but it was better than none. "You're staying here," he announced.

"Like hell I am."

"I'm your boss now. You'll do as I say." Chancy walked on. "Look after the herd until I get back."

"Hold on," Jelly said, hobbling to catch up. "You can't take Krine on by yourself. He's too quick on the shoot. Maybe even quicker than me."

"Then it doesn't make a difference which ones of us braces him, does it?" Chancy deliberately walked faster.

Hobbling furiously, wincing with every step, Jelly declared, "This ain't right, damn it. Leaving me to twiddle my thumbs while you put your hide at risk."

"You won't have time to twiddle," Chancy said over his shoulder. "You're to look after the longhorns and try not to let too many stray off."

"Likely as not they'll stay put until daylight," Jelly said, "so there's no reason not to let me tag along."

"Your leg," Chancy said.

"I can manage."

"I've made my decision," Chancy said firmly.

The commotion and din of gunfire had made the horses nervous. Several pranced and sought to pull free.

"Look after these too," Chancy said. "The ladies can use them on the drive to Wichita."

"You still intend to let a flock of doves lend us a hand?"

"Unless you can pull five or six cowpokes out of your pocket, I do." Chancy picked a sorrel that was standing quietly. A saddle was still on it. Patting its neck, he led it a little way from the rest and forked leather.

Jelly hobbled after him. "I'm begging you. Don't do this. We've lost too many as it is."

"If you're going to be my top hand from here on out," Chancy said, "you should show more respect." He leaned down. "If I don't make it back, I expect you to see to the herd. Get it to the railhead, no matter what. Some would say it's impossible. Prove them wrong."

"Your top hand?"

"Lucas Stout had Ben Rigenaw. I have you."

"Well, I'll be," Jelly said, and smiled. "I'm beginning to see why Stout picked you and not one of us others. He must have seen something in you I didn't."

Chancy raised the reins.

"Wait. How will you find him in the dark?"

"He'll likely head north," Chancy speculated. "All his men have been wiped out and his town burned. There's nothing for him to go back to."

"Makes sense."

"If I haven't caught up by, say, noon tomorrow, I'll turn around and come back."

"If you do catch up," Jelly said, "don't take chances."

"As if I would."

"Don't go at him straight up or he'll gun you for sure," Jelly advised. "Shoot him from ambush. In the back if you have to. Whatever it takes."

"I'm not no back-shooter," Chancy said indignantly, and tapped his heels to the sorrel. The gall, to suggest he commit so cowardly an act.

"Would you go at a grizzly straight on?" Jelly yelled. "No. You'd shoot it from far off to be safe."

"Not the same," Chancy shouted back.

"You're too pigheaded for your own good! Do you know that?"

Chancy didn't answer. He fixed on the North Star and willed himself to relax. It might be a long ride. Krine would probably seek to cover as much distance as he could before sunrise.

The miles fell behind him, the wind strong on his face.

Chancy couldn't stop yawning. He was sore and weary and would dearly love to catch some sleep. In a real bed with a soft pillow, and a quilt to keep him warm and snug. He'd curl up and not stir for a week. Just thinking about it made his eyelids grow leaden and his chin start to droop.

With a sharp toss of his head, Chancy sat straighter. He couldn't afford to doze off. He was alone in the middle of the vast prairie. A single mistake could cost him his life.

Ahead, dark bumps appeared, swelling to become a line of hills.

Chancy climbed the first. From the crest he had a sweeping view of the benighted land ahead. He half hoped that Krine had stopped and kindled a fire, but there wasn't a glimmer of light to be seen.

"Knew it wouldn't be that easy," Chancy said to the sorrel, and headed down the other side.

In half an hour he was out of the hills and crossing a tableland. The wind was even worse, and got dust into his eyes.

Chancy grew despondent. He was searching for the proverbial needle in a haystack. For all he knew, Krine had gone west or east instead of north.

Chancy was acting on a hunch, nothing more. It could be a complete waste of his time. He was tempted to rein around and head back to the herd, but since he had come this far, he figured he'd stick to his original plan and push on until at least daybreak. If he didn't come across sign of Krine by then, he'd call it quits.

The idea of Krine getting away didn't sit well, though. Not after all the man had cost them. All the lives lost. All the suffering. If ever a man deserved an early grave, it was Artemis Krine.

Chancy would give anything to see him dangling from the end of a rope. Barring that, a slug to the head would suffice.

He chuckled at how bloodthirsty he'd become. Not a week ago he would have said that killing was wrong. Not anymore. There were times when it had to be done, when a person had to set personal feelings aside and do what needed doing.

Chancy consoled himself with the thought that if Krine did get away, he could always go after him later. After the herd was sold, and he had turned the proceeds over to the Flying V's owner. He would make the rounds of the cow towns and ask every bartender and barber if they'd seen a gent answering to Krine's description. It was a long shot, but it might work.

Suddenly a dry wash spread before him.

Chancy slowed to a walk to descend. The last thing he needed was for the sorrel to take a spill and maybe break a leg. He reached the bottom and was about to goad the sorrel up the other side when he distinctly heard the metallic click of a gun hammer being cocked.

"Any fast moves and you're dead."

Chapter 72

Chancy drew rein and imitated a statue. His hands were in front of him. To try to draw would be futile.

A horseshoe pinged on rock, and a horse came up next to the sorrel.

"Well, look who it is," Artemis Krine said. "The boy who's caused me so much trouble. If this isn't fitting, I don't know what is."

Chancy slowly turned his head and stared into the muzzle of the Starr revolver. "You came north after all."

"I have a new gang to recruit," Krine said, "and the towns in Kansas are full of hard cases."

"How did you know I was after you?"

"I didn't," Krine said. "I came down here to get out of the wind and to rest my animal." He patted his bay. "Good thing I did."

Chancy suspected he had mere minutes to live. Krine wasn't the kind to toy with him, like a cat with a mouse. Krine would simply shoot him dead and push on. Frantic to save his skin, he said, "I'm not alone."

"Liar."

"We spread out to cover more ground," Chancy said. "You shoot and they'll hear and come on the run."

Krine rose in the stirrups but couldn't see over the rims on either side. "I don't believe you," he growled, but he didn't sound entirely confident.

"Then squeeze that trigger and see what happens," Chancy bluffed, shifting slightly.

Krine tilted his head, listening. "I don't hear anything. I still think you're a damn liar."

Chancy shifted a little more. "That's your problem. You've underestimated us all along."

"I had your outfit licked," Krine said. "You burned down my town and killed a lot of my men, but I beat you."

"We've taken the herd back," Chancy said to keep him talking. "You haven't beaten anyone."

"I wish you and that damn herd never showed up," Krine said bitterly.

"For what it's worth, the feeling is mutual." Chancy shifted farther, only an inch or so. He'd made up his mind he wouldn't die meekly. He would try to get off a shot. Even if he missed, it was better than just sitting there.

"I wouldn't have reckoned it possible. A bunch of cowpokes against some of the worst bad men in the territory, and you licked us."

"We were fighting for the brand," Chancy said.

"It was more than that. Others fought us. But they weren't shucks compared to you. From your trail boss on down, you were as salty as Comanches."

Yet again Chancy shifted. Now he was almost facing Krine. "You prod a man, you have to expect him to prod back."

"There are men and there are men." Krine gestured with his Starr. "How about you climb down? I still don't believe you're alone, but I've learned not to push my luck with your outfit."

"You have to back off," Chancy said. "I can't swing down with your horse so close."

"Slide off," Krine said. "Real slow."

Chancy was hoping he'd say that. He slid his boot out of the stirrup and started to raise his leg over the saddle horn. All he had to do was swing it over and he could slide off as Krine wanted. Instead, when his leg reached its highest point, he let go of the reins and swung his leg at Krine's gun hand. The Starr went off, but the shot missed.

Startled, the sorrel wheeled away from the bay, and Chancy was nearly unhorsed. Clinging to the saddle horn, he jabbed his heels.

The sorrel bolted up out of the gully and came to a gallop with its mane flying.

Another shot boomed. Hugging his saddle, Chancy fled for his life. Or that was the impression he wanted to give.

Krine gave chase.

Chancy couldn't have planned it better if he'd tried. He was no match for Krine with a six-gun, but he'd match his riding ability against anyone else's any day of the week. Krine had made the blunder a lot of bad men made: he was too confident by half.

Lashing his reins, Chancy maintained his lead. Twenty, forty, fifty yards, they covered. Chancy reckoned that was enough. With a silent prayer, Chancy did the last thing Krine would expect. Drawing his Remington, he clutched it tight and launched himself from the saddle.

Cowboys took spills all the time. It was a common hazard of the job. Which was why some of them, Chancy included, learned how to fall without breaking their necks, or worse. Chancy knew to loosen his body and to turn so his shoulder and side bore the brunt. He came down hard enough that it knocked the breath from his lungs, but otherwise he was unhurt. Rolling, he pushed to his knees.

The bay came abreast of him, Krine intent on the still-moving sorrel.

Chancy extended his six-shooter, cocking it as he did, and centered the barrel on the mass in the bay's saddle, the best he could do given the dim starlight. He fired, thumbed the hammer, fired again. There were answering blasts, and it felt as if his head were kicked by a mule. The next moment he was on his back, the stars spinning crazily overhead, his hat gone.

Chancy thought he heard a thud, and blacked out.

As if he had popped out of a black hole, Chancy was suddenly awake and aware, his eyes open. He lay still, afraid his wound was mortal. There wasn't much pain, but he'd heard that sometimes was the case. The Remington was still in his right hand. Gingerly he flexed the fingers of his left and raised it to his head. He was bleeding, but not a lot. The slug had only grazed him, taking off skin and flesh and hair, and sparing his brainpan.

Thank you, God, Chancy thought, and went to raise his head to look around. Pain pounded fiercely at his skull. Stifling a groan, he stayed still until the pain subsided.

He was about to try again when a strange sound intruded on the stillness of the night.

A slight scraping noise, as if something were being dragged along the ground. He couldn't make sense of it.

The sound stopped and after a bit began again.

Suddenly Chancy knew. It wasn't something being dragged. It was someone crawling.

It was Krine.

Stalking him.

Chapter 73

Chancy's first impulse was to heave to his feet and run. Except that would draw more lead. Instead, he eased onto his side, which provoked more pounding in his head. It was difficult to concentrate. He strained his eyes searching for Krine but didn't see him.

The scraping had stopped again, which didn't help.

Chancy tried to swallow but his mouth was too dry. He needed to change position. Krine might have some idea of where he was. Accordingly he inched to his right. Every movement brought more pain, and after only a few feet he stopped and sagged. He had no strength at all. His head wound must be worse than he thought. Or maybe it was the shock of being hit.

Chancy moistened his mouth and wet his lips. He was about to cock the Remington, but didn't. The click might give him away. He looked for the horses, but neither was near.

Here he was, alone and hurt and pitted against a hard-as-nails killer who was incredibly quick and accurate.

Chancy almost chuckled at the absurdity of it all. All he ever wanted was to cowboy, to tend cattle and not bother anyone and not have anyone impose on him. To have a simple life, where the worst that might happen was being gored by a longhorn or being thrown by a mustang.

How did a man get into these fixes? Chancy asked himself. The answer was obvious. "Life."

The renewed sound of scraping brought Chancy out of himself. He jerked his head up, and paid for it with more agony. He peered into the dark until he thought his head would explode, but nothing. Krine was out there, but where? He was shocked when Krine gave him the answer.

"Gantry? Are you still breathing?"

Chancy didn't respond. He pegged the voice as coming from thirty or forty feet to the west.

"Did I get you or are you playing possum?"

Chancy bit his lip. It was a trick. It had to be. An outlaw as crafty as Krine wouldn't give himself away unless it was a ruse.

"You can answer me, boy. I'm about done in. You caught me good with one of your shots."

Chancy doubted it. But even if it was true, the fact that Krine could crawl about, and talk, was proof he could shoot too.

"I never thought it would be like this. Done in by a cowpoke, of all things. And one barely old enough to shave."

Chancy was older than that. He just looked young.

"You've beaten me. I'm a goner. It won't be long now and there will be just you."

Was it Chancy's imagination, or did the voice come from a different spot each time? He realized Krine was quietly moving as he talked. To keep him distracted while Krine closed in?

"You Texans. You die hard, and that's a fact. Ives was a Texan. Did you know that? From down San Antonio way."

Chancy was sure now. The talk was to distract him. He crawled a few feet and flattened on his belly.

"Come on, boy. Talk to me."

Chancy held his tongue.

"All right. You think you're so smart. But you're not. I lied. I'm not done in. You hit me, but I'll live. I can't say the same for you. Make peace with your maker, boy. Your time has come."

A vague shape moved at the limit of Chancy's vision. It had to be Krine. Chancy pointed the Remington but waited. He must be absolutely certain. If he missed, he would have given himself away. Krine would see his muzzle flash, and Krine was a better shot.

Chancy broke out in a sweat. It felt as if a swarm of centipedes were crawling around inside him. He grew clammy and cold. But he didn't move. He didn't twitch. He would wait until hell froze over if he had to.

The shape moved again. Not toward him, though. Krine was crawling to the north. Or maybe circling, trying to pinpoint where he was.

Chancy debated with himself. If he waited too long, Krine would crawl out of sight. There might not be another chance. Against his better judgment, he slowly thumbed the hammer back. He braced for a shot, but none came. Holding his breath, he stroked the trigger.

The night exploded with gunfire. Two, three, four shots. Lead smacked the ground close to Chancy. A slug whistled overhead.

Then quiet fell.

Chancy let out his breath. Wonder of wonders, he hadn't been hit. He lay there a long time, perfectly still. The shape didn't move again. A battle of nerves, he reckoned, and he'd be damned if he'd break before Krine did.

A new sound reached him, that of someone struggling for each breath. Or pretending to. Krine wanted him to think he was hurt bad when he probably wasn't.

A single word came out of the night, a wet, bubbly sound, as if Krine were speaking underwater. "God."

Chancy raised his head. If Krine was faking, he was good.

"Gantry?" The bubbling was worse.

Chancy still didn't reply.

"Gantry? I'm dying."

Good for you, Chancy thought.

"I don't want to die alone."

Chancy would have laughed except Krine would hear.

"I'm getting rid of my gun."

The shape moved and something arced and fell to the earth with a thump. Metal glinted dully.

Every nerve screaming at him not to, Chancy crawled toward it. When he reached it, he blinked in surprise. It was the Starr.

"Gantry?" Krine said again, weaker than before.

Chancy rose into a crouch.

"Gantry, I'm begging you."

Pointing the Remington, thinking he was the worst fool in all creation, Chancy edged forward.

Artemis Krine was on his back, his right arm outflung, his left arm bent with his hand under him. His mouth and chin were dark with blood. He was staring at the sky, and gasping.

"Serves you right," Chancy said.

Krine twisted his head. "You've done me in, boy. As green as you are. I can't hardly believe it."

Chancy covered him, watching the arm under Krine's back.

"You must carry a four-leaf clover around, the luck you have. You should be a gambler."

"Die, already," Chancy said.

"What, you can't spare a few words for the man you killed?" Krine gurgled. "It's the decent thing to do."

"What do you know of decent?"

"Not a lot. I always thought to be decent was to be weak." Krine turned his body a little. "You want something in this world, you have to be strong. You have to take it."

"Quit playacting," Chancy said.

Krine stared, blood bubbling from his mouth.

"You don't have long. It's now or never."

"I reckon so."

Chancy was ready when Krine jerked a derringer from behind his back. He shot Krine in the chest, cocked the Remington, shot him in the face, cocked the Remington, stepped up, jammed the muzzle to Krine's forehead, and blew his brains out. "You made a mistake," he said to the body. "Decent can be strong too when it has to be."

Suddenly so tired he could barely stand, Chancy shuffled a couple of steps. He thought about Missy Burke and looked up at the stars and said, "Thank you."

EPILOGUE

Most herds arrived in Wichita without fanfare. But word had spread up the trail that some loco Texans and a bunch of women were bringing in fifteen hundred head, and people thronged to the cattle yard to witness the spectacle. It even made the front page of the *Wichita Eagle* under the banner headline

SEEING IS BELIEVING!
FIRST FEMALE DROVERS
BRING HERD TO TOWN!

Chancy Gantry oversaw the sale, deposited the money in the Wichita Bank, sent word to the Flying V, and with Missy Burke on his elbow, hunted up a parson and had him officiate their "I do"s.

In attendance at the hasty nuptials were Jelly Varnes, wearing his ivory-handled Colt, and Laverne Dodger, his empty sleeve pinned to his side. Ollie Teal, who had to use crutches, served as best man. The doves from Prosperity were maids of honor, and each and every one wept as the vows were exchanged, Della Neece sobbing so loudly the parson had to shush her.

A month later there was another wedding. Ollie Teal and Margie Hampton tied the knot. By then Ollie had recuperated enough to get around without crutches. It was Margie who'd tended him on the long trail drive. She'd hovered at his side day and night, waited on him hand and foot. She'd changed his bandages, fed him, washed him.

And whenever any of the other ladies offered to take her place, she'd shoo them off. "Ollie is mine to take care of," she'd tell them. It got so that Ollie and she were inseparable. When they reached Wichita they took adjoining rooms for propriety's sake, but no one was fooled.

Chancy had never seen his pard so happy as the day Ollie said his vows. After the ceremony, at a small reception at a restaurant, Ollie took him aside and pumped his hand and said he was sorry but he had a new pard now.

"That's all right," Chancy said. "I have one too."

Ollie glanced over at where Margie and Missy and the other ladies were laughing and eating. "And I owe it all to nails."

"How's that again?" Chancy said.

"If those owl-hoots hadn't nailed me to that wall, I never would have needed nursing. And if Margie hadn't nursed me, she'd never have taken a liking to me like she did, and been willing to be my wife."

"Life is full of surprises."

"I'll say." Ollie beamed happily. "My pa told me once not to let it upset me if I never got hitched. He said that women can be fussy when it comes to who they marry, and there might not be one willing to tie her star to the likes of me." Ollie stopped, and his brow knit. "Say, how do you tie a star anyhow? They're so far up in the sky, you can't lasso one if you tried."

"It's a figure of speech, I think they call it."

"Well, my pa was wrong. Margie says I'm just the kind of man she's been looking for. I asked her if it was because I have a small nose and she'd mentioned once how she likes small noses better than big noses, but she said that wasn't it."

"Not many ladies marry over noses," Chancy said.

"Margie said she'd marry me because I'm the only purely innocent man she ever met. What did she mean by that, do you reckon? I'm not more innocent than the next fella. I cuss sometimes. And I have bad thoughts now and then."

"You have a good heart, pard. That's what she meant."

"All I know is I'll do my best by her."

"That's all any man can do."

Ollie lowered his voice. "Can I ask you a favor?"

"Anything. Anytime," Chancy said.

"It's about tying. Not stars, though. Diapers."

"Aren't you getting ahead of yourself?"

"Margie says she wants to have kids. Lots and lots of kids, was how she put it. I don't know the first thing about it. Take diapers, for instance. If you tie a diaper too loose, it'll fall off. If you tie it too tight, you'll strangle the baby's gut. It has to be just right, like that bear's porridge."

"Oh, Ollie."

"What?"

Ollie and Margie Teal went on to have nine children. They stayed in Wichita the rest of their days. Ollie worked as a store clerk and Margie as a seamstress. One night about five years after they were married, she asked him if he missed being a cowboy and Ollie replied that he didn't miss it as much as he'd thought he would. When she asked why that was, he smiled and kissed her and said that she looked a lot better in a dress than a cow ever could.

Laverne Dodger finished medical school and became a full-fledged sawbones. He hung his shingle out in Topeka and lived a long life devoted to relieving the suffering in others. Over two hundred people attended his funeral, and his tombstone was chiseled to read HERE LIES DOC DODGER, BELOVED HEALER AND FRIEND.

Jelly Varnes returned to Texas. He stayed at the Flying V for several years, then drifted to the border country. A certain senorita was the lure. He met her on a trip to Dallas, where she was visiting a sister. He stayed in the border country for ten years but never married, and was involved in several shooting scrapes. The most notorious was an incident in a saloon in which he shot and killed three vaqueros.

A Texas Ranger happened to be in the vicinity, and investigated the killings. He interviewed a number of witnesses. They all agreed the shooting was over a woman, apparently the same senorita. They also agreed that one of the vaqueros, "an hombre of vicious temperament," as one witness put it, started the affray when he became "too friendly" with the senorita and she objected. When the vaquero slapped her, Jelly knocked him down. The vaquero rose and went for his six-shooter, and Jelly drew and shot him in the face before he cleared leather. Witnesses said the other two tried to unlimber their own revolvers, and that Jelly shot both "as quick as lightning."

Jelly didn't stick around. Even though he could have claimed self-defense, he not only left the border country; he left Texas.

Next he turned up working for John H. Slaughter in Arizona. He stayed at the Slaughter Ranch not quite five years, and left after yet another shooting.

Jelly was in Galeyville when a drunk pistol-whipped a freighter who refused to drink with him. Jelly told the drunk to leave the man be, and the drunk went for his six-gun. They buried him in an unmarked grave.

The next anyone heard the name Jelly Varnes was in California. An old man who went by that handle lived in a cabin on a bluff overlooking the ocean. He made the local newspaper when he saved two children being set on by a rabid dog. The old man had an ivory-handled Colt hidden under his shirt, and killed the dog with a shot to the head. He was arrested for carrying a concealed firearm but released after an uproar over the unfairness of it.

The brother and sister took a liking to the old man, and treated him as the grandfather they'd never had. They brought him sweets and fruit, and he'd regale them with tales of the cattle years. He had a flair for storytelling, but he would only ever share his stories with them.

When Jelly passed on, they were the only ones who stood by the hole as his coffin was lowered, and the girl placed flowers on his grave.

As for Chancy Gantry, he and his wife moved to Salina, where they opened a dry goods store and ran it until they were old enough for rocking chairs. Missy bore them seven children and those seven gave them sixteen grandchildren.

The family had a tradition that, come hell or high water, they got together once a year, on Independence Day. Missy wanted it to be on Thanksgiving, but Chancy pointed out that winter weather often struck by late November, and some of their brood had a long way to travel. In the summer the weather was better.

For twenty wonderful years the family held those get-togethers, and Chancy was never happier as when he had everyone under one roof and all of them safe and well. He delighted in rocking his grandchildren on his knee and playing hide-and-seek.

Chancy and Ollie paid each other visits now and then. They'd take a jug and sit in the shade of a tree and share their latest doings. Chancy noticed early on that Ollie always wore shirts with longer sleeves than usual, even in the hottest weather. He never asked why. He noticed too that when Ollie raised an arm, those sleeves never slid far enough to show Ollie's scars.

Ollie also refused to ever touch a hammer or nails. Any building that had to be done around his place, he hired it out. He wouldn't even allow a hammer in his house.

When Ollie eventually passed on, it was remarked by many that he was the most "beloved man in the county."

Finally, of the original outfit, only Chancy was left. One evening he and Missy stood in their yard watching the sun set and admiring the spectacular colors.

Missy, her hair now white but her smile still as bright, turned to Chancy and asked if he ever missed the old days.

"When we got married and started our life together?"

"Before that," Missy said. "The Flying V. The trail drive. Prosperity."

"Have you been conked on the head?" Chancy joked.

"We wouldn't have met if not for that."

"I'd as soon forget it, thank you very much," Chancy said. "Not the part where I met you. The rest of it. The killings and all."

Missy squeezed his hand. "I'm sorry I brought it up. But every now and then you get a look to your eyes. As if you're remembering."

"The memories do bubble up now and then," Chancy admitted.

"You only did what you had to in order to protect people you cared about. Can any of us ever do more than that?"

"I reckon not," Chancy said.

"Then smile for me, you lunkhead."

"Yes, ma'am," Chancy said, and did.

Read on for an excerpt from

PHANTOM HILL

by Carlton Stowers.
Available in March 2016 from Signet in paperback and e-book.

Coy Jennings was limping almost as badly as his horse when, in the distance, he saw chimney smoke lazily climbing into the clear morning sky. From a small rise he could see a couple of clapboard buildings, a few small houses, and a lengthy row of tents. The wind carried the sounds of people hurrying about, dogs barking, a rooster crowing, and a blacksmith's hammer making a steady clanging.

Phantom Hill didn't look like much of a town.

"I reckon if we don't fall flat on our faces," he said to the hobbling bay, "we're gonna make it."

The trip took far longer than Jennings had planned. What he had figured would be a two-day ride turned into more than a week, after his horse had startled a rattlesnake, which then had bitten him just above the hoof on his back leg. Coy hadn't even bothered to kill the snake, instead dismounting immediately and cutting away a length of rein to tie above the small marks left by the rattler's fangs. He'd quickly tethered his mount to a mesquite tree, taken out his knife, and begun cutting small X's above the wound. Kneeling in front of the startled animal, he'd sucked the bloody poison from the leg. Once that was done, he'd made a small fire and boiled water to bathe the cuts. He'd then made a mushy plaster of tobacco and placed it on the leg, wrapping it tightly with a strip of cloth ripped from his shirt.

But it still swelled, and soon became feverish. Through the remainder of the day and into the night, Jennings had tended the bay, a gentle animal that his pa had given him when he was still in his teens. He'd ridden him to the schoolhouse and town dances, then during his days as a Confederate soldier. He was the only horse Jennings had ever owned and he refused to consider the idea that it might become his responsibility to put the animal down and relieve him of his misery.

The only time he had left the horse's side was to walk to a nearby spring for water and to whisper a prayer. *Lord, you know I'm not one for asking favors. Likely as not, I'm not deserving of any. Last time I recall reaching out to you was when that Union soldier shot me in the leg and you saw to it I didn't die. What I'm asking this time is if you could see your way clear to do the same for my horse. Rodeo's his name and he's lived a good and honorable life. More than me; that's for sure. I'd thank you kindly for anything you can do to help him get better.*

On the third morning he woke long before sunup to find Rodeo standing, chewing on mesquite beans. Though he wasn't putting weight on the affected leg, the swelling had gone down. The horse's eyes were clear as he looked down at his owner.

"Appears you're feeling better," Coy said, climbing to his feet to stroke Rodeo's flank. He filled his hat with water from his canteen and held it for the horse to drink. "Let's rest for another day or so, then see if you can walk the rest of the way. Maybe we'll find someone who can provide you proper doctoring."

The going was difficult, Rodeo slowly trailing his owner, who carried his saddle over his shoulder. Neither could travel more than a mile before stopping to rest. It was well past noon before they reached Phantom Hill and located the livery.

The blacksmith, shirtless with tobacco juice caked in his graying beard, eyed them as they approached. "Can't rightfully figure out which of you two looks worse," he said before bursting into a thundering laugh. "Name's Giles Weatherby. Welcome to Phantom Hill, Texas, such as it is. I call it the Gateway to No Place."

Jennings said, "Ya'll got a doctor in this town?"

"You ailing?"

"My horse is."

Weatherby glanced at the Colt holstered on the visitor's hip. "You wouldn't be some gunslinging outlaw come to stir up trouble, would you?"

"Nope."

"Didn't really think so. If you've got fifty cents you can board him inside. There's hay and oats and a watering trough. Looks like you could do with some time out of the sun yourself. Get settled while I go see if I can fetch Doc Matthews. He tends man, beast, and babies . . . when he's sober enough."

He was chuckling to himself as he turned to hurry down the only street in the dusty little settlement.

In the cool darkness of the stable, Jennings filled a bucket with oats as Rodeo drank from the trough. Every muscle in his body ached as he let the saddle slip from his shoulder onto a bale of hay. Pushing his hat high on his head, he sat against the wall as the horse ate and was asleep and snoring loudly when the doctor arrived half an hour later.

"Much louder and the rafters of this fine establishment would be falling in," Doc Matthews said. One hand was on Jennings's shoulder, shaking him awake. In the other he held a small leather bag.

Coy rubbed his eyes and shook his head. "My apologies. You a doctor?"

"Son, I'm *the* doctor. Only one for miles around. It's my understanding that you've got a horse needing some manner of attention."

He was already peeling away the bloodstained wrap as Jennings explained about the snakebite and what he'd done in an attempt to halt the spread of the venom. "I'd say you've done a good job," the doctor said. "Aside from a bit of infection in a couple of the places where you took a knife to him, I'd say he's doing as well as could be expected. 'Bout all I can do is clean the leg, do a little sewing up, and put some salve on the wounds. Then we'll give him time to rest and see how things look."

"He going to be okay?"

"Yes, sir, that's my professional judgment." The doctor rose and looked at Jennings. "You, on the other hand, are another matter. Seems to me if you don't get yourself a hot bath, some food, and a considerable amount of rest, you're not gonna be worth shooting." He sniffed. "Wouldn't hurt to have those clothes you're wearing laundered either."

Standing nearby, the blacksmith broke into another of his booming laughs.

"Tell you what," the doctor said. "You go get cleaned up and something to eat, and I'll take care of what needs to be done here. I 'spect Mr. Weatherby or his stableboy can give me a hand, if needed.

"Oh, and I'll be requiring a dollar in payment before you go."

For the first time in days Coy Jennings smiled as he reached into his pocket and pulled out a coin.

After a pat to Rodeo's muzzle he took the short walk past a small general store and a saloon that appeared to have been so hastily built that it still had stitched-together tent canvases serving as a roof toward Miss Mindy's Fine Eatery and Bathhouse. A small hand-painted sign near the entrance displayed a sparse menu that included venison stew, cold-water corn bread, and collard greens.

A small dog lying in the doorway lifted its head only slightly, apparently too tired or disinterested to bother to growl or bark. Jennings stepped over him and entered a room where there were four empty tables.

"Lemme guess, mister. You'll first be needing something to eat, then considerable time in a tub to wash all that trail grime away." The small woman stood less than five feet, with red hair that was a tangle of curls. She wore overalls and a flannel shirt and was smoking a cigar. "I'm Mindy. The stew's still hot on the stove and has plenty of potatoes and beans mixed into it. I've got corn bread, but all the greens are gone. Does that tempt your appetite?"

"Ma'am, just about anything that don't bite back does," Jennings said.

"Then take yourself a seat next to the window and enjoy the view—what there is of it—and I'll be off to the kitchen."

She soon returned with his food and a tin cup filled with coffee, pulled up a chair across the table from him, and took a seat without asking for an invitation. "Not that I'm the nosy sort," she said, "but it isn't often we get strangers visiting. What brings you to this godforsaken part of Texas?"

"Looking for work," Jennings replied as he dipped a slice of corn bread into the sweet-smelling stew. "I heard there was a ranch hereabouts that's hiring."

"That, I suppose, would be Lester Sinclair's spread," she said, "being as it's the only ranch we've got. Just about everybody else—them not employed by Sinclair—tries to farm."

"And what can you tell me about Mr. Sinclair?"

"Not much aside from the fact that he's not one of my favorite people. Truth is, I also work for him. He's the actual owner of this place despite the fact that it bears my name. The saloon down the street is his as well."

With that she rose and wiped her hands on her apron. "This ain't a hotel, mind you, but I do have a couple of rooms out back if you're needing a place."

"I reckon I'll be staying down at the livery," he said, "but I could do with that hot bath you mentioned."

"In that case, I'll go out back and start heating up the water. While you're waiting, feel free to help yourself to the coffee. No charge, since it's likely getting a bit bitter. You'll find the pot on the stove behind that door. I s'pose you'll be wanting your clothes washed as well."

Jennings nodded.

"Then plan to soak in your bath for a considerable time."

Sitting in the tub of hot water did wonders for his tired and aching muscles, and he took another nap. The clean smell of his sunshine-dried clothes lifted his spirits almost as much as the doctor's having said that Rodeo was going to be fine. He was hardly limping as he left Miss Mindy's, and he decided on a walk through the town before returning to the livery.

There wasn't much to see and only a few people were moving about. A couple of wagons slowly passed, loaded with provisions, and one driver waved. When Jennings tipped his hat in return, he realized that Miss Mindy had dusted it clean while he bathed.

He briefly considered visiting the saloon for a beer but decided his dwindling finances spoke against such an indulgence. Instead he stopped into the general store and purchased a small pouch of tobacco to replace what he'd used doctoring his horse.

The blacksmith was waving as he approached. "My, my, don't you look a sight better? You could go courtin', all cleaned up as you appear to be. Did Miss Mindy offer you some of that sweet-smelling lilac water to put in with your bath? If so, I'd better put out a warning to the womenfolk."

Coy responded with a slight smile.

"Your horse is in the far stall, all mended and doing well," Weatherby said. "I hung your saddle on the wall next to him."

"Appreciate it."

"Just part of the friendly service. Course, I must inform you that if you're gonna be bedding down here tonight it'll cost you another twenty-five cents."

Jennings paid him and walked inside to check on Rodeo.

As he entered the dimly lit stable, he was aware of someone speaking in a low voice near his horse. He approached to find a young man combing burrs from Rodeo's mane, talking gently as he did so.

Jennings stood watching and listening awhile before he spoke. "Who might you be?"

The young man jumped, then turned to face him. "My . . . my name's Ira. Ira Dalton. I help Mr. Weatherby some. I been talking with your horse."

Jennings nodded. "And what is it you two have been talking about?"

"Just things, you know. Gettin'-acquainted talk. Best I can figure, he's right proud you doctored his leg and brung him to shelter. I'm of a mind that 'cause you treat him so kindly he must admire you greatly."

"He told you that, did he?"

"In his way, yeah, he did. He's a mighty handsome animal."

"His name's Rodeo."

"Seems a fine name to me. Did I tell you I'm Ira . . . Ira Dalton?"

Jennings extended his hand. "That you did," he said. "Pleased to know you, Ira Dalton. My name's Coy . . . Coy Jennings."

As they shook, Dalton smiled. "That seems a fine name too. I'm gonna be sure to remember it. *Mr. Coy Jennins . . . Coy Jennins . . .*"

"Just Coy will do."

At the sound of his owner's name, Rodeo lifted his head and placed his muzzle beside Jennings's face, causing his freshly cleaned hat to fall to the hay-strewn floor.

"Yes, sir, Mr. Coy Jennins," the young man said, "I'd say he likes you a lot."